A desperate colonel writing his own rule book in a last-ditch effort to conquer the moon for man, in—

PROJECT NURSEMAID

Six generations of gallant voyagers in one of the most breathtakingly imaginative space adventures ever written—

DAUGHTERS OF EARTH

A young girl and her brother stranded as orphans on a planet whose inhabitants have the power to take over their minds, in—

HOMECALLING

Three superlative SF novels
by the one and only
JUDITH MERRIL

DAUGHTERS
OF EARTH

THREE NOVELS

by Judith Merril

A DELL BOOK

Published by
DELL PUBLISHING CO., INC.
750 Third Avenue
New York, New York 10017

Reprinted by arrangement with
Doubleday & Company, Inc.
Garden City, New York

Printed in the U.S.A.

First Dell printing—July 1970

CONTENTS

PROJECT NURSEMAID

I

THE GIRL IN the waiting room was very young, and very ill at ease. She closed the magazine in her lap, which she had not been reading, and leaned back in the chair, determined to relax. It was an interview, nothing more. If they asked too many questions or if anything happened that looked like trouble, she could just leave and not come back.

And then what . . . ?

They wouldn't, anyhow. The nurse had told her. She didn't even have to give her right name. It didn't matter. And they wouldn't check up. All they cared about was if you could pass the physical.

That's what the nurse had said, but she didn't *like* the nurse, and she wished now that she had bought a wedding ring after all. Thirty-nine cents in the five-and-ten, and she had stood there looking at them, and gone away again. Partly it was knowing the salesgirl would think she was going to use it for a hotel, or something like that. Mostly, it was just—*wrong*. A ring on your finger was supposed to mean something, even for thirty-nine cents. If she had to lie with words, she could, but not with . . . That was silly. She should have bought it. Only what a ring meant was one thing, and what Charlie had meant was something else.

Everybody's got to learn their lesson sooner or later, honey, the nurse had said.

But it wasn't like that, she wanted to say. Only it was. It was for Charlie, so what difference did it make what *she* thought?

She should have bought the ring. It was silly not to.

'I still say, it's a hell of a way to run an Army.'

'You could even be right,' said the Colonel, and both of

7

them smiled. Two men who find themselves jointly responsible for a vitally important bit of insanity, who share a strong, if reluctant, mutual respect for each other's abilities, and who disagree with each other about almost everything, will find themselves smiling frequently, he had discovered.

The General, who was also a politician, stopped smiling and added, 'Besides which, it's downright immoral! These girls—*kids!* You'd think . . .'

The Colonel, who was also a psychologist, stopped smiling too. The General had a daughter very much the same age as the one who was waiting outside right now.

'It's one *hell* of a way to run an Army.'

The Colonel nodded. His concept of morality did not coincide precisely with the General's, but his disapproval was not one whit less vehement. He had already expressed his views in a paper rather dramatically entitled 'Brave New World???' which dealt with the predictable results of regimentation in prenatal and infantile conditioning. The manuscript, neatly typed, occupied the rearmost position in a folder of personal correspondence in his bottom desk drawer, and he had no more intention of expressing his view now to the General than he had of submitting the paper for publication. He had discovered recently that he could disapprove of everything he was doing, and still desire to defend his right to do it; beyond doubt, it was better than supervising psych checks at some more conventional recruiting depot.

'A *hell* of a way,' he agreed, with sincerity, and glanced meaningfully at his appointment pad.

Thursday was apparently not the General's day for accepting hints gracefully from junior officers; he sat down in the visitor's chair, and glared. Then he sighed.

'All right, so it's still the way we have to run it. Nobody asked you. Nobody asked me. And I'll say this, Tom, in all fairness, you've done a fine job on one end of it. We're getting the babies, and we're delivering them too . . .'

'That's more your work than mine, Hal,' the Colonel lyingly demurred.

'Teamwork,' the General corrected. 'Not yours or mine, but both of us giving it everything we've got. But on this other business, now, Tom—' His finger tapped a reprimand on the sheaf of papers under his hand. '—Well, what comes first, Tom, the chicken or the egg? All eggs and no hens, it just won't work.'

The General stopped the chuckle, and the Colonel followed suit.

'The thing is, now we've got the bastards—and I mean no disrespect to my uniform, Colonel. I'm using that word literally—now we've got 'em, what're we going to do with 'em?'

His fingers continued to tap on the pile of reports, not impatiently, but with emphasis.

'I don't say it's your fault, Tom, you've done fine on the other end, but if you're going to bounce everybody who can pass the physicals, and if everyone who gets by you is going to get blacked out by the medics, well—I don't know, maybe the specs were set too high. Maybe you've got to—well, I don't want to tell you how to do your job, Tom. I don't kid myself about that; I know I couldn't fill your shoes if I tried. All I can do is put it squarely up to you. You've got the figures there in front of you. *Cold figures,* and you know what they mean.'

He stopped tapping long enough to shove a neatly typed sheet an inch closer to the other man. Neither of them looked at the sheet; both of them knew the figures by heart. 'Out of three hundred and thirty-six applicants so far, we've accepted thirty-eight. We've had twenty-one successful Sections to date,' the General intoned. 'And six of those have been successfully transported to Moon Base. Three have already come to term, and been delivered, healthy and whole and apparently in good shape all around.

'Out of one hundred and ninety-six applicants, we have so far accepted exactly *three*—one, two, three—foster parents. Only one of those is on the Base now. She's been on active duty since the first delivery—that was August 22, if I remember right, and *that* makes twenty-five days today that she's been on without relief.

'Mrs. Kemp left on the rocket this morning. She'll be on Base—let's see—' He shuffled rocket schedules and Satellite-Moon Base shuttles in his mind. '—Wednesday, day after tomorrow. Which makes twenty-*seven* days for Lenox. If Kemp's willing to walk in and take over on a strange job, Lenox can take a regular single leave at that point; more likely she'll have to wait for the next shuttle—thirty-one days on duty, Tom, and most of it carrying full responsibility alone. And *that's* not counting the two days she was there before the first delivery, which adds up to—let's see—thirty-three altogether, isn't it?'

The Colonel nodded soberly. It was hard to remember that the General happened to be right, and that the figures he was quoting were meaningful, in terms of human beings. Carefully, he lowered mental blinds, and managed to keep track of the recital without having to hear it all. He knew the figures, and he knew the situation was serious. He knew it a good deal better than the General did, because he knew the *people* as well as how many there were . . . or weren't.

More women on more rockets would make the tally-sheet look better, but it wouldn't provide better care for the babies; not unless they were the *right* women. He waited patiently for a break in the flow of arithmetic, and tried to get this point across. 'I was thinking,' he began. 'On this leave problem—couldn't we use some of the Army nurses for relief duty, till we catch up with ourselves? That would take some of the pressure off and I'd a lot rather have the kids in the care of somebody we didn't know for a few days than send up extra people on one-year contracts when we do know they're not adequate.'

'It's a last resort, Tom. That's just what I'm trying to avoid. I'm hoping we *won't* have to do that,' the General said ominously. 'Right now, this problem is in our laps, and nobody else's. If we start asking for help from the Base staff, and get *their* schedules fouled up—I tell you, Tom, we'll have all the top brass there *is* down on us.'

'Of course,' he said. 'I wasn't thinking of that angle . . .' But he let it go. No sense trying to make any point against the Supreme Argument.

'Well, that's my job, not yours, worrying about things like that,' the General said jovially. But all the time, one finger, as if with an independent metronomic existence of its own, kept tapping the pile of psych reports. 'But you know as well as I do, we've got to start showing better results. I've talked to the Medics, and I'm talking to you. Maybe you ought to get together and figure how to . . .

'No, I said I wouldn't tell you how to do your job, and

'You're quite sure?' he said politely. 'It's not *necessary;* but it does work to the advantage of the child, if we have as much information as possible.'

'I'm sorry,' she said tightly. 'He—' She paused, and made up her mind. 'He doesn't know about it. We're both still in school, Colonel. If I told him, he'd think he had to quit, and start working. I can't tell him.'

It sounded like the truth, almost, but her face was too stiffly composed, and the pulse in her temple beat visibly against the pale mask. Her words were too precise, when her breath was coming so quickly. She wasn't used to lying.

'You realize that what you're doing here is a real and important contribution, Mrs. Barton? Don't you think he might see it that way? Maybe if I talked to him . . . ?'

She shook her head again. 'No. If it's that important, I guess I better . . .' The voice trailed off, almost out of control, and her lips stayed open a little, her eyes wide, frightened, not knowing what the end of that sentence could possibly be.

The Colonel pushed the printed sheet away from him, and looked at her intently. It was time for the last question.

'Mrs. Barton— What do people call you, anyway? Cecille? Cissy? Ceil? Do you mind . . . ?'

'No, that's all right. Ceil.' It was a very small smile, but she was obviously more comfortable.

'All right, Ceil. Now look—there's a line on the bottom there that asks your reason for volunteering. I wish it wasn't there, because I don't like inviting lies. I know, and everybody connected with this project knows, that it takes some pretty special motivation for a woman to volunteer for something like this. Occasionally we get someone in here who's doing it out of pure and simple—and I do mean simple—patriotism, and then I don't mind asking that question. I don't think that applies to you . . . ?'

She shook her head, and tried a smile.

'Okay. I wanted to explain my own attitude before I asked. I don't care why you're doing it. I'm damn glad you are, because I think you're the kind of parent we want. You'll go through some pretty rugged tests before we accept you, but by this time I can usually tell who'll get through, and who won't. I think you will. And it's in the nature of things that if you *are* the right kind, you'd have to have a pretty special personal reason for doing this . . . ?'

He waited. Her lips moved, but no sound came out. She tried again, and when she swallowed, he could almost feel in his own throat the lump that wouldn't let her lie come out. He pulled the application form closer to him, and wrote quickly in the last space at the bottom, then shoved it across, so she could see:

> *I think I'm too young to raise a child properly, and I want to help out.*

'All right?' he asked gently. She nodded, and there were tears in her eyes. He opened the top drawer and got her some Kleenex. Again she started to say something, and swallowed instead; then the dam broke. He wheeled his chair over to her, and reached out a comforting hand. Then her head was on his shoulder, and she was crying in loud snuffly childish sobs. When it began to let up, he gave her some more Kleenex, and got his chair back in position so he could kick the button under the desk and dim the light a little.

'Still want to go through with it?' he asked.

She nodded.

'Want to tell me any more?'

She did; she obviously wanted to very much. She kept her lips pressed firmly together, as if the words might get out in spite of herself.

'You don't have to,' he said. 'If you want to, you understand it stops right here. The form is filled out already. There's nothing else I have to put on there. But if you feel like talking a little, now that we're—' he grinned, and glanced at the damp spot on his shoulder, '—now that we're better acquainted—well, you might feel better if you spill some of it.'

'There's nothing to tell,' she said carefully. 'Nothing you don't already know.' Her face was expressionless; there was no way to tell what she meant.

'All right,' he said. 'In that case, sit back and get comfortable, because *I've* got some things to tell you. The Colonel is about to make a speech.' She smiled, but it was a polite smile now; for a minute, she had warmed up, now they were strangers again.

He had made the same speech, with slight variations, exactly 237 times before. Every girl or woman who got past him to the medics heard it before she went. The wording and the manner changed for each one, but the substance was the same.

All he was supposed to do was to explain the nature and purposes of the Project. Presumably, they already knew that when they came in, but he was supposed to make sure. He did. He made very sure that they understood, as well as each one was able, not only the purposes, but the nature: what kind of lives their children might be expected to lead.

It never made any difference. He knew it wouldn't now. Just once, a woman had come to them because she had been warned that carrying a child to term would mean her death and the baby's, both. She had listened and understood, and had asked soberly whether there were any similar facilities available privately. He had had to admit there were not. The process was too expensive, even for this purpose, except on a large-scale basis. To do it for one infant would be possible, perhaps, for a Rockefeller or an Aga Khan—not on any lesser scale. The woman had listened, and hesitated, and decided that life, on any terms, was better than no life at all.

But this girl with her tremulous smile and her frightened eyes and her unweathered skin—this girl had not yet realized even that it was a human life she carried inside herself; so far, she understood only that she had done something foolish, and that there was a slim chance she might be able to remedy the error without total disaster or too much dishonour.

He started with the history of the Project, explaining the reasons for it, and the thinking behind it: the psychosomatic problems of low-grav and null-weight conditions; the use of hypnosis, and its inadequacies; the eventual recognition that only those conditioned from infancy to low-grav conditions would ever be able to make the Starhop . . . or even live in any comfort on the Moon.

He ran through it, but she wasn't listening. Either she knew it already, or she just wasn't interested. The Colonel kept talking, only because he was required to brief all applicants on this material.

'The problem was how to get the babies to the Base. So

far, nobody has been able to take more than four months of Moon-grav without fairly serious somatic effects, or else a total emotional crackup. It wasn't practical to take families there, to raise our crop of conditioned babies, and we couldn't safely transport women in their last month of pregnancy, or new-born babies, either one.'

She was paying attention, in a way. She was paying attention to *him,* but he could have sworn she wasn't hearing a word he said.

'The operation,' he went on, 'was devised by Dr. Jordan Zamesh, of the Navy . . .'

'I'm sorry,' she said suddenly, 'about your uniform.'

'Uniform . . . ?' He glanced at the spot on his shoulder. 'Oh, that's all right. It's almost dry, anyhow. Dacron.' *Damn!* He'd miscalculated. She was too young to stew over a brief loss of control this way—but she'd been doing it anyhow, and *he hadn't noticed.* Which was what came of worrying about your boss when you were supposed to have your mind on the customers. *Damn!* And double it for the General. She might have been ready to talk, and he'd rushed into his little speech like an idiot while she sat there getting over the sobbing-spell. All by herself. Without any nice sympathetic help from the nice sympathetic man.

'I guess,' she was saying, 'I suppose you're used to that?'

'I keep the Kleenex handy,' he admitted.

'Does *every*body—?'

'Nope. Just the ones who have sense enough to know what they're doing. The high-powered patriots don't, I guess. All the others do, sooner or later, here or some place else.' He looked at her, sitting there so much inside herself, so miserably determined to sustain her isolation, so falsely safe inside the brittle armour of her loneliness. She had cried for a minute, and cracked the armour by that much, and now she hated herself for it.

'What the hell kind of a woman do you think you'd be?' he said grimly. 'If you'll pardon my emphasis—what the hell kind of woman could give a baby away without crying a little?'

'I didn't have to do it on your uniform.'

'You didn't have to, but I'm glad you did.'

'You don't have to feel . . .' She caught herself, just in time, and the Colonel restrained a smile. She had almost forgotten that there wasn't any reason to feel sorry for *Mrs. Barton.*

She smoothed out her face, regained a part of her composure. 'I'm sorry,' she said. 'All I do is apologize, isn't it? Now I mean I'm sorry, because I wasn't really listening to you. I was too embarrassed, I guess? I'll listen now.'

He'd lost her again. For a moment, there had almost been contact, but now she was gone, alone with her shell of quiet politeness. The Colonel went on with his speech.

'. . . the operation is not dangerous,' he explained, 'except insofar as any operation, or the use of anaesthesia, is occasionally dangerous to a rare individual. However, we have managed to cut down on even that narrow margin; the physical exams you'll get before the application is approved will pretty well determine whether there is any reason why you should not undergo operative procedure.

'Essentially, what we do is a simple Caesarian section. There are modifications, of course, to allow the placenta and membrane to be removed intact, but these changes do not make the operation any more dangerous.

'There is a certain percentage of loss in the postoperative care of the embryos. Occasionally, the nutritive surrogate doesn't "take", whether because of miscalculations on our part, or unknown factors in the embryo, we can't tell, but for the most part, the embryos thrive and continue to grow in normal fashion, and the few that have already been transported have all survived the trip—'

'Colonel . . . ?'

He was relieved; he hadn't *entirely* misread her. She was a nice girl, a good girl, who would be a good wife and mother some day, and she interrupted just where she ought to.

'Yes?' He let himself smile a little bit, and she took it the right way.

'Does— Is— I mean, you said, the operation isn't dangerous. But what does it do as far as—having babies later goes?'

'To the best of our knowledge, it will not impair either your ability to conceive or your capacity to carry a baby through a normal pregnancy. Depending on your own healing potential, and on the results of some new tech-

niques we're using, you *may* have to have Caesarians with
any future deliveries.'

'*Oh!*'

As suddenly as it had happened before, when she cried,
the false reserve of shame and pride and worry fell away
from her. Her eyes were wide, and her tongue flickered out
to wet her upper lip before she could say, '*There'll be a
scar!* Won't there? This time, I mean?'

There were two things he could say, and the one that
would comfort her would also seal her away again behind
the barrier of proper manners and assumed assurance. He
spoke slowly and deliberately:

'Perhaps you'd better tell your husband beforehand,
Ceil. . . .'

She stared at him blankly; she'd forgotten about the husband again. Then she sat up in her chair and looked
straight at him. '*You know I'm not married!*' she said. She
was furious.

The Colonel sat back and relaxed. He picked up the
application blank he had filled out, and calmly tore it down
the centre.

'All right,' she said tiredly. She stood up. 'I'm sorry I
wasted your time.'

'You didn't,' he said quietly. 'Not unless you've changed
your mind, that is.'

Half-way to the door, she turned around and looked at
him. She didn't say anything, just waited.

He took a fresh form out of his drawer, and motioned
to the chair. 'Sit down, won't you?' She took a tentative
half-step back towards him, and paused, still waiting. He
stood up, and walked around the desk, carefully not going
too close to her. Leaning on the edge of the desk, he said
quietly, in matter-of-fact tones:

'Look, Ceil, right now you're confused. You're so angry
you don't care what happens, and you're feeling so beat,
you haven't got the energy to be mad. You don't know
where you're going, or where you *can* go. And you don't see
any sense in staying. All right, your big guilty secret is out
now, and I personally don't give a damn—except for one
thing: that it *had* to come out before we could seriously
consider your application.'

He watched the colour come back to her face, and her

eyes go wide again. 'You mean——?' she said and stopped. Looked at the chair; looked at the door; looked at him, waiting again.

'I mean,' he said, 'bluntly, that I used every little psychological trick I know to get you to make that Horrible Admission. I did it because what we're doing here is both important and expensive, and we don't take babies without knowing what we're getting. Besides which, I think you're the kind of parent we want. I didn't want to let you get away. I hope you won't go now.' He reached out and put a hand on her arm. 'Sit down, won't you, Ceil? It won't hurt to listen a while, and I think we can work things out.'

This time he pretended not to notice the tears, and gave her a chance to brush them away, and get settled in the chair again, while he did some unnecessary rummaging around in his closet. After that it went smoothly. They stuck to the assumed name, Barton, but he got her real name as well, and the college she was going to. She lived at school; that would make the arrangements easier.

'We can't do it till the fifth month,' he explained. 'If everything goes all right till then, we can probably arrange for an emergency appendectomy easily enough. You'll come in for regular checkups meanwhile; and if things start to get too—*obvious*, we'll have to work out something more complicated, to get you out of school for a while beforehand. The scar is enough like an appendix scar to get away with,' he added.

The one thing he had really been disturbed about was her age, but she insisted she was really nineteen, and of course he could verify that with the school. And the one thing she wouldn't break down about was the father's name. He decided that could wait. Also, he left out the unfinished part of his speech: the part about the training the children would have. For this girl, it was clear, the only realities were in the immediate present, and the once-removed direct consequences of present acts. She was nineteen; the scar mattered, but the child did not. Not yet.

He took her to the outer office and asked Helen, at the desk, to make an appointment for her with Medical and to give her the standard literature. Helen pushed a small stack of phone messages over to him, and he riffled through. Just one urgent item, a woman in the infirmary with a fit of postoperative melancholia. *They're all in such a damn hurry to get rid of the babies,* he thought, *and then they want to kill themselves afterwards!* And this nice girl, this pretty child, would be the same way. . . .

Helen had Medical on the phone. 'Tell them I'll be right down,' he told her, 'for Mrs. Anzio. Ten-fifteen minutes.'

She nodded, confirmed the time and date for Ceil's appointment, and repeated the message, then listened a minute, nodding.

'All right, I'll tell him.' She hung up, pulled a prepared stuffed manila envelope out of her file, and handed it to the girl. 'Four-fifteen, Friday. Bring things for overnight. You'll be able to leave about Sunday morning.' She smiled professionally, scribbling the time on an appointment-reminder slip.

'I'll have to get a weekend pass—to stay overnight,' the girl said hesitantly.

'All right. Let us know if you can't do it this weekend, and we'll fix it when you can.' The Colonel led her to the door, and turned back to his secretary inquiringly.

'They said no rush, but you better see her before you leave today. They're afraid it might get suicidal.'

'Yeah. I know.' He looked at her, smart and brisk and shiny, the perfect Lady Soldier. She had been occupying that desk for three weeks now, and he had yet to find a chink or peephole in the gleaming wall of her efficiency. *And for an old Peeping Tom like me, this is going some!* The thought was indignant. 'You know what?' he said.

'Sir?'

'This is a *hell* of a way to run an Army!'

'Yes, sir,' she said; but she managed to put a good deal of meaning into it.

'I take it you agree, but you don't approve. If it will make you feel any better, I have the General's word for it. He told me so himself. Now what about this Browne woman?'

'Oh. She called twice. The second time she told me she wants to apply for FP. I told her you were in conference, and would call her back. She was very—insistent.'

'I see. Well, you call her back, and make an appointment for tomorrow. Then . . .'

'There's another FP coming tomorrow afternoon,' she reminded him. 'A Mrs. Leahy.'

'Well! Two in one day. Maybe business is picking up. Put Browne in first thing in the morning. Then call the Dean of Women at Henderson, and make an appointment for me—I'll go there—any time that's convenient. Sooner the better. Tell her it's the Project, but don't say what about.' There were three more messages; he glanced at them again, and tossed them back on her desk. 'You can handle these. I better go see that Anzio woman.'

'What shall I tell General Martin, sir?' She picked up the slip with the message from his office, and studied it with an air of uninformed bewilderment.

The Perfect Lady Soldier, all right, he decided. *No bucks passed to her.* 'Tell his *secretary* that I had to rush down to Medical, and I'll ring him back when I'm done,' he said, and managed to make it sound as if that was what he'd meant all along.

II

IN THE MORNING, very slightly hung over, he checked first with the Infirmary, and was told that Mrs. Anzio had been quiet after he left, had eaten well, and had spent the night under heavy sedation. She was quiet now, but had refused breakfast.

'She supposed to go home today?'

'That's right, sir.'

'Well, don't let her go. I'll get down when I have a chance, and see how she sounds. Who's O.D. down there? Bill Sawyer?'

'Yes, sir.'

'Well, tell him I'd suggest stopping sedation now.'

'Yes, sir.'

He hung up and buzzed Helen. 'You can send Miss Browne in now.'

Miss Browne settled her bony bottom on the edge of the visitors' chair. She was dressed in black, with one smart-looking gold pin on her lapel to show she was modern and broad-minded—and a mourning-band on her sleeve, to show she wasn't *too* forgetful of the old-fashioned proprieties. She spoke in a faintly nasal whine, and used elegant, refined language and diction.

It took about 60 seconds to determine that she could not be seriously considered for the job. It took another 60 minutes to go through the formality of filling out an application blank, and hearing her reasons for wanting to spend a year at Moon Base in the service of the State. It took most of the rest of the morning to compose a report that might make clear to the General just why they could not use an apparently healthy woman of less than thirty-five years, with no dependents or close attachments (her father had just died, after a long illness, during which she had given up '*everything*' to care for him), with some nursing experience, and with a stated desire to 'give what I can for society, now that there is nothing more I can do for my beloved father.'

Give, he thought. *Give till it hurts. Then give ·a little more, till it hurts as much as possible.* It was inevitable that this sort of job should attract the martyr types; inevitable, but still you wondered, when nine-tenths of the population had never heard of the Project, just how so *many* of this kind came so swiftly and unerringly to the waiting room.

He wrote it down twice for the General: once with psychological jargon, meant to impress; and again with adjectives and examples, and a case history or two, meant to educate. When he was done, he had little hope that he had succeeded in making his point. He signed the report and handed it to Helen to send up.

Mrs. Leahy, in the afternoon, was a surprise.

She walked into his office with no sign of either the reluctance-and-doubt or the eagerness-and-arrogance that marked almost every applicant who entered there. She sat down comfortably in the visitors' chair, and introduced herself with a friendliness and social ease that made it clear she was accustomed to meeting strangers.

She was a plump—not fat—attractive woman, past her first youth, but in appearance not yet what could be called middle-aged. He was startled when she stated her age as forty-seven; he was further startled when she stated her occupation.

'Madam,' she said, and chuckled with pleasure when he couldn't help himself from looking up sharply. 'You don't know how I've been waiting to see your face when I said that,' she explained, and he thought wearily, *I should have known. Just another exhibitionist.* For a few minutes, he had begun to think he had one they could use.

'Do you always show your feelings all over your face like that?' she asked gleefully. 'You'd think, in your job— The *reason* I was looking forward to saying it was—well, two reasons. First, I figured you'd be one of these suave-faced operators, professionally unshockable, and I wanted to jolt you.'

'You did, and I am,' he said gravely. 'Usually.'

She smiled. 'Second, I'm not often in a position to pull off anything like that. People would disapprove, and what's worse, they'd refuse to wait on me in stores, or read me lectures, or—anyhow, it seemed to me that here I could just start out telling the truth, seeing that you'd find out anyhow. I don't suppose the people you accept get sent up before you've checked them?'

'You're right again.' He pushed his chair back, and decided to relax and enjoy it. He liked this woman. 'Tell me some more.'

She did, at length and entertainingly. She was a successful businesswoman. She had proved that much to her own satisfaction, and now she was bored. The house ran itself, almost, and was earning more money than she needed for personal use. She had no real interest in expanding her operations; success for its own sake meant nothing to her. She had somehow escaped the traditional pitfalls of Career; maybe it was the specialized nature of her business that never let her forget she was a woman, and so preserved her femininity of both viewpoint and personality.

It was harder to understand how she had managed to escape the normal occupational disease of her world: the yearning for respectability and a place in conventional society. Instead she wanted new places, new faces, and something to do that would make use of her abilities and give scope to her abundant affections.

'I've never had children of my own,' she said, and for the first time lost a trace of her aplomb. 'I—you realize, in my business, you don't start out at the top? A lot of the girls are sterile to start with, and a lot more get that way. Since I started my own place, the girls have been almost like my own—some of them, the ones I keep—but . . . I think I'd like to have some real babies to take care of.' Her voice came back to normal: 'Getting to grandmother age, I guess.'

'I see.' He sat up briskly, and finished the official form, making quick notes as she parried his questions with efficient quiet answers. When he was done, he looked up and met her eyes, unwillingly. 'I may as well be frank with you, Mrs. Leahy—'

'Brush-off?' she broke in softly.

He nodded. 'I'm afraid so.' She started to get up, and he reached out a hand, involuntarily, as if to hold her in her seat. 'Don't go just yet. Please. There's something I'd like to say.'

She sat still, waiting, the bitterness behind her eyes veiled with polite curiosity.

'Just . . .' He hesitated, wanting to pick the right words to get through her sudden defences. 'Just that, in my personal opinion, you're the best prospect we've had in six months. I haven't got the nerve to say it in so many words, when I make my report. But I didn't fill out that form just to use up more of your time. If it were up to me, you'd be on your way down for a physical exam right now. Unfortunately, I am not the custodian of moralities in this Army, or even on Project.

'What I'm going to do is send in a report recommending that we reserve decision. I'll tell you now in confidence that we're having a hard time getting the right kind of people. The day *may* come—' He broke off, and looked at her almost pleadingly. 'You understand? I can't recommend you, and if I did, I'd be overruled. But I wish I could, and if things change, you may still hear from us.'

'I understand.' She stood up, looking tired; then, with an effort, she resumed her cheerful poise, and took his offered hand to shake good-bye. 'I won't wish you bad luck, so—good-bye.'

'Good-bye. And thank you,' he said with sincerity, 'for coming in.'

Then he wrote up his report, went down to see the Anzio woman, cleared her for release, and went home where a half-empty bottle waited from the night before.

There was no summons from the General waiting for him in the morning, and no friendly, casual visit during the hour before he left to see Dean Lazarus at Henderson. He didn't know whether to regard the silence as ominous or hopeful; so he forgot it, temporarily, and concentrated on the Dean.

He approached her cautiously, with generalizations about the Project, and the hope that if she were ever in a position to refer anyone to them, she would be willing to co-operate, etc., etc. She was pleasant, polite, and intelligent for half an hour, and then she became impatient.

'All right, Colonel, suppose we come to the point?'

'What point did you have in mind?' he countered warily.

'I have two students waiting outside to see me,' she said, 'and I imagine you also have other business to attend to. I take it one of our girls is in what is called "trouble"? She came to you, and you want to know whether I'll work with you, or whether the kid will get bounced out of school if I know about it. Stop me if I'm wrong.'

'Go on,' he said.

'All right. The answer is, it depends on the girl. There are some I'd grab any chance to toss out. But I'd guess, from the fact that she wound up coming to you, she either isn't very experienced or she *is* conscientious. Or both.'

'I'd say both, on the basis of our interview.'

She looked him over thoughtfully. *Lousy technique,* he thought, and had to curb a wicked impulse to ham up his role and confuse her entirely; it wasn't often he had a chance to sit in the visitors' chair.

That studying look of hers would put anybody on the defensive, he thought critically, and then realized that maybe it was meant to do just that. Her job didn't have the same requirements as his.

'Let me put it this way,' she said finally. 'I'm here to try to help several hundred adolescent females get some education into their heads, and I don't mean just out of books.

I'm *also* here to see to it that the college doesn't get a bad reputation: no major scandals or suicides, or anything like that. If the girl is worth helping, and if you want my co-operation in a plan that will keep things quiet and respectable, and make it possible for her to continue at school—believe me, you'll have it.'

That left it squarely up to him. Was that girl 'worth helping'? or rather: would Dean Lazarus think so?

'I think,' he said slowly, 'I'll have to ask you to promise me first—since your judgment and mine may not agree—that you won't use any information you get from me *against* the girl. If you don't want to help, when you know who it is, you'll just sit back. All right?'

She thought that over. 'Providing I don't happen to acquire the same information from other sources,' she said.

'Without going *looking* for it,' he added.

'I'm an honest woman, Colonel Edgerly.'

'I think you are. I have your word?'

'You do.'

'The girl's name is Cecille Chanute. You know her . . . ?'

'*Ceil!* Oh, my God! Of course. It's always the ones you don't worry about! Who's the boy? And why on earth don't they just get married, and . . . ?'

He was shaking his head. 'I don't know. She wouldn't say. That's one thing I thought you might be able to help me with. . . .'

He left shortly afterwards. *That* part, at least, would be all right. Unless something unexpected turned up in the physical, the only problem now was getting the necessary data on the father.

When he got back to the office, the memo from the General was on his desk.

TO: *Edgerly*
FROM: *Martin*

[No titles. Informal. That meant it wasn't the death-blow yet. Not quite.]

RE: *Applicants for PN's and FP positions.*
   After reading your reports of yesterday, 16/9, and after giving the matter some thought, bearing in mind our conversation of 15/9, it seems to me that we

*might hold off on accepting any further PN's until the
FP situation clears up. Suggest you defer all further
interviews for PN's. Let's put our minds to the other
part of the problem, and see what we can do. This is
urgent, Tom. If you have any suggestions, I'll be glad
to hear them, any time.*

It was signed, in scrawly pencil, H. M. Just a friendly
note. But attached to it was a detailed schedule of PN acceptances, operations, shipments, and deliveries to date,
plus a projected schedule of operations, shipments, and
theoretical due dates for deliveries. The second sheet was
even adjusted for statistical expectation of losses all along
the line.

What emerged, much more clearly than it had in the
General's solemn speechmaking, was that it would be
necessary not only to have one more Foster Parent trained
and ready to leave in less than three months, but that
through January and February they would need at least
one more FP on every bi-weekly rocket, to take care of the
deliveries *already* scheduled.

Little Ceil didn't know how lucky she was. *Just in under
the wire, kid.* She was lucky to have somebody like that
Lazarus dame on her side, too.

And *that* was an idea. People like Lazarus could help.

He buzzed Helen, and spent most of the rest of the day
dictating a long and careful memo, proposing a publicity
campaign for Foster Parent applications. If the percentage
of acceptances was low, the logical thing to do about it was
increase the totals, starting with the applications. Now that
he'd have more time to devote to FP work, with the cur-
tailment on PN, he might fruitfully devote some part of it
to a publicity campaign: discreet, of course, but designed to
reach those groups that might provide the most useful material.

The Colonel was pleased when he had finished. He spent
some time mapping out a rough plan of approach, using
Dean Lazarus as his prototype personality. Social workers,
teachers, personnel workers—these were the people with
the contacts and the judgment to provide him with a steady
stream of referrals.

Five women to find in two months—with this programme, it might even be possible.

The reply from the General's office next morning informed him that his suggestion was being considered. For
some weeks, apparently, it continued to be considered, without further discussion. During that time, the Colonel saw
Ceil Chanute again, after her Med report came through
okayed, and then went to see Dean Lazarus once more.

Neither of them had had any luck finding out who the
boy was. They worked out detailed plans for Ceil's 'appendectomy', and the Dean undertook to handle the girl's family. She felt strongly that they should not be told the truth,
and the Colonel was content to let her exercise her own
judgment.

At the end of the two weeks, another applicant came in.
The Colonel tried his unconscientious best to convince himself the woman would do; but he knew she wouldn't. This
time it took less than an hour for an answer from the General's office. A phone call, this time.

'. . . I was just thinking, Tom, until we start getting
somewhere on the FP angle—I notice you've got six PN's
scheduled that aren't processed yet. Three-four of them,
there are loopholes. I think we ought to drop whatever we
can . . . ?'

'If you think so, sir.'

'Well, it makes sense to me. There's one the Security
boys haven't been able to get a complete check on; something funny there. And this gal who won't tell us the
father's name. And the one who was supposed to come in
last week and postponed it. We can tell her it's too late
now . . . ?'

'Yes, sir. I'll have to see them, of course. These women
are pretty desperate, sometimes. They—well, I think it
would be better to consider each case separately, talk to
each one— There's no telling what some of them might do.
We don't want any *un*favourable publicity,' he said, and
waited for some response to the pointed reminder.

There was none. 'No, of course not. You use your judgment, Tom, that's all, but I'd like to have a report on each
one—just let me know what you do about it. Every bit of
pressure we can get off is going to help, you know.'

And that was all. Nothing about his Memo. Just a gentle warning that if he kept on being stubborn, he was going to be backed up a little further—each and *every* time.

He got the file folders on the three cases, and studied two of them. The 'Barton' folder he never even opened. He found he was feeling just a little more stubborn than usual.

Sergeant Gregory came in, and he dictated a letter of inquiry to the woman who had failed to keep her appointment, then instructed the Sergeant to call the other one, and make an appointment for her to come in and see him. 'But first,' he finished, 'get me Dean Lazarus at Henderson, will you?'

III

WAITING OUT THERE in the room with the Wac and the mirror was almost as it had been the first time. Something was wrong. Something had happened to spoil everything. It had to be that, or he couldn't have got her called out of class. Not unless it was *really* important. And how did he explain it to Lazarus anyhow?

She sat there for five minutes that seemed like hours, and then the door opened and he came out with a welcoming smile on his lips, and all of a sudden everything was all right.

'Hi. You made good time, kid. Come on in.'

'I took a cab. I didn't change or anything.' It *couldn't* be very bad; if he looked so calm.

'Well, don't change next time either,' he said, closing the door behind them. 'Jeans are more your speed. And a shirt like that coming in here once in a while does a lot to brighten up my life.'

The main thing was, he had said *next time*. She let out a long breath she didn't know she'd been holding, and sat down in the big chair.

'All right,' he said, as soon as he had gone through the preliminary ritual of lighting cigarettes. 'Now listen close, kid, because we are in what might be called a jam. A mess. Difficulties. Problems.'

'I figured that when you called.' But she wasn't really worried any more. Whatever it was, it couldn't be *very* bad. 'I was wondering—what did you tell the Dean?'

'The Dean . . .? Oh, I told her the truth, Ceil. About two days after you first came in.'

'You *what?*' Everything was upside down; *nothing* made sense. She had been asked to one of Lazar's teas yesterday. The old girl had been sweet as punch today about the call, and excusing her from classes. *'What* did you say?' she asked again.

'I said, I told her the truth, away back when. Now, listen a minute. You're nineteen years old and you're a good girl, so you still respect Authority. Authority being people like Sarah Lazarus and myself. Only it just so happens that people like us are human beings too. I don't expect you to *believe* that, just because I say it, but try to pretend for a few minutes, will you?' There was a smile playing around the corners of his mouth. She didn't know whether to be angry or amused or worried. 'I went in to see Mrs. Lazarus in the hope that she'd co-operate with us in planning your "appendectomy". It turned out she would. She thinks a lot of you, Ceil, and she was glad to help.'

'You took an awful chance,' she said slowly.

'No. I made sure of my ground before I said anything. A lot surer than I am now. I think when you get back, you better go have a talk with the lady. And after that, you better remember that she's keeping her mouth shut, and it would be a good idea if you did the same. You realize the spot *she'd* be on, if other girls found out . . .?'

She flushed. 'I'm not likely to do much talking,' she reminded him, and immediately felt guilty, because Sally knew. It was Sally who had sent her to that doctor. . . .

'Everybody talks to *some*body,' he said flatly. 'When you feel like you have to talk, try to come here. If you can't, just be careful who it is.'

His voice was sharp and edgy; she'd never heard him talk that way before. *I didn't do anything,* she thought, bewildered. He cleared his throat, and when he spoke again, his voice sounded more normal.

'All right, we've got that out of the way. Now: the reason I asked you to come in such a hurry—well, to put it bluntly, and without too much detail, there've been some policy changes higher-up here, and there's pressure being put on me to drop as many of the PN's coming up as I can find excuses for.'

PN's? she wondered, and then realized—*Pre Natal.*

'. . . I didn't want to do this. I hoped you'd tell me in your own time.' She'd missed something; she tried to figure it out as he went along. 'If you didn't—well, we've handled two-three cases before where the father could not be located.'

Oh!

'Till now,' he went on, 'I thought if we couldn't convince you that it was in the best interests of the child for you to let us know, we might be able to get by without insisting. But now I'm afraid I'm going to have to ask you to tell me whether you want to or not. I'll promise to use every bit of tact and discretion possible, but—'

'I *can't*,' she broke in.

'Why not?'

'Because . . . I can't.' If she told the reason, it would be as bad as telling it all.

'Not even if it means you can't have the operation?'

That's not fair! There was nothing she could say.

'Look, Ceil, if it's just that you don't want him to know, we might be able to work it that way. Most people have physical exams on record one place or another, and the little bit more that we like to know about the father, you can probably tell us—or we can find out other ways. Does that change the picture any?'

She bit her lip. Maybe they *could* get all the information without—not without going through the Academy, they couldn't. It was there, *that* was true enough. Charlie wouldn't have to know at all—not till they kicked him out of school, that is! She shook her head.

'Look,' he said. He was pleading with her now. Why didn't he just tell her to go to hell and throw her out, if it was all that important? Why should it matter to *him?* 'Look, I'm supposed to be sending you a regretful note right now. But the fact is, if I can put in a report that you came in *today*, before I could take any action, and that you voluntarily cleared up the problem . . . do you understand?'

'Yes,' she said. 'I think I do.'

'You're thinking that this is a trick? I tricked you once before, so that you told me what you didn't mean to. Now I'm doing it again? Is that it?'

'Aren't you?'

'No.' His eyes met hers, and held there. She *wanted* to believe him. He had admitted it the other time—but not till after he found out what he wanted to know.

'Maybe I don't *know*,' she said spitefully. That was silly, a childish thing to say. Suddenly she realized he hadn't spoken since she said it, and—

Migod! Suppose he believes it! She looked up swiftly, and found a smile on his lips.

'Why on earth would you tell me a thing like that?' he asked mildly. 'Are you feeling wicked today?'

All right, she thought, *you win.* But she needed a few minutes; she had to think it out. 'Thank you,' she said, stalling, but also because she meant it.

'You're welcome I'm sure. What for?'

'At the doctor's I went to—they asked me *if* I knew who it was.'

The Colonel smiled. 'You're a nice girl, Ceil. Don't forget it. You're a nice girl, and it shows all over you, and anybody who can't see it is crazy. That doctor should have his head examined.'

'That explains it.' When he grinned like that, he seemed hardly any older than she was.

'You mean she was just being—well, *catty?*'

'That's one way of putting it.' He opened his bottom desk drawer, and pulled out a round shaving mirror, with a little stand on it. She took the mirror hesitantly, when he handed it to her. *Jonathan Jo had a mouth like an O, And a wheelbarrow full of surprises* . . . or a desk drawer. She held the mirror gingerly, not sure what it was for.

'I'm sorry,' she giggled. 'I don't shave yet. I'm too young.'

He smiled. 'Take a look.'

She didn't want to. She looked quickly, and tried to hand it back, but he didn't take it. He left it lying on the desk. 'All right,' he said. 'Now: do you remember what the other lady looked like? The nurse?'

'She was blonde,' Ceil recalled slowly. 'Dyed-blonde, I mean, and her skin was sort of—I guess she had too much powder on. But she was kind of good-looking.'

'Was she? How old do you think she was?'

'Oh, maybe, I don't know—forty?'

'*And why do you suppose she was working in a place like that?*'

She sat there, and tried to think of an answer. What kind of reason would a woman have for working for that kind of a doctor? All she could think of was what her mother would have said: *Well, you know, dear, some people just don't care. I don't suppose she thinks about it, just so long as she earns a living. They're well paid, you know.*

That's what was in the back of her own mind, too— until she stopped to think about it; and then she couldn't figure out an answer. She couldn't think of *any* reason that could make *her* do it.

She looked at him hopelessly, like a child caught unprepared in grammar school, and she saw he was grinning at her again. Not in a mean way; it was more as if he were pleased with her for *trying* to answer than making fun because she couldn't.

Maybe the important thing was just to try. That's what he'd been trying to tell her. That was the way *he* thought about people, all the time.

'I can't tell you his name,' she said, and took a deep breath and let out a rush of words with it, all run together: 'He's-a-cadet-at the-Space-Academy-they'd—' She had to stop and breathe again. 'They'd throw him out.'

'I don't think so,' he said thoughtfully. 'I think we could manage it so they . . .' His voice trailed off.

'You don't know how tough they are there—' she insisted, and then stopped herself. 'I guess you do.'

He was silent for a moment, and then he said unexpectedly, 'Nope. You're right.' His voice was bitter. 'That's *exactly* what they'd do.' He sat and thought some more; then he smiled, looking very tired. 'All right. All we really care about with the father is the physical exam. If you want to get in touch with him yourself, and ask him to come in, using any name he wants, that would do it. Or if you'd rather, you can tell me, off the record, and I'll get in touch. But either way, you have my word his name won't get any farther than this chair without your permission.'

She thought about that. She ought to do it herself, but . . . 'I'd trust *you*,' she said. If that's all right. If you don't mind. I'd—just as lief not—I don't really want to see him, if I don't have to.'

'Any way you want it, kid.' He wrote down the name, when she told him, on a piece of paper from his memo pad. *Charles Bolido*. He drew a line slowly under the two words; then he looked up at her, and down at the pad again, and drew another line, very dark and swift, beneath the first.

'Look, Ceil, it's none of my business if you don't want to talk about it, but—well, are you sure you know what you want to do? Before I get in touch with the boy—well, put it this way: are you giving *him* a fair break? I gather you're not on very good terms any more, and you say he doesn't know about the baby. Maybe—'

'*No,*' she said.

He smiled. 'Okay, kid. It's your life, not mine. Only one thing: what do I do if *he* wants to see *you?* Suppose he *wants* to quit school and get married?'

'He won't,' she said, but she had to clear her throat before the words came out right. 'He won't.' And she remembered. . . .

. . . the grass was greener than any grass had ever been, and the water was bluer, and the sky was far and high above and beyond while he talked about the rockets that would take him on top of the fluffed-out clouds, and away beyond the other side of the powder-puff daytime moon. The sun trailed across the vaulting heaven, and the shade of the oak tree fell away from them. They were hot and happy, and he jumped up, and took her hands, and she stood up into his arms.

'Love you, babe,' he whispered in her ear.

She leaned back and looked up at him and in the streaming sunlight he seemed to be on fire with beauty and strength and youth and she said, 'I love you, Charlie,' savouring the words, tasting them, because she had never said them before.

She thought a frown crossed his face, but she wouldn't believe it, not then. He took her hand, and they ran together down into the water.

It wasn't till later, in the car, that she had to believe the frown; that was when he began explaining carefully, in great detail, what his plans were, what a Spaceman's life was like, and why he could not think about marriage, not seriously about any girl.

He never even knew it had been the first time for her, the only time. . . .

She couldn't explain all that. She sat still and looked at the man across the desk, the man with the nice smile and the understanding eyes and the quiet voice. *Charlie has wavy black hair,* she remembered; the Colonel's was sandy-coloured and straight, crew-cut. Charlie had broad shoulders and his skin was bronzed and he had a way of tilting his head so that he seemed to be looking off into the distance, too far for *her* to see. The Colonel was nice enough looking, but his skin was pale and his shoulders a little bit round—from working indoors, at a desk, all the time, she supposed. Only, when he looked at you, he *saw* you, and when he listened, he understood. She couldn't explain the whole thing, but of course she didn't have to . . . not to him.

'He won't want to,' she said quietly; she had no trouble talking now. 'If he says so, he won't really mean it. He—he *couldn't* give up the Space school. That's all he ever wanted. It's the only thing that matters to him.' She said it evenly, in a detached objective way, just the way she wanted to, and then she sat absolutely still, waiting for what he'd say.

He tapped his pencil, upside down, on the top of the desk. She couldn't see his face at all. Then he looked up, and he had a made-up smile on his face this time, a smile he didn't *mean*. He nodded his head a little. 'I see.' Then he stood up, and came around to the side of the desk where she was sitting, and put both his hands on her shoulders, and with his thumbs against the sides of her jaw, he tilted her face up, so she was looking straight at him.

'You're a good girl, Ceil.' He meant *that*. 'You're a hell of a good girl, and the chances are Charlie is a lot better than you give him credit for. *There*fore—' He laughed, and let go of her shoulders, and leaned back against the desk. '. . . I am *not* going to give you the the fond paternal kiss I had in mind a moment ago. You might misunderstand.' He grinned. 'Or you might *not*.'

He wanted her to go now. She stood up, but there was a feeling of something more she had to say. 'I wish you had,' was what she said, and she was horrified. She hadn't even *thought* that.

'All right,' he said. 'Let's pretend I did. Didn't you wear a coat?'

'I had a jacket. I guess I left it outside.'

He had the door open. 'I'll let you know how it turns out,' he promised her, and then he turned around and started talking to the Wac.

He didn't even see her out of the other door.

IV

ONCE EACH MONTH, on the average, a Miracle came to pass, and a woman entered Colonel Edgerly's office who seemed, in his judgment, emotionally fit to undertake a share of the job of giving 200 homeless, motherless, womb-less infants the kind of care that might help them grow up to be mature *human* beings.

He had thought the Miracle for this month was used up when Mrs. Leahy came in. It was a Major Miracle, after all, when one of these women could also pass the Medical and Security checks, as well as his own follows-ups with the formal psych tests. To date, in almost nine months of in-terviewing, there had been only three such Major Miracles.

Mrs. Serruto, the colonel suspected, was not going to be the fourth. But if she failed, it would likely be in Medics; meantime, he could have the satisfaction at least of turning in one more favourable preliminary report.

She came in the morning after his interview with Ceil, without an appointment, and totally unexpected—a gift, he decided, directly from a watchful Providence to him. Virtue had proved an inadequately self-sufficient reward through a restless night; but surely Mrs. Serruto had been Sent to make recompense.

Little girls with big blue eyes should keep their trans-ferences out of my office, he wrote rapidly on a crisp sheet of white paper. He underlined it, and added three large ex-clamation points. Then he filed it neatly in his bottom desk

drawer—the same one that held his unpublished article—
and turned to Mrs. Serruto with a smile. She was settled
and comfortable now, ready to talk; and so was he. He
pulled over an application pad, and began filling things in,
working his way to the bottom, and the important personal
questions.

He paused a moment at OCCUPATION—but it couldn't
happen twice. It didn't. 'Housewife,' she said quietly; then
she smiled and added, 'but I think I'm out of a job. That's
why I came.'

He listened while she told him about herself and her
family, and he actually began to hope. Her son was in the
Space Service already, on the Satellite. He'd just passed
his year of Probationary, and now the daughter-in-law had
qualified for a civilian job up there. The young wife and
the two grandsons had been living with her; the grandmother kept house, while the mother went to school, to
learn astronomical notation.

Now the girl was going up to be with her husband and
to work as an Observatory technician and secretary; the
boys would go to Yuma, to the school SpaServ maintained
for just that purpose.

'We weren't sure about the boys,' Mrs. Serruto explained.
'We talked it over every which way, whether they'd be
better off staying with me, or going to Yuma, but the way
they work it there, the children all have a turn to go up
Satellite on vacations, and they have an open radio connection all the time. And of course, it's such a wonderful
school. . . . It was just they seemed awfully young to be
on their own, but this way they'll be closer to their own
parents than if they were with me.'

'What made you decide on a Foster Parent job, Mrs.
Serruto?' *Let her just answer right once more,* he prayed, *to
whatever Providence had sent her there. Just once more*
'Most of the applicants here are a good deal younger than
you are,' he added. 'It's unusual to find a woman of your
age willing to start out in a strange place again.' He smiled.
'A *very* strange place.'

'I—Oh, it's foolish for me to try to fool you, isn't it?
You're a trained psychologist, I guess? Well, all the reasons
you'd think of are part of it: I'm not young, but I still have
my strength, thank the Lord, and I kind of *like* the idea

of something new. Lots of people my age feel that way; look at all the retired people who start travelling. And keeping house in the same town for thirty-two years can kind of give you a yen to see the world. But if you want the honest answer, sir, it's just that I *heard,* I don't know if it's true, but I heard that if you get one of these jobs, you spend your leaves on Satellite . . . ?'

She was watching him anxiously; he had to restrain his own satisfaction, so as not to mislead her. She wasn't in yet, by a long shot—but he was going to do everything he could to get her there.

'That's right,' he told her. 'In theory, you get four days off out of every twenty. The shuttle between Base and Satelitte is on a four-day schedule, and one FP out of every five is supposed to have leave each trip. Actually, that only gives you about 45 hours on the Satellite, allowing for shuttle-time. And at the beginning, you may not get leave as regularly as you will later on.' He realized what he was doing, and stopped himself, switching to a cautious third-person-impersonal. 'There's been a good deal of research done on what we call LGT, Mrs. Serruto—that's short for Low Gravity Tolerance. We don't know so much yet about no-grav, but they're collecting the data on that right now. There's a pamphlet with all the information we have so far; you'll get a copy to take home with you, and then if you still want to apply, and if you can pass the tests, there's a two-months' Indoctrination Course, mostly designed to prepare the candidate for the experience of living under Moon-grav conditions.

'The adjustment isn't easy, no matter how much we do to try and simplify it. But the leave schedule we're using has worked out, for regular SpaServ personnel. That is to say, we've cut down the incidence of true somatic malfunctions—'

She made a funny despairing gesture with hands and shoulders. He smiled. 'Put it this way: Low-grav and no-grav do have some direct—call it *mechanical* effects on the function of the human body. But most of these problems are cumulative. It takes—let's see, at Moon-grav, which is about one-sixth of what you're used to, it takes from ten to twelve months, in the average case, for any serious mechanical malfunctions to show up—I should have let you read the pamphlet first,' he said. 'They've got it all explained there, step by step.'

He paused hopefully, but she obviously didn't want to wait; she wanted to hear it now. 'Anyhow,' he went on, 'we found, by experimenting, that the total tolerance could be extended considerably by breaking up the period. To put it as simply as possible: the lower the gravity, the shorter the time before serious "structural" malfunctions begin to appear—you understand? When I say "structural" I mean not only that something isn't working right, but that there's been actual physical damage done to the body in some way, so that it *can't* work right.'

The faint frown went away, and she nodded eagerly.

'All right. The lower the gravity, the quicker the trouble. Also, the shorter the time-span, the more you can take. That is, a person whose total tolerance at any particular low gravity is, say, six weeks—taken at a stretch—can take maybe ten or twelve weeks if he does it a few days at a time with leaves spent at normal, or at least higher, gravity.

'The reason for this last fact is that even before the structural malfunctions begin to appear, most people start suffering from all kinds of illnesses—usually not serious, at first, but sometimes pretty annoying—and these are *psychogenic. . . .*'

He looked at her inquiringly, and she nodded, a little uncertainly.

'Very few of the body functions actually *depend* on gravity,' he explained. 'I mean *internal* functions. But all of us are *conditioned* to performing these functions under a normal Earth-gravity. A person's digestive system, for instance, or vasc—circulatory system, will work just as well with low gravity, or none; but it has to work a little differently. And the result is a certain amount of confusion in the parts of the brain that control what we call "involuntary" reflexes: so that the heart, for instance, tries to pump just as hard as it should to suit the environment it's in—and *at the same time* it may be getting messages from the brain to pump just as hard as it's used to doing.

'When that happens you *may*—or anyone may—develop a heart condition of some kind; but it's just as likely that the patient might come up with purely psychological symp-

toms. *Or* any one of the various psychogenic diseases that
result from ordinary internal conflicts, or anxiety states,
may develop instead—'

Now she was shaking her head in bewilderment again.
'Look,' he said. Enough was enough. 'This is all in the
reading matter you'll get when you leave today. And it's a
lot clearer than I can make it. For now, just take my word
for it, on account of the psych end of it, four months has
been set as the limit of unbroken Moon duty. However,
we've found that people can take up to a year there with
no bad effects at all, *if* they get frequent enough leave.
That's why it's set up the way it is now.'

'You mean one year is all?' she asked quickly. 'That's the
most?'

He shook his head. 'No. That's the standard tour of duty
on the present leave system. Here's how it works: You
sign a year's contract, which is really for sixteen months,
except the last four months are Earth leave. During the
twelve months on the moon, you get twenty per cent Satellite leave. That means you spend one-fifth of your time at
a higher gravity. Not Earth-normal: the Satellite's set at
threequarters—you know that?'

She shook her head. 'I didn't know. I knew it was less
than here on Earth, but the way Ed described things there,
I thought it was a lot less than that.'

'It probably would be,' he told her, 'if we didn't use the
Satellite for leaves for Base personnel and people from the
asteroid stations. Down to about one-half-grav, the bad effects are hardly noticeable, and there are technical reasons
why we'd prefer to have to maintain less spin on Satellite.
But threequarters is just about optimum for the short
leaves: high enough to restore your peace of mind, and low
enough to make it comparatively easy to readjust each
time.

'We used to have less frequent longer leaves on Earth—
usually a fifty per cent system, one month there, one here.
We changed it originally so as to avoid having our LG
people constantly exposed to high-grav in acceleration, as
well as to save rocket space, and travel time, and things
like that. Afterwards, we found out that we were getting
much easier adjustments back to LG after the short leave
at threequarters, instead of the longer one on Earth.'

'That makes sense,' she said thoughtfully. 'If you were picking the people who could take the low gravity best, they'd maybe have the most trouble with the acceleration.'

'Yes and no. Strictly, physiologically, it tends to work that way; psychologically it's just the opposite, usually. And all this is in the prepared literature too.' He smiled at her, and determinedly changed the subject. 'Now what we've got to do is arrange for your physical. If it's all right with you, I'd like to get an appointment set up right away, for as soon as possible. Frankly, that's going to be your toughest hurdle here. If you get past that, I don't think we'll have too much more to worry about. But don't kid yourself that it's going to be easy.'

'I'm pretty healthy, Colonel.' She smiled comfortably. 'My people were farmers, over there and over here; I think they call it "peasant stock"? And I've been lucky. I always lived good.'

'For fifty-two years,' he reminded her gently. 'That's not *old*—but forty is old in SpaServ. Remember, the whole reasoning behind this Project is that if we catch 'em young enough, we think we can train the kids to get along under no-grav conditions. And at your age, even acceleration can be a problem. Anyhow—'

He stood up, and she started gathering her coat and purse together. She was wonderful, he thought, almost unbelievable, after most of the others who came in here: a woman, no more, no less—a familiar, likable, motherly, competent, womanly kind of woman. When it came to psych tests (*if* it got that far, he had to remind himself, as he'd been trying to remind her), he knew she'd come up with every imaginable symptom and psychic disorder . . . in small, safe quantities. A little of this, and a little of that, and the whole adding up to the rare and 'balanced' personality.

'Anyhow,' he said, 'there's no sense talking any more till after you see the Medics.' He led her out to Helen's desk, got her appointment lined up, and made sure she was provided with duly informative literature. Then he saw her out, and went back to his desk, to plot.

The routine report he kept routine. That was no place to urge special allowances or special treatment. He mentioned the SpaServ connections, of course, but did not emphasize them. If the General read carefully, that would be enough. But he had to be *sure*.

He laid out his strategy with care, and found two items pending in his files that would serve his purpose: neither very urgent, either capable of assuming an appearance of immediate importance. Satisfied, he went out to lunch, and from there over to Henderson College to see the Dean again. He outlined to her his conversation with Ceil the day before—or at least some of it. The only part of that interview that concerned Sarah Lazarus was in connection with the young man at the Academy.

'When I thought it over,' he explained, 'it seemed to me it might cause some embarrassing questions all around if I were to approach the boy myself. I'm not in a position to say, "Personal", and not be asked any more. So I wondered if you . . .' He let it slide off, waiting to see what she'd offer.

'What was it exactly you wanted me to do?' she hedged.

'Write to him. That's all that would be necessary. They don't censor incoming mail there. Or if you'd rather not have anything down on the record, a phone call could do it.'

She nodded thoughtfully. 'I suppose . . .' she began slowly, then made up her mind. 'Of course. I'll take care of it. What's the young man's name?'

'I'm afraid,' he smiled, 'we'll have to get Ceil's permission before I tell you that. I made some powerful promises yesterday.' ‾

'I know,' she said, and he looked at her, startled. 'Cecille came in to see me yesterday evening,' she explained, enjoying her moment of superior knowledge. 'She said she wanted to thank me for—for "being so wonderful", I think she said. I believe she *meant* for not tossing her out on her ear as soon as I had heard the *awful truth*.'

'She comes from a—rather old-fashioned family?'

'That's one way of putting it. Her father is a very brilliant man in his line of work, I understand—something technical. He is also a boss-fearing, Hell-fearing, foreigner-fearing, bigoted, narrow-minded, one-sided, autocratic, petty, self-centred domestic tyrant. He spoils his wife and daughter with pleasure, as long as they abide by his principles—and his wife is a flexible, intelligent, family-loving woman who decided a long time ago that his principles had better be hers. Yes—I'd say it was an old-fashioned family. A fine family, if you stick to the rules.'

He nodded. 'That's about the way I figure it.'

The Dean cleared her throat. 'Anyhow, Cecille spent an hour or more with me last night, and after she got done telling me how wonderful *I* was, she started on what *really* interested her.'

'She's already told you about him? Well, good. That makes it easier.'

'No.'

Again he was startled, but only for an instant. He knew what was coming now, and he had time to cover his responses. Her technique was still lousy—but maybe it worked on her students.

'No,' she said. 'The rest was all about *you*.' She was watching him closely—of course. 'I suppose,' she asked thoughtfully, 'that happens fairly often? A girl in trouble comes to see you, and finds you a sympathetic saviour, and promptly decides she's in love?'

'Sometimes,' he admitted. 'I didn't think Ceil had quite reached that stage yet. I was even hoping she might avoid it.'

'She didn't put it that way herself.'

'It's annoying most of the time,' he told her. 'Sometimes, it's flattering as all hell.' He grinned, and refused further comment; when she laughed, he thought he detected a note of relief. He hoped he had said enough, and not too much.

'If you want to wait a minute,' she said, 'I'll get her up here now, and we can get this settled.'

He glanced at his watch. 'Fine!' And it was. Ceil came up, looked in horror from one to the other, and, as soon as she could breathe out again, asked, pleading, *'What's wrong?'*

His own laughter and the Dean's mingled, and when the girl had gone again, much relieved, the faint edge of doubt or suspicion between the man and the woman was gone too. He promised to get in touch with her as soon as he heard from the boy, and got back to his own office in plenty of time for the afternoon's carefully mapped campaign.

About 3:30, and for an hour afterwards, there was usu-

ally a lull in the General's afternoon. At 3:45, the Colonel
went upstairs with his knotty-looking little problem, and
got his expected sequence of responses: irritation at being
bothered when no bother was looked for, followed by the
gratification at having so easily solved a really minor difficulty the Colonel had apparently been unable to untangle
for himself.

'Takes the organizational mind, Tom,' the General said
jovially. 'I guess you have to get older, though, before you
begin to get the broad view most of the time.' He took his
4 o'clock cigar from the humidor, and offered one to the
Colonel.

'No thanks. I think I'll have to get older to appreciate
those, too.' He lit himself a cigarette, and held the lighter
for the other man.

'You'll get there,' the General puffed. 'See you finally
broke down,' he added, grunting around the fat cigar. 'Let
one of those ladies get past you.'

'I got tired of saying *no*. I'm afraid she won't get too far,
though.'

The General raised an inquiring eyebrow. 'Haven't studied the report yet, but looked okay, quick glance.' Fragrant
smoke rolled over the words, and swallowed up some of
them.

'She's not *young*,' the Colonel said hesitantly. 'I—well,
frankly, I was making some allowance for the fact that her
son and daughter are stationed in Satellite—'

'Oh? SpaServ?' He was interested now.

'The boy is. Five-year hitch, I think. I thought it might
make her more likely to stick with us, if she lasts out one
year.'

'Tom, you got a positive *tal*ent—' The General even took
the cigar out of his mouth to indulge himself in the lately
rare luxury of using the faintly Southern-Western-home-
folks manner that had done so much to put him where he
was today. '—a *tal*ent, I tell you, for seein' things wrong-
end hind-to.'

Edgerly made the politely inquiring sound that was indicated.

'Naturally, I mean, we want re-enlistments. But that's
next year, and frankly, Tom, off the record, by the time we
can get her up there and she's worked a year and had her

four months' leave, you and me, we're going to be wearing the skin off our backsides some place else *al*together. But don't get me wrong.' He chuckled warmly, and reinserted the cigar. 'You wan' make 'lownces, you make 'em, *any* reason you want.'

The Colonel stayed a few more minutes, till his cigarette was finished and he could politely leave. But on the way home, he stopped down in Medical, and dragged Bill Sawyer out with him for a drink.

It took two before Bill got around to it.

'That dame you called us on today—what's her name, Sorrento?'

'Serruto.'

'Yeah. Did you put a bug in the Old Man's ear, or what?'

'Me? What kind of bug?'

'Oh, he was dropping gentle hints all over me this afternoon. Real gentle. One of them hit my toe, and I think the bone's broken. He thinks she ought to pass her Medic.'

'She's not *young*,' Edgerly said judiciously.

'No. But she's got a son in SpaServ, and after all, we *do* try to make some allowances, keep family together—hell, *you* know!'

The Colonel grinned. 'What you need is a drink.'

'You know, I never thought of that!' The doctor chuckled. 'Hey! Remember that babe you were all steamed up about? Canadian. She'd lost her forearm . . . ?'

'Yeah, Buonaventura. And I still don't see what damn difference sixteen inches of good honest plastic and wire instead of flesh and blood could make on the Moon.'

'Regulations, son, regulations. That's what I was thinking about. Maybe if you could fix it for *her* to get a son into SpaServ . . .'

'About twenty years from now, you mean?'

'Well, she wasn't exactly a knockout, but she wouldn't be hard to take. Maybe I'd co-operate myself.'

'Leave those little things to us bachelors,' the Colonel said sternly. 'No married man should have to sacrifice that way for the Service.'

The waiter came with fresh drinks, and they concentrated on refreshing themselves for a short time. 'Just the same,' Edgerly said seriously, 'I wish we could get more young ones like that. . . . I guess it's six of one and you-

know-what of the other. The young ones wouldn't want
to stay more than a year or maybe two . . . this Buonaventura gal, for instance. You know, her husband was
killed in the same accident where she lost her arm. Honeymoon and all that. So she wanted to go be real busy for a
while, till she could start thinking about another man. But
any *young* woman who was healthy enough in the head to
trust up there would just be putting in time, the same
way . . .'

'Okay, but these grandmas you're sending up aren't going to be able to take any more than one or two tours,
anyhow,' Sawyer put in.

'That's what I meant. You can't win.'

'What you need,' said the doctor, 'is a drink.'

'You know, that's an idea. . . .'

V

FOR A LITTLE while, there was the illusion that things were
improving, all around. Tuesday, the same day Serruto was
winding up her 38-hour session in Medic, there was a letter from one Adam Barton, asking if an appointment for
the necessary examinations could be arranged sometime
between November 27 and 30. Thanksgiving leave, the
Colonel realized, and phoned down himself to set it up.
They'd been trying to keep the weekend free for the staff,
but this one would have to go through.

He managed to keep himself from asking about Mrs.
Serruto; they wouldn't have a final answer till late afternoon. Then, on impulse, he phoned Sarah Lazarus, and
asked her to have lunch with him.

'Celebration. Space Service owes you something,' he explained.

'More than you know,' she replied, but wouldn't say any
more on the phone, except to suggest that in her own opinion she was entitled to a *good* lunch.

Over hors d'oeuvres, and the remains of a ladylike Du-
bonnet, she explained: she had neither written nor tele-
phoned to Barton-Bolido; she had gone to see him instead.

'When I thought it over, it seemed too awkward any other way,' she said. 'It's only about a three-hour drive, and I understood they had visiting Sunday afternoon.'

'We can reimburse you for the expense,' the Colonel offered. 'We have a special fund for that kind of thing. . . .'

'So do *we*,' she said. 'The expense was the least of it. If you could reimburse me for the—what do they call it— "mental agony" . . . ?'

'I take it you had something of a heart-to-heart talk?' He was very genuinely curious. 'Is Ceil's impression of him anywhere near accurate?'

'*I* don't know what Ceil's impressions are,' she said drily. 'Which kind of evens the score, doesn't it?' She attacked a casserole of beef-burgundy sauté, with apparent uninterest in continuing the conversation.

'All right,' he laughed. 'I surrender. One betrayal deserves another. *He* wouldn't be very likely to talk to *me*, you know.' He told her what the girl had said, and she nodded.

'That's about it—except he happens to be crazy about her, so this bit of news has really got him in a tizzy. He'd managed to "forget" about her, he said, since the summer —convincing himself that it was best to let the whole thing drop—don't see her any more, don't write—*you* know? And it makes sense. He does have his handsome little heart set on SpaServ—see, I'm learning the lingo? I'll have the pastry,' she told the waiter, with no change of tone or tempo. 'Anyhow, he can't marry for the next two years, till he graduates. And after that, there's a four-year . . . hitch?'

He nodded soberly.

'Hitch, before he can even *hope* to get permission to have his family with him, wherever he is—provided it's some place where he can *have* a family.'

'It will be,' he told her. 'Policy is shaping up that way. They're encouraging wives to go up Satellite now, and any station with enough gravs for moderate good health will be opened for families as fast as possible. The boys seem to last longer that way, and work better.'

She was interested. He would have liked to hear more about Charles, but that was personal curiosity, which would in any case be satisfied later on. There was more urgent business for this luncheon, and it was already getting late. He answered her questions, more or less completely but always with a direction in mind, and eventually they came round to the Foster Parent problem.

'I'm sweating one out today,' he told her. 'Maybe that's why I decided to use you as an excuse for a good lunch. It's not easy to find the right people, and half the time, when I do get someone I'm satisfied with, she can't get past the Medics. Stands to reason: the kind I want are likely to have led pretty busy lives, and mostly they run to older women—*old,* that is, in SpaServ terms—forty and fifty. The one I'm waiting to hear about is fifty-two. If her heart will stand up to blast-off acceleration, she *may* make it. But you never know what kind of ruination those boys can pull out of their infernal machines.'

'What you need is a good old-fashioned diagnostician,' she said, laughing. 'The kind that looked you over and told you in five minutes what was wrong—and turned out to be right.'

He shook his head sadly. 'We're not even allowed to do *that* in psych clinics any more. If you can't tab it up on IBM or McBride cards, it just ain't so.' He sipped at his coffee, which was cold, but—by design—not yet empty. 'I'll tell you what we *do* need, though,' he said seriously.

'What?'

'More Foster Parents.'

She gave him that studying look again. 'Just what is it you're trying to tell me, Colonel?'

'Nothing at all,' he said steadily, returning her look. 'Just chitchat over lunch. I *did* have a notion about how to publicize our problem in the quarters where it might do the most good: educators, social workers, people like that. But I haven't been able to get official authorization for it yet, so . . .'

Deliberately, he paused and sipped again at the cold coffee. '. . . so naturally, this is all just idle talk. I'm not *trying* to tell you anything; I'm just answering your questions.'

She was sipping her own coffee when he tried to get a look at her face. When he dropped her off at the College, she hadn't revealed any reaction. They said a friendly goodbye, and he thanked her again for her efforts with the young man, then drove back fast. It was mid-afternoon already, and the report on Mrs. Serruto—

The report was on his desk when he got back. He read it through, and sank back in his chair to find out what it felt like to relax.

The General had given him till October 9 to find a satisfactory FP. Today was the seventh.

He swivelled his chair around to look out of the window, at the wide sweep of the mountain range, the dark shapes, green-blue and purple, pushing up into the pale-blue sky of the mesa country. Life was good. For some minutes, he did nothing at all but fill his vision with colour and form, and allow his excellent lunch to be digested. Finally he turned back to the desk and riffled through papers in the *Hold* basket till he found the Schedule that had come with the General's last memo.

Mrs. Serruto would be ready for the rocket on December 9. They didn't have to have another one till January 6. After that, one on each bi-weekly shipment, at least through February.

January 6, less two months' training, left him 30 days. Serruto had been blind luck; he couldn't count on that again. He buzzed Helen, and dictated a brief memo for the General, asking for a conference, soon, on his proposals about publicity. Half-way through, the phone rang in the outer office. He picked it up on his desk, and it was Sarah Lazarus.

God is on my side, he thought. He had hardly expected to hear from her so soon, after her stubbornly non-committal silence during lunch.

She had enjoyed the luncheon, she said, and wanted to thank him again.

'You earned it,' he told her. 'Besides which, the pleasure was at least half mine.' *Or will be, when you get around to what's on your mind. . . .*

'The other thing I wanted to ask you about,' she said, 'was whether Thanksgiving weekend would be all right for our girl's visit?'

Not with the Medics it wouldn't, but he assured her it would. They had the boy coming in that Friday anyhow. The Colonel mentally apologized to God for his presumption.

'You said five days, I think?'

"Fi—oh, for the . . . *visit*. Yes. She ought to be here two days ahead of time, and then it's usually best to wait at least two days afterwards.'

'Well—maybe she'd better come in at the beginning of the week. That will give her a chance to get dramatically ill in class. And it will work out better when I tell her parents, I think.'

'Any way you want it,' he assured her. 'It's far enough ahead so the schedule's pretty open. Especially with our present curtailments. . . .' He waited.

'Oh, yes,' she said. 'That's right. I'd forgotten.' Then, very sweetly, she asked him if he would care to come to dinner at her home on Saturday evening.

It's your deal, lady, he thought; all he could do was pick up the cards and play them as they came.

'Cocktails start at six,' she said, and gave him an address. He hung up, trying to remember whether he had ever heard any reference to a *Mr.* Lazarus. That cocktail-chatter sounded like a big party, but her tone of voice didn't. He shrugged, and turned back to his secretary, who was waiting with an inevitable expression of intelligent detachment.

'Make a note, Sergeant. Remind me to buy a black tie. I'm in the social whirl now.'

She made the note, too. Nothing he could do now would save him from being reminded. He favoured the Perfect Lady Soldier with a look of mingled awe, horror, and affection, and got on with the business of dictating his reminder to the General. . . .

Brigadier General Harlan Foley Martin, U.N.S.S., resplendent in full uniform, with the blazing-sun insignia of SpaServ shining on his cap, was conducting a party of visitors through his personal domain: the newest, cleanest, finest building in the entire twenty-seven acres that made up the North American Moon Base Supply Depot—which was beyond doubt the biggest, cleanest, fastest and generally bestest Depot anywhere on Earth.

It was of particular importance that these (self-evident) facts should be brought to the attention of the visitors, against the time when they returned to their respective Depots in South Africa, North Asia, and Australia, to establish similar centres in which to carry out their share of the important and inspiring work of Project Nursemaid.

Half a dozen duly humble seekers after knowledge followed at his heels (metaphorically speaking; in actual practice, the General politely ushered them ahead of him through doors and narrow passageways), drinking in wisdom, observing efficiency, and uttering appropriate expressions of admiration.

The General felt it was time for a bit of informality, and there was no better way than in a display of that indifference to rank and protocol for which the Normerican Section was famous. Accordingly, he headed straight for the office of his Psychological Aide, Colonel Edgerly. There were times when it was possible to place a good deal of faith in the Colonel's judgment and behaviour.

Edgerly rose to the occasion. He showed them through his Department, explained the psych-testing equipment in three languages, and excused himself from accompanying them further on account of the press of his own work.

In the waiting-room, as they took leave of the Colonel, the General drew the attention of the visiting gentlemen away from the admirable example of Normerican soldiery behind the reception desk with a typical display of typical Normerican informality.

'Oh, by the way, Tom, before I forget it—I've been too busy the last day or two, but I saw your memo on that idea of yours, and I want the two of us to get together some time and talk it over. Some time *soon*. . . .' He smiled, and the Colonel smiled back.

'Well, let's set up a date now.' Edgerly turned to the Sergeant behind the desk.

'Oh, no need for that, Tom. Just give me a ring, or I'll drop in on you. Any time, any time at all. . . .'

The General and his party proceeded to examine the hospital facilities on a lower floor.

Colonel Edgerly reknotted his tie, adjusted the angle of his cap, and stepped out of his car in front of one of the city's better apartment houses. A doorman led him to the proper elevator, and pushed the appropriate button for him. He stepped out into a foyer done in walnut wood and cream-coloured plaster. As the elevator door closed, a chime rang softly in a room behind the floral-printed draperies, and he had hardly time to savour the nostalgia the decor had produced before his hostess pulled the drapes aside and asked him in.

She was wearing a black dinner dress that displayed, among other things, a rather different personality from the one she wore in her office. However, there *was* a Mr. Lazarus, and five or six other guests besides.

They drank cocktails and engaged in party conversation until one more couple arrived. The dinner was well-cooked and well-served, and eaten to the accompaniment of some remarkably civilized table talk, plus an excellent wine and subdued background music. Afterwards, three more couples came in, and by the time the last of them arrived, the Colonel's opinion of his hostess—already improved by her home, her dress, her food and drink—had reached a peak of admiration and appreciation. Out of thirteen persons present that evening, every one except three escorting husbands—*every* other one was an upper-echelon executive of some social service agency, woman's club, child care organization, or adult educational centre.

The Colonel did not proselytize, nor did he mention any specific difficulties the Project was having. There was no need to do either. The guests that evening had come specifically to meet him, because they were curious and interested and felt themselves inadequately informed about Project Nursemaid. He had nothing to do but answer eager intelligent questions put to him by alert and understanding people—and in the course of answering, it took no more than an occasional shift of emphasis to convey quite clearly that the Project's capacity for handling PN's must necessarily depend in large part on its success in finding satisfactory Foster Parents.

'Did you say before that you preferred older women for these jobs, Colonel?' He looked around for the questioner: a slim tailored woman with a fine-drawn face and clean, clear skin; she looked as though she belonged on a country estate with dogs and horses and a prize-winning garden. For the moment, he couldn't remember her name, or which outfit she was connected with.

'No. Not at all. If I mentioned anything like that, it should have been by way of complaint. The fact is that most of the people who satisfy our other requirements *are* older women—older in SpaServ terms, anyhow. Most of our candidates are, for that matter. Women under the age of forty, if they're healthy, well-balanced personalities, are either busy raising their own families, or else they're even busier looking for the right man to get started with. From the Medical viewpoint, we'd a lot rather get younger people. And for that matter, I think they might suit our purposes better all around—the right kind, that is.'

'I see. I was particularly interested, because we've been doing some intensive work lately on the problem of jobs for women over thirty-five, and I thought if we knew just what you wanted . . . ?' She let it drift off into a pleasant white-toothed smile, one feathery eyebrow barely raised to indicate the question-mark at the end. He remembered now —Jane Somebody, from Aptitudes, Inc., the commercial guidance outfit. He struggled for the last name.

'I think Miss Sommers has a good point there, Colonel.' This was the dumpy little woman with the bright black eyes, sitting on the hassock across from him. *Sommers, that's right! Next time I'll put Sergeant Gregory in my pocket to take notes.* 'I hate to pester you so much on your night out, but I think several of us here might be able to send you people occasionally, if we knew a little more about just what you want.'

This one he remembered: she was the director of the Beth Shalom Family Counselling Service. 'Believe me, Mrs. Goldman, I can't think of any way I'd rather be pestered. I just wish I'd known beforehand what I was getting into. I'd have come prepared with a mimeographed list of requirements to hand out at the door.' With complete irrelevance, the thought flashed through his mind that the Sergeant never *had* reminded him about that black tie. *You're slipping, old girl!* he thought, and smiled at Mrs. Goldman. 'As it is—well, it takes about a week to complete the testing of an applicant. If I tried to tell you in detail what we want, Mrs. Lazarus might get tired of our company after a while. I think you probably know in general what personality types are suitable for that kind of work. Beyond that, probably it would work better for you to ask any specific questions you have in mind, and let me try to answer them.'

'Well, I *was* wondering—are you only taking women, or are you interested in men too? There's one couple I had in mind; they're young and healthy and what psychological problems they've got are all centred on the fact that they can't have any kids of their own, and because he's a freelance artist with no steady income, they can't adopt one. I think they might like to go, for a year or two . . . ?'

There was no point in telling her that the chances were a thousand to one they'd never pass the psychs. Nobody had ever proved that most cases of sterility were psychogenic, but the Project had, so far, built up some fascinating correlations between certain types of sexual fears and childlessness; and then the 'free-lance artist' . . . He satisfied himself with answering the question she'd asked, and the other important one implied in her last sentence.

'We'd be delighted to have couples, if we can get them. We haven't taken any men so far, but we've got a couple on our reserve list. We want them later on, but for the immediate future, we need women in the nursery. One other point, though . . . what you said about "a year or two".

'We're signing people up for one-year contracts. One year's duty, and four months' leave, that is. We're doing it that way for several reasons: we want to be able to re-test everyone medically before we renew contracts; and we want to check actual records of behaviour on duty and psychosomatic responses against our psych tests. A few other things, too, but all of 'em boil down to the fact that we *think* we know what we're doing, but we're not sure yet. However—

'If it weren't for the special problems of LGT, we'd— well, obviously, if it weren't for those problems, the Project wouldn't be necessary at all—but since it is necessary, we're still hampered by the same limitations. We'd like to provide permanent Foster Parents for each group of children. We can't do that, for the same reason we can't just send whole families up there: the adults can't take it that long. Even with the present leave system, five years is prob-

ably going to be the maximum—five years' duty, that is,
with four-month intervals on Earth between each tour.

'Right at this point, we're just not in a position to in-
sist that anyone who goes should agree to put in the
maximum number of tours—I mean whatever maximum
the Medics decide on for the individual person. We can't
do it, because it's more important just to get people *up*
there. But we would if we could.'

He broke off, uncomfortably aware that he was monop-
olizing the floor. 'I'm sorry. I seem to be making a
speech.'

'Well, go ahead and make it,' Mrs. Lazarus said easily.
'It's a pretty good one.'

'I'm just letting off steam,' he laughed. 'This is my pet
frustration. Right now, the Project, or our division, has
the specific job of supplying personnel, and we're not supposed to worry about the continuation of the Project five
or ten years from now. But I'm the guy who's supposed to
pick the right people to do the job—and I *can't* pick them
without thinking in terms of what will happen to those
kids when they're five years old and fifteen and twenty.'

'I think I understand your difficulty a little bit, Colonel.'
It was a quiet, very young-sounding voice from across the
room. 'We have something of the same problem to face.' He
picked her out now: the nun, Mother Mary Paul. One of
the orders specializing in social work; Martha . . . ? Yes:
Order of Martha of Bethany. 'Some of the children who
come to us are orphans; others are from homes temporarily
unable to care for them; some are day students; some are
students who live in the convent. Most of them, in one way
or another, are from homes where they have not received—
well, quite as much as one might hope a happy home could
provide. We want to give them the *feeling* of having a
home with us—and yet, we know that most of them will be
leaving us and going to their own families, or adopted
families, or other schools. It's—rather a harder job, I think,
to give a small child a sense of security and of *belonging*,
when you know yourself that the time will come when the
child must be handed over to someone else's care. I know I
tend to demand a good deal more of the sisters going into
orphanage work than a family qualifying for adoption.'

'You've said that better than I could have—' What were

you supposed to call her? Not *Sister;* he gathered she was too high up in her order. *Mother? Your Reverence?* He compromised by omitting any title, and hoped the omission was not an offence. 'About the sense of belonging. Ideally, of course, the children should be in families, with permanent adoptive parents. But we have to juggle the needs of the children against the limitations of the adults. The kids need permanence; but the grown-ups just can't last long enough under the conditions. So to even up the books, an FP, Foster Parent, has to be something pretty special: a mature woman with the health of a young girl—a sane and balanced personality just sufficiently off keel to want to go to the Moon—someone with the devotion of a nun, who has no very pronounced doctrinal beliefs . . . I could go on and on like that, but what it all comes down to is that the kind of people we want are useful and productive right here on Earth, and mostly much too busy to think about chasing off to the Moon.'

There was a general laugh, and people started moving about, shifting groups, debating the wisdom of one more drink. The Colonel debated not at all. He took a refill happily, and turned away from the bar to find himself being converged upon. Mrs. Goldman, Mother Mary Paul, and a Dr. Jonas Lutwidge, pastor of the local Episcopal Church, and a big wheel of some kind in the city's interdenominational social welfare organization.

They did not exactly all speak at once, but the effect was the same: What, they wanted to know, had he meant by 'no pronounced doctrinal beliefs'?

The Colonel drank deeply, and began explaining, grateful that this had come up, if it had to, in a small group, and equally glad that he had thoughtfully provided himself with a double shot of whisky in this glass.

The broad view first: '. . . you realize that there will be, altogether, one thousand babies involved in this Project. Two hundred of them will come through our Depot. The rest will be from every part of the world, from every nationality, every faith, every possible variation of political and social background. The men and women who care for them, and who educate them, will not necessarily be from the same backgrounds at all. . . .' And world governments being still new, and human beings still very much creatures of habit and custom, there was no guarantee that bias and discrimination could be ruled out in the Project except by the one simple device that would make anything of the sort *impossible*.

From the individual viewpoint: 'These kids are going to grow up in an environment almost entirely alien, from the Earth viewpoint. They'll spend their time half on Moon Base, and half on the no-grav training ship. They won't have parents, in the sense in which we use the term, or families, or any of the other factors that go to forming the human personality. Maybe we could grow us a thousand supermen this way, but frankly we don't want to find out. We might not *like* them; they might even not like *us*. . . .' Therefore every effort was going to be made to provide a maximum of artificial 'family' life. The babies would be assigned, shortly after birth, to a group of five 'brothers and sisters'; Foster Parents in the group would necessarily change from time to time, but whenever a contract was renewed, the parent would go back to the same group. There would be a common group-designation, to be used as a last name; even first names were to be given by the first FP to assume the care of each baby. 'It's all part of what you were saying before, Mother,' he pointed out. 'We want the Foster Parents to *feel and act* as much as possible as if these were their own children; unfortunately, the physical setup is such that the opportunities to create such situations are few enough. We have to use every device we can.'

Obviously, under these circumstances, religious training could not be given in accordance with the child's ancestry. The solution finally decided upon had been to invite all religious groups to select representatives to participate in the children's education. They would all be exposed to every form of religious belief, and could choose among them. A compromise at best—and one that could work only by a careful system of checks and balances, and by making certain, insofar as possible, that the proselytizing was done *only* by the official representatives, and not by evangelical Foster Parents.

Mother Mary Paul and Mrs. Goldman both seemed tentatively satisfied with the explanation. Dr. Lutwidge was

inclined to argue, but Sarah Lazarus came to the Colonel's
rescue with a polite offer of coffee which drew their attention to the noticeable absence of the other guests.

It was almost one o'clock when Edgerly got home, in a
glow of pleased excitement, and in no mood for bed. He
stalked through the four rooms of his bachelor cottage,
surveying everything with profound distaste, and sat up for
an hour more, making sketches and notes about the im-
provements he meant to effect. Next morning, on his way
to work, he stopped at a florist's for the brown jug and
yellow roses that he had felt, all evening, should have been
on the table in that foyer. Briefly, he debated drawing on
the Special Account to cover the cost, and decided against
it; he had made his gesture now towards Better Living, and
could leave his own home alone.

Within a week, the number of FP applicants in his office
began to increase; within three weeks, he had another successful candidate. His working day, which had for a short
time been quiet and peaceful, resumed its normal pace, an
hour or two behind schedule. And if the General still had
failed to authorize the publicity campaign which the Colonel had already *unofficially* initiated, at least the Old Man
had done nothing to impede it, and was showing a remarkable tendency to stay entirely out of the Psych Dept.'s hair.

This was good, up to a point. But by the middle of November, when the first rush of applicants referred by the
Dean's friends had begun to diminish and he had found
only one more acceptable candidate, the Colonel began to
feel the need of an official authorization that would make it
possible to carry his campaign farther abroad. The people
he'd met were all local; some had state-wide influence,
others only in the immediate area. The Depot represented
a territory that covered all of what had once been Canada,
Alaska, and the U.S.A., plus part of Mexico.

The Colonel chafed a while, then sent another memo,
asking for a conference on his suggestions of five weeks
ago. For some days afterwards, he watched and waited for
a response. Then another satisfactory applicant turned up,
and he was busy with psych-tests and briefing interviews for
the better part of a week. He checked off the second
January rocket on his schedule, and offered up a brief

prayer to whatever Deity had been looking out for him, that another such woman should come his way before the third of December.

And then it was Thanksgiving week.

VI

MONDAY AFTERNOON, Ceil Chanute was admitted to the Project infirmary. Tuesday morning, Dean Lazarus called to report that she had informed the girl's family of her illness, and had successfully headed off any efforts at coming out to visit her. Wednesday morning, the day her operation was scheduled, the Colonel came in early and had breakfast with Ceil in the Med staff-room. He saw no reason to tell her that this was standard practice whenever possible, and when he went upstairs he was basking in the glow of her evident pleasure at what she thought a special attention.

He spent most of the morning dealing swiftly and efficiently with correspondence; the only time he hesitated was over one handwritten letter, from a town a hundred miles away. This he read carefully, then slid it into his pocket, to handle personally later on.

At 4:30 that afternoon Ruth Mackintosh came in. She was the most recent of his successful candidates, now in her first week of regular training, and part of the process was a daily hour in his office, mostly to talk over any problems or questions of hers—partly to allow him continuous observation of her progress and her attitudes.

At five-oh-four the sergeant, out at the desk, buzzed him with the news that the operation on the Chanute girl was completed, without complications, and she would be coming out of anaesthesia shortly. The Colonel repeated the news for his visitor's benefit, explaining that he might have to leave in a hurry, if Ceil began to wake up.

'Oh, of course—maybe you'd rather go down now?'

He would. For some idiotic reason, he said instead; 'It'll be ten or fifteen minutes anyhow.'

'I wish I'd known,' she said. 'I was going to ask you if I could see an operation before I went up.'

That was a new one. 'Have you ever watched an operation before?'

'Well, I used to be a practical nurse; I've seen plenty of home deliveries, and I saw a Caesarian done once—oh, you mean, will it upset me? No.' She laughed. 'I don't think so.'

That wasn't what he'd meant. 'Why do you want to see it?' he asked slowly. With some people the best way to get an answer was to ask a direct question.

'I don't know—I just want to see as much as I can, know as much as I can about the babies and what's happened to them already, and where they come from, and—if you people weren't so obviously oriented in the opposite direction, I'd want to meet the mothers, too, as many as I could.'

Wonderful—if true. He scribbled a note to check over certain of her tests for repressed sadistic leanings, and told her, 'We're not oriented the other way *entirely*. In fact, we've changed our feeling about that several times already. Just now, I don't think it would be possible for you to meet any of the parents, but I think we can manage a pass to see a section performed. I'll check.'

He reached for the phone, but it buzzed before he could get to it. He listened, and turned back to Mrs. Mackintosh.

'I'm afraid I am going to have to run out on you.' He stood up. 'The kid downstairs is coming out of it now—you understand?'

'Of course.' She stood up, and followed him to the door. 'Do you want me to wait, or . . . ?'

'If you'd like to. Check with Sergeant Gregory here. She'll give you all the dope about getting that pass. And if you want to wait, that's fine, unless the Sergeant says I'm going to be busy. She knows better than I do.' He wanted to get out of the other door and downstairs. The feeling of urgency was unreasonable, but it was there. 'Helen,' he said briskly, 'you get things worked out with Mrs. Mackintosh. I'll be downstairs if you want me. Sorry to rush off like this,' he told the other woman again. 'Helen'll set up another appointment for us. Or wait if you want.' *That's the* third *time I said that*, he thought irritably, and stopped trying to make sense, or to say anything at all.

He had the satisfaction, at least, as he went out of the door, of one quick glimpse of the Perfect Lady Soldier, out of control. Helen was flabbergasted . . . and it showed.

Waiting for the elevator, he wondered what she thought. Going down in the elevator, he was sure he knew. And striding down the corridor on the hospital floor, he was dismayed to consider that she might possibly be right.

He had some news for Ceil Chanute, tucked away in his jacket pocket—news he had withheld all morning, uncertain what effect it might have on her, and therefore unwilling to deliver it before the operation. True enough, he ought to be on hand when she woke up; it *might* be what she'd want to hear. True, but *not* true *enough*—not enough to warrant his indecent haste.

He made himself slow down before he reached the nurse's cubicle outside the Infirmary. When he went inside, he had already made up his mind that his concern about his own behaviour was ridiculous anyhow. An occasional extra show of interest in an individual case—*any* case— was *not* necessarily the same thing as an unprofessional personal involvement.

Not *necessarily,* echoed a sneaky, cynical voice in the back of his mind.

He reached the bed, and abandoned introspection. She was awake, not yet entirely clear-minded, but fully conscious. He sat down on the chair right next to her head, and picked up her limp hand.

'How's the girl?'

'I'll live.' She managed a sort of a smile.

'Feeling bad?'

'All right . . .'

'Hungry?'

She shook her head.

'Thirsty?' She hesitated, then nodded. 'Water? Tea? Lemonade? Ginger ale?' She just smiled, fuzzily. The nurse, standing at the foot of the bed, looked to him for decision. 'Tea,' he said, but the girl shook her head. 'Something cold,' she murmured.

The nurse went away, and the Colonel leaned back in the chair, to an angle where he could watch her face without making her uncomfortably aware of it. 'I've got some news for you,' he said.

She turned her head to look at him, suddenly worried.

'Take it easy, kid. If it was anything bad, I wouldn't tell

you *now*. Just that you'll have some company tonight—*if* you want to.'

'Company . . . ?' Her eyes went wide, and she seemed to come out of the post-operative daze entirely. '*Not my mother!*'

'Nope. Gentleman who gave his name as Adam Barton.'

It took her a moment to connect; then she gasped, and said uneasily, 'How did he know—? But how could he get here *tonight?* Isn't he at school? How—'

'One at a time. He's coming for his physical on Friday. I guess Dean Lazarus told him you were being operated on today. I had a note from him this morning.' He took it out of his pocket, and held it out, but she shook her head in vigorous refusal. 'Look, kid: he's leaving there at five this evening; left already. He'll be here about eight, and he's going to phone when he gets in. He'd like to see you.'

She didn't say anything, but he could see the frowning intensity of her face. 'Do you want to see him, Ceil? It's up to you, you know. I thought—in case you wanted to, you might like to know about it right away, when you woke up. But . . .'

'*No!*'

'Whatever you want, gal. I wouldn't decide right away, if I were you. He'll phone when he gets in. I'll tell the nurse to check with you then.'

'No,' she said again, less violently, but just as certainly. 'No. She doesn't have to ask me. Just tell him no.'

'Okay. If you change your mind, tell her before eight. Otherwise, she'll tell him *no,* just like the lady said. Here's your drink.' He took the cold glass from the nurse's hand, and put it on the table. 'Can you sit up?' She tried. 'Here.' He lifted her head, cradling her shoulders in his arm, and helped her steady the glass with his other hand. It didn't feel like anything special. She was female, which was nice, and well-shaped, which was better. Otherwise, he couldn't find any signs of great emotion or excitement in himself. He eased her down gently, and stood up.

'I'll be around till six if you want me,' he said. 'Anything you get a yen for, tell the nurse. If she can't fix you up, she'll call Colonel Edgerly, of the Special Services Dept. We aim to please. The patient is always right. If you want to get sat up some more, you can use the nurse, but it's more fun if I do it.'

She giggled weakly, and the nurse produced a tolerant smile. Out in the hall, he left instructions about the phone call. 'She may change her mind,' he finished. 'Nobody says *no* that hard unless they meant to say *yes* at the same time. Let me know if she has any sudden change of mood—up *or* down. I'll be at my home phone all evening, if you want me—of if she does.'

Going back in the elevator, he didn't worry about his own emotions; he pondered instead on what 'Adam Barton's' must be.

She lay flat on her back in the neat hard white bed, and felt nothing at all. Delicately, she probed inside herself, but there was no grief and no gladness; not even anger; not even love. It was all over, and here she was, and that was that. After a while, she'd be getting up out of the bed, and everything would be just the same as before.

No. Not quite everything. They had taken out more than the—the baby. She thought the words, thought them *as* words. *Baby*. They had taken out more than that, though. Whatever it was Charlie had meant, that was gone too. Out. Amputated. Cut away.

She couldn't see him, because he would be a stranger. She didn't know him. She wouldn't know what to say to him, or how to talk. What had happened long ago had happened to a different girl, and to some man she didn't know.

Adam Barton!

Her hand came down hard on the mattress, and jarred her, so that she became aware of pain. That was a relief. At least she could feel *some*thing. She saw the clenched fist of the hand, and was astonished: it hadn't *fallen* on the bed; she'd *hit* the mattress with her fist!

Why?

She couldn't remember what she was thinking about when she did it. The pain in her pelvis was more noticeable now, too, and no longer something to be grateful for.

She didn't remember calling the nurse, but somebody in a white uniform handed her a pill, and lifted her head so she could sip some water.

He was right. It was more fun when *he* did it. She wished he would come back. She wanted him to stroke her head, the way her daddy used to do when she was very little, and then she was waking up, and very hungry.

The nurse came in right away; she must have been watching through the glass at the end of the room. But when she brought the tray, there was nothing on it except some junket and a glass of milk. When she insisted she was still hungry, the nurse agreed doubtfully to some orange juice. Then she lay there with nothing to do but dream about a full meal, and try to sort out memories: The terrible moment when they put the cone over her face in the operating room—the dazed first wakening—the Colonel . . .

'Nurse!'

The white uniform popped through the door.

'What time is it?'

'Seven twenty-four.'

'Oh. Is—Colonel Edgerly wouldn't be here now, would he?'

'No. But he left word for us to call if you wanted him.'

'Oh, no. It's not important. It can wait.' It *wasn't* important; it wasn't even *anything*. I was just—just wanting to know if he was here. No, it wasn't, because she felt better now. It was wanting to know he hadn't *forgotten* about her. *Well, he didn't!* she scolded herself happily. He wouldn't, either. He wasn't the kind of man who took on responsibilities and then walked out on them, like . . .

Like I *did*, she thought suddenly.

The telephone out in the nurse's room was ringing. It cut off half-way through the second ring. She listened, but you couldn't hear the nurse's voice through the wall. He could be calling to find out how she was. Or her father—if her *father* knew . . .

She giggled, because her father would bawl her out for daydreaming and 'woolgathering'. That's what he called it when he talked to her, but she'd heard him telling her mother once, when he didn't know she could hear, 'Mental masturbation, that's all it is! Poking around inside herself till she wears herself out. There's no satisfaction in it, and all it does is make you want more of the same. Plenty of good men, men with *ability*, starving to death right now be-

cause they couldn't stop themselves from doing just that.'
It was funny how she remembered the words, and just the
way he'd said them; it was years and years ago, and she'd
hardly understood it at the time. 'If that girl spent half
the time thinking about *what she's doing* than she does worrying about what she already did and dreaming about what
she's going to do,' he'd finished indignantly, 'then *I*
wouldn't worry about her at all!'

He was right, she thought tiredly, and a moment later
she thought it again, more so, because she remembered
that it was Charlie who had called. She should have talked
to him; she could have done that much, at least. She'd been
lying here thinking he was the kind of person who walked
out on his responsibilities, and that wasn't fair, because
she didn't know what he would have done if she'd told him.

Well, why didn't *I tell him?* she wondered, and . . .

Stop it! she told herself. *If you have a toothache, you
won't make it better by worrying it with your tongue all the
time.*

Her father had said *that,* too, she remembered, and suddenly she was furious. *That's not what I was doing,* she told
him coldly, but she didn't try to explain, not to him. Only
there was a difference. She wasn't just worry-warting or
daydreaming now; she was trying to find out *why*—a lot
of *why's.*

That was the way *he* thought, all the time: *Why?* It was
thinking that way that made him the kind of person he
was. . . .

She giggled again. Every time she thought about him,
she thought *he,* and never a name. *Colonel* didn't fit at
all, and *Mister* wasn't right, and just plain *Edgerly* was
silly, and she didn't dare think *Tom.*

The nurse came to give her a pill.

'Is that to make me go to sleep?' she asked warily.

'It's a sedative,' the nurse said, as if that was different.

'I slept all day,' she said. 'Will it bother anybody if I
read a while?' She didn't want to read, especially, but she
didn't want to sleep yet either. The nurse handed her the
pill, and held out the water, and obediently, because she
didn't know how to argue about it, she lifted her head and
swallowed twice. When she moved like that, she remembered what it was she was trying so hard not to think about.

It didn't hurt so much any more, but there was a kind of *empty-ache*.

The nurse turned on her bed light, and got some magazines from the table across the room. 'If you want anything, the bell's in back of you,' she said.

Ceil let her hand be guided to the button, but there was something she wanted right now. 'Was it—' she started, and tried again. 'What was it?'

'It's a boy,' the nurse said, and laughed. 'Or anyhow, it *will* be, we think. You can't always tell for sure so soon.'

Is . . . will be . . .

Her head was swimming, from the pill probably.

Not *was. Will be.*

It's alive, she thought. *I didn't kill it.* She smiled, and sank back into the pillow, but when she woke up she was crying, and she couldn't stop.

VII

THE PHONE WOKE him at 3:43, according to the luminous figures on the dark clock-face. By the same reckoning, he had had exactly one hour and fifty-eight minutes of sleep. It was not enough.

He drove down to the Depot at a steady thirty-five, not trusting his fuzzy reflexes for anything faster; he made up for it by ignoring stop signs and traffic signals all along the way. The streets were empty and silent in the darkest hour of a moonless night; in the clear mountain air, the rare approach of another set of headlights was visible a mile or more away. He drove with the window down and his sports shirt opened at the neck, and by the time he got there he was wide awake.

They had taken her out of the infirmary into one of the consultation rooms, where the noise would not disturb the other woman who was waiting for an operation the next day. She was crying uncontrollably, huddled under a blanket on the couch, her shoulders trembling and shaking, her face turned to the wall, her fingers digging into the fabric that covered the mattress.

He didn't try to stop her. He sat on the edge of the couch, and put a hand on her shoulder. She moved just enough to throw it off. He waited a moment, and rested the same hand on her head. This time there was a hesitation, a feeling of preparation for movement again, and then she stayed still and went on crying.

After a little while he began stroking her head, very softly, very slowly. There was no visible or audible reaction, yet he felt she wanted him to continue. He couldn't see his watch. The dial was turned down on the arm that was stroking the girl's hair, but he thought it must have been a long time. He began to feel overwhelmingly sleepy. The sensible thing would have been to lie down next to her, and take her in his arms, and both of them get some sleep. . . .

No, not sensible. Sensible was what it wouldn't be. What it *would* be was pleasant and very reasonable—but only within the limits of a two-person system of logic. From the point of view of the Depot, the General, the nurse, the Space Service's honour, and the civilized world in general, it would be an unpardonable thing to do. *If I were in uniform,* he thought sharply, *it would never have occurred to me!*

She hadn't quite stopped crying yet, but she was trying to say something; the words got lost through the sobs and the blanket, but he knew what they would be. Apologies, embarrassment, explanations. He stood up, opened the door, called down the corridor for the nurse and asked for some coffee.

If I were in uniform, she'd have said, 'Yes, sir!' clickety, clack.

When he turned back, Ceil was sitting up on the couch, the blanket wrapped around her, covering everything but her face, which was a classical study in tragi-comedy: tear-stained and grief-worn, red-nosed and self-consciously ashamed.

'I—I'm sorry. I don't know what—I don't *know* what was the matter.'

He shrugged. 'It happens.' When the coffee came, he

could try to talk to her some, or get her to talk. Now he was just tired.

'They woke you up, didn't they?' She had just noticed the sports shirt and slacks; she was looking at him with real interest. 'You look different that way. N—' She cut it off short.

'Nicer?' he finished for her. 'How do? My name is Tom. I just work here.'

'I'm sorry I made you get out of bed,' she said stiffly.

No you're not. You feel pleased and important and self-satisfied. He shrugged. 'Too much sleep would make me fat.'

'What time is it?'

He looked at his watch. 'Ten to five.' The nurse came in with a tray. 'Time for breakfast. Pour some for me, will you? I'll be right back.'

He followed the nurse down the corridor, out of earshot of the open door. 'Did the kid call last night—Barton?'

'Not since I've been on; that was midnight.'

He walked back to the little cubicle with her and found the neat notation in the phone log at 2003 hours, with a telephone number and extension next to the name. He turned to the nurse, changed his mind, and picked up the phone himself. There was a distinct and vengeful satisfaction in every twirl of the dial; and a further petty pleasure when the sleepy, resentful voice at the other end began to struggle for wakefulness and a semblance of military propriety as soon as he said the word 'Colonel.'

'I'm not certain,' he said briskly, 'but if you get out here fast, Ceil just might want to see you this morning.'

'Yes, sir.'

'You have a car?'

'Yes, sir, I dr—'

'Well, it should be about twenty minutes from where you are. Come to the main gate at the Depot. You have any identification, *Mister Barton?*'

'I . . . no, sir. I didn't think about . . .'

'All right. Use your driver's licence.'

'But that has my own na—'

'Yeah, I know. You're permitted civvies on leave, aren't you?'

'Yes, sir.'

'Okay. You ask for me. Personal visit. I'll leave word at the gate where they can find me. You know how to get out here?'

'I think so, sir.'

'Well, let's make sure.' He gave careful instructions, waited for the boy to repeat them, and added a final reminder: 'You'll only need identification to get in the main gate. Understand?'

'Yes, sir.'

The Colonel hung up and picked up the other phone, the inside system. He left word at the gate that he was expecting a visitor, and could be found in the Infirmary. Then he went quickly back to the little room where Ceil waited, before the creeping dark edge of a critical conscience could quite eclipse the savage glow of his ego.

With a cup of coffee steaming in his hands and the comfort of an armchair supporting him, he decided it was certainly unjust, but not at all unreasonable, for a man who had barely napped all night to take a certain irritable delight in awakening another man at five—even if there was no element of masculine competition—which of course there wasn't, really. This last point he repeated very firmly to himself, after which he could give his full attention to what Ceil was saying.

She was talking in a rambling steady stream; words poured through the floodgates now with the same compulsive force that had produced the violent tears and wracking sobs of an hour earlier. He didn't have to answer; he didn't even have to listen, except to satisfy his own interest. *She* had to talk; and she would have to do a lot more of it, too. *But not all at once,* he thought drowsily, *not all of it at five o'clock in the morning.*

Sometimes it happened this way. A single shock—and having one's abdomen cut open is always a shock—was enough to jolt an individual over a sudden new threshold of maturity. Ceil had been crying for a double loss: her own childhood, as well as the baby she hadn't known she wanted till it was gone. Now she had to discover the woman she was becoming. But *not* all in the next half-hour.

The nurse came to the door with a meaningful look. He stood up, realizing he had waited too long to tell the girl, uncertain now which way to go. The nurse retreated from the doorway, and he stepped over to the couch, sat down on the edge, and put his hand on Ceil's arm.

'Look, kid, I have to go see somebody now. . . .'

'Oh, *I'm* sorry!' She didn't look sorry; she looked relaxed and almost radiant, under the tousled hair and behind the red eyes. 'That other woman . . . she's being operated on today, isn't she?'

'Yes.' And he'd damn near forgotten that himself. 'Yes, but that's not . . . There's somebody here to see *you*, really.'

This time she didn't think of parents. This time she knew.

'Charlie . . . !'

'*Adam.*' He smiled.

'I don't . . . I don't *know* . . . ?'

He didn't smile, but it was an effort. 'Well, you'll have to decide. I've got to go talk to him anyhow.' He stood up and reluctantly left his half-full cup of coffee on the tray. At the door he turned back and grinned at her. 'While you're making up your mind—we might be a few minutes —you'd have time to comb your hair a little if you wanted to, and things like that. . . .'

He watched her hands fly, dismayed, to her head, and saw her quick horrified glance in the wall mirror. Her mind was made up. . . .

The boy was in the waiting room, at the end of the corridor, standing with his back to the door, staring out of the window. He was tall—taller than Edgerly—and built big; even in rumpled tweeds there was an enviable suggestion of the heroic in his stance and the set of his shoulders. Empathy, the Colonel decided, was going to be a bit harder to achieve than usual. He took a step into the room, a quiet step, he thought, but the boy turned immediately, stepped forward himself, then paused.

Eagerness turned to uncertainty in his eyes, and then to disappointment. He started to turn back to the window.

'Barton?' the Colonel asked sharply, and as the boy started forward again, the man was suddenly genuinely annoyed with himself. Of course the kid didn't know who he was; you don't spring to attention and salute a lounging figure in wrinkled slacks and open-necked shirt. For that matter, they were *both* in civvies. His irritation had been based on something else altogether.

'I'm Colonel Edgerly,' he said, and was gratified to hear

the trained friendliness of his own voice. 'I've been looking forward to meeting you.' *A little stiff, but all right . . .* He extended a hand, and the boy took it, doubtfully at first, then with increasing eager pressure.

'It's a pleasure to meet you, sir. Mrs. Lazarus told me about you and how much you'd done for—for Ceil. I was hoping I'd get to see you while I was here.'

'Nothing much to see now but an empty shell.' The Colonel produced a smile. 'Ceil will see you in a few minutes, I think. Might as well sit down and take it easy meanwhile. . . .' He dropped into an overstuffed chair, and waved the boy to another. 'I've been in there with her since three o'clock, or somewhere around there. You'll have to excuse it if I'm not at my brightest.' *Sure, excuse it. Excuse me for being fifteen years older and two inches shorter. Excuse her for being seductive as all hell with a red nose. Excuse you for being so damn handsome! Excuse it, please. . . .*

'Is she . . . is everything all *right?*' The kid was white under his tan. 'They said last night she was resting comfortably. Did anything . . . ?'

'She's fine. She had a fit of the blues. It happens. Better it happened so quickly, while she was still here. . . .' He hesitated, not sure what to say next. The boy on the other chair waited, looking polite, looking concerned, looking intelligent.

A regular little nature's nobleman! the Colonel thought angrily, and gave up trying to generate any honest friendliness; he would be doing all right if he could just keep *sounding* that way.

'Now look,' he said, 'there are a couple of things I ought to tell you before you go in. First of all, she didn't ask to see you. It was my own idea to call you. I thought if you were here, she'd be—glad.'

'Thank you, sir. I appreciate that.'

Quite all right. No favours intended. As long as he allowed himself full inner consciousness of his resentment, he could maintain a proper surface easily. 'I don't know how she'll act when you go in. She's been having a kind of crying jag, and then a talking spell. If she wants you to stick around, you can stay as long as the nurse lets you, but you ought to bear in mind that she didn't have much sleep last night, and she needs some rest. It might be better if you just checked in, so to speak, and let her know you're available, and come back later for a real visit—if she wants it. You'll have to decide that for yourselves. She . . .'

He stopped. There was so *much* the boy ought to know, so much more, in quality and subtlety both, than he could convey in a short talk in the impatient atmosphere of a hospital waiting room—or perhaps more than he could possibly convey to this particular person in any length of time anywhere. And he was tired—much too tired to try.

'Look,' he said. 'There's another patient I have to see while I'm here. The nurse will come and get you as soon as Ceil's ready for company. Just—sort of take it easy with her, will you? And if I'm not around when you're done, ask the nurse to give me a ring. I'd—like to talk to you some more.'

'Yes, sir.' The boy stood up. There was an easy grace in his movements that the Colonel couldn't help enjoying. 'And—well, I mean, thank you, sir.'

The Colonel nodded. 'I'll see you later.'

He spent half an hour being professionally reassuring at Nancy Kellogg's bedside, while she ate her light preoperative meal. With a clinical ear, he listened to her voice more than her words, and found nothing to warrant the exertion of a more personal and demanding kind of listening. As soon as he could, he broke away and went upstairs to his office, striding with determined indifference past the little room where Ceil and Charlie were talking.

There was a spare uniform in his closet. He showered and shaved in the empty locker room at the Officers' Club, and emerged feeling reasonably wide-awake and quite unreasonably hungry. It was too early yet for the Depot cafeteria to be open—not quite seven.

The Infirmary had its own kitchen, of course. . . . *So that's it!* More understandable now, why he was so hungry. He usually got along fine on coffee and toast till lunch; and lunch was usually late—a good deal more than four or five hours after he woke up.

He stood undecided in the chill of the mountain-country morning, midway between the Officers' Club, the Nursemaid building, and the parking lot. All he had to do was get into his car and drive downtown to a restaurant. Not even downtown: there was an all-night joint half a mile down the road.

On the other hand, he *ought* to be around, for the Kellogg woman as much as Ceil. . . .

The Psychologist, the Officer, the Man, and a number of identifiable voices held a brisk conference, which came to an abrupt conclusion when the Body decided it was too damn cold to argue the matter out. The composite individual thereupon uttered one explosive word, and Colonel Edgerly headed for the Infirmary.

The nurse said, Yes, sir, they could get him some breakfast. Yes, sir, Mrs. Barton had seen Mr. Barton, and she was now back in bed, asleep or on her way to it. Yes, sir, Mr. Barton was waiting. In the waiting-room. She had tried to call the Colonel, but he was not in his office. Mr. Barton had decided to wait.

'I told him you'd probably gone home, sir, and I didn't know if you'd be back today or not, but . . .'

Home? There was more about the boy insisting that the Colonel wanted to see him, but he lost most of it while the realization dawned on him that it was Thanksgiving Day. He was officially not on duty at all. He could have . . .

He could have gone away for the weekend; but not having done so, he couldn't have refused the call in the middle of the night; *nor* could he leave now, with Young Lochinvar waiting to see him, and Nancy Kellogg expecting him to be around when she was done in the operating room.

'. . . anything in particular you'd like to have, sir?'

Breakfast, he remembered. He smiled at the nurse. 'Yeah. Ham and eggs and pancakes and potatoes and a stack of toast. Some oatmeal maybe. Couple quarts of coffee.' She finally smiled back. 'Anything that comes easy, but lots of it,' he finished, and went off to find Barton.

Colonel Edgerly put his coffee cup down, lit a cigarette, and sank back into the comfortable chair, savouring the fragrance of the smoke, the flavour of food still in his mouth, the overall sense of drowsy well-being.

On the edge of the same couch where Ceil had huddled

under a blanket earlier the same morning, Ceil's young man sat and talked, with almost the same determined fluency. But this time, the Colonel had no desire at all to stop the flow.

He listened, and the more he heard, the harder it got to maintain his own discomfort, or keep his jealous distance from the boy. Barton-Bolido was a good kid; there was no way out of it. And Ceil, he thought with astonishment, was another. A couple of good kids who had bumped into each other too soon and too hard. In a couple of years—

No. That's how it could have been, if they hadn't met when they did, and if the whole train of events that followed had never occurred. The way it was now, Charlie would be ripening for marriage in two or three more years; but Ceil had just this early morning crossed into the country of maturity—unaware and unsuspecting, but no longer capable of turning back to the self-centred innocence of last summer or last week.

Briefly, the Colonel turned his prying gaze inside himself and noted with irritation, but no surprise, that the inner image of the Ceil-child was still vividly exciting while the newer solider Ceil evoked no more than warm and pleasant thoughts. Well, it wasn't a new problem, and unless he started slapping teen-age rumps, it wasn't a serious one. He returned his attention to the young lady's young man, and waited for a break in the flow of words to ask:

'I take it you and Ceil are on . . . speaking terms again?'

'*Yes,* sir.'

'Good. It was important for her, I think.'

'How do you mean, sir?' The boy looked vaguely frightened now.

'Just—oh, just knowing that you came, that you give a damn. . . .'

'I guess she had a pretty low opinion of me,' the boy said hesitantly.

'I wouldn't put it that way,' the Colonel told him, professionally reassuring.

'Well, she did. And I'm not so sure she was wrong. Frankly, sir, I'm glad it turned out the way it did. I mean, if she had to—to get *pregnant,* I'm glad she came here. I don't know what I would have . . .'

'Well, we're glad too,' the Colonel interrupted. 'And right now, it doesn't really matter what you would have done, if things worked out any other way. You could be a blue-dyed skunk or a one-eyed Martian and the only thing that would make any real difference is what Ceil *thought* you were. She's gone through a tough experience, and her own opinion of herself, her ability to pull out of this thing, is going to depend a lot on whether it all seemed worth-while—which means, in part, her opinion of *you*.' He stood up. 'Well, I suppose as long as I'm here, I might as well get some work done. . . .'

'I didn't mean to take up so much of your time, sir.'

'You didn't take it. I donated it. You going back to the hotel, or stick around here?'

'I'd like to stay around if it's all right.'

'All right with me. Major Sawyer—*Dr*. Sawyer to civilians like you, boy—should be in soon. If he kicks you out, you'll have to go. Otherwise, don't get in the nurse's way, and I don't imagine anyone will care. I'll be down later myself.'

He was in the doorway, when the boy called, 'Colonel . . .'

He turned back.

'Colonel Edgerly, I just wanted to say—I guess I said it before, but—I want to thank you again. In case I don't see you later. Ceil—Ceil told me how much you've done for her, and how you arranged for Dean Lazarus to get in touch with me, and—well, I want you to know I appreciate it, sir.'

'Aw 'twarn't nothin'.' The Colonel grinned, and added, 'After all, that's what I'm here for.' He went on down the corridor to the elevators, and up to his office, comfortably aware of a full stomach and a fully distended sense of virtue. Everybody would live happily ever after, and to top it all, he had a full day ahead to catch up on the neglected paper work of months behind.

The phone was ringing when he entered the office. He had heard it all the way down the corridor, buzzing with tireless mechanical persistence.

'Hello. Edgerly speaking.'

'Oh, Tom. Good. They told me you were in, but switchboard couldn't find you. Told 'em to keep ringing till they got you. Could you run up for a minute? Couple things to talk over.'

'Yes, sir. I'm free now, if you'd like . . .'

'Fine. Come right up.'

The Colonel looked at the overstuffed *Hold* basket, and smiled. The paper work could wait. He didn't know what the General was doing there on Thanksgiving Day, and he didn't care. This conference was long past due.

VIII

THE GENERAL WAS doing the talking; the Colonel sat in stunned silence, listening. Not the smallest part of his shock was the realization that the General not only sounded, but really was, sincere.

'. . . when you're running an outfit like this, Tom, the biggest thing is knowing who to put the pressure on and when to ease up. You're a psychologist. You're supposed to be able to see something like this, even when you're the one who's concerned. These last couple months, now, you had a pretty free hand. You realize that?'

The Colonel nodded. It was true. He hadn't thought of it that way. He'd been champing at the bit, waiting for some kind of recognition. But it was true.

'Okay, I think I did the right thing. I told you what we had to have, and I told you I wasn't going to tell you how to do it. I put some pressure on, and then I left you alone. I got the results I wanted. We had three successful applicants the first nine months, and three more in less than nine weeks afterwards.

'I didn't ask how you were doing it, and I didn't want to know. It's your job, and the only time I'll mess around with what you're doing is when you're *not* getting results. The only trouble was, I didn't ask for enough, or I didn't do it soon enough. I should have allowed for a bigger margin of safety, and I didn't. That was my fault, not yours—but we're both stuck with it now.'

Again the Colonel nodded. There were questions he

should ask, ideas he should generate, but all he could feel at the moment was overpoweringly sleepy.

The General surprised him again.

'I take it you had a rough night. Suppose you take a copy of the transcript with you. Look it over. If you get any ideas, I'll be right here. I've got to have an answer Monday morning, and it better be a good one.'

The Colonel took the stapled set of onionskins, and stood up.

'Sorry to spoil your holiday,' the General rumbled.

The Colonel shrugged. 'At least the holiday gives us a few days to figure things out.'

The General nodded, and they both forgot to smile.

Back in his office, with a container of coffee getting cold on his desk, the Colonel read the transcript of the telephone conversation all the way through, carefully, and then through again.

The call had been put through to the General's home phone at 7:28 that morning, from the Pentagon in Washington. Apparently there had been some sleepless nights on that end too, after the arrival of the Satellite Rocket the evening before.

The conversation ran to seven typed pages. The largest part of it was a gingerbread façade of elaborately contrived informalities and irrelevancies. Behind the façade of jovial threats and ominous pleasantries, the facts were these:

For reasons as yet unknown, there had been three 'premature' deliveries of PN's on the Base: that is, the babies had come to term and been delivered from their tanks, healthy and whole, several weeks in advance of the expected dates. The three 'births', plus two that *were* expected, had all occurred within a 36 hour period, at a time when only two or three FP's were on Base. Mrs. Harujian was on Satelleave; and to complicate matters, Mrs. Lenox, the first one to go up, was suffering at the time from an attack of colitis, a lingering after-effect of her first long unrelieved spell of duty.

Army nurses had had to put in extra time, spelling the two women in the nursery. The extra time had been sufficient to foul up the Satelleave schedule for the regular

Army staff on Base. A four-star General who had gone on the rocket to Satellite, for the especial purpose of conferring with a Base Captain, whose leave was cancelled without notice, inquired into the reasons therefor, and returned on the rocket without having accomplished the urgent business for which he had submitted his corpulent person to the discomforts of blast-off acceleration.

The rocket had hardly touched ground, before the voice of the four stars was heard in the Pentagon. Channels were activated. Routine reports were read. Special reports analysing the reports were prepared—and somewhere along the line, it became known that the PN schedule at the Depot was not what it should be.

The phone call to General Martin therefore informed him that on Monday morning a small but well-starred commission would set forth from Washington to determine the nature of the difficulties at the Depot, and make suggestions for the improvement of conditions there.

For some time the Colonel sat in his office digesting these pieces of information. At noon he went down to the infirmary; said hello to Ceil, who was awake and looking cheerful; spent half an hour talking to Mrs. Kellogg, who was being prepared for the operating room; left word that he would be with the General, if not in his own office, when she came out of anaesthesia; declined, with thanks, an invitation from the staff to join them in Thanksgiving dinner; and went upstairs to see his boss.

The conference was shorter than he had expected. The General had also been doing some thinking, and had arrived at his conclusions.

'We took a gamble, and we lost, that's all,' he said. 'I figured by the time the shipments began to fall off enough so anybody would notice, we'd be back on a full schedule of operation again. Somebody noticed too soon, that's all. Now we have to get back to schedule right away. As long as we do that there won't be any heads rolling . . .

'Now this Serruto woman is ready to go on the next trip, that right?'

The Colonel nodded, waiting.

'Then you've got, what's-er-name, Breneau? She's scheduled for January 6, that right? And Mackintosh just started training, she goes January 20? Okay, I want those two accelerated. I'll give you any facilities or help you need, but I want them ready for December 23 and January 6 instead.'

The Colonel did some quick figuring, and nodded. 'We can manage that.'

'Okay. The next thing is, I want somebody else started right away. You got a back file of maybe nineteen-twenty names that are open for reconsideration. Couple of 'em even had medicals already. I want one started next week. She goes up with Mackintosh January 6.'

'You realize, sir, you're asking me to send up a woman I've already rejected as unsatisfactory, and to do it with only five weeks' training instead of two months?'

'I'm not asking you. I'm telling you. That's an order, Colonel. You'll get it in writing tomorrow.'

'Yes, sir.'

'Oh, hell, Tom, take it easy, will you? I'm sorry I had to put it that way, but I'm taking responsibility for this. You don't have to agree; all you have to do is produce. You give me what I want, I give them what *they* want, and after things settle down, you can get things going more the way you want 'em.'

'May I say something, sir? Before I start doing what I'm told?'

'Sure. Go ahead.'

'You were talking about a margin of safety. I'm worried about the same thing. You want to make sure we have enough people up there to handle a normal scheduled flow of shipments. I want to see the same thing. But sending up ten or twenty or fifty unqualified women *isn't going to give us any margin* . . . sir.'

'I'd tell the Pentagon boys what we're doing, and why, and stick with it. I wouldn't start more PN's till we're sure we have enough FP's. And I'd start doing some scouting around for the FP's.'

'Oh, we got back to that? The publicity campaign?'

'I still think it's a good idea.'

'Okay, Tom, let's get a couple of things straight. You made a suggestion, and I didn't pay any attention, and you went ahead and tried it out anyhow. Yeah, sure I know about it. What do you think I meant this morning about knowing when to put on pressure? You did it the right way. You were discreet and sensible, and it worked—a one-man campaign, fine.

'But what you could do that way wasn't enough, so you sent me another little note, because you wanted to get it set up officially, and expand it. Well, look, Tom, I don't want to sound insulting. I know you know a lot about people, that's your job. But you know 'em one-at-a-time, Tom, and it's been *my* business for a hell of a long time to know them all-in-a-bunch, and believe me—

'You start a big full-scale publicity campaign on this thing, and we'll be out of business so fast, you won't know what hit you. The American people won't stand for it, if they know what's going on here.'

'They know now, sir. We're not Secret.'

'Yeah. They know. If they subscribe to *The New York Times* and read the science column on page thirty-six. Sure we're not Secret; the Project is part of the knowledge of every well-informed citizen. And how many citizens does that include? Look at the Satellite itself, Tom. It was no secret. The people who read the small print knew all about it way back some time in the 1940's when it was mentioned in a congressional budget. But it sure as hell surprised the citizens when it got into the sky—and into the headlines. We can't risk the headlines yet. If people knew *all* about us . . . well, probably we could win over a good majority. But if all they see is the headlines and the lead paragraphs and the editorials in the opposition papers . . . and don't think they aren't going to make it sound as if the government was running a subsidized abortion ring! Does that make it any clearer?'

'Yes, sir. A lot clearer.'

'Okay. I'll get official orders typed up in the morning, and a new schedule for trainees. Now you might as well knock off, and enjoy what's left of the holiday. Start worrying tomorrow. . . .'

Colonel Edgerly sat in a chair by the head of a hospital bed and listened to fears and complaints, and was grateful that Nancy Kellogg was really married, and had three children and a husband at home, and was not going to go off any deep ends in the immediate future. He made little jokes and reassuring noises, and held the little pan for her when she was sick the second time.

With the surface of his mind he listened to everything she said and could have repeated a perfect catalogue of all her aches and pains. When she moved on to the subject of previous deliveries, he asked interested questions at appropriate intervals. She wanted to talk, and that was fine, because as long as he kept the top surface busy he didn't have to pay attention to what was going on farther down.

When she began to get sleepy, he went and found Ceil, who was watching television out in the staff-room. She turned off the set and started a stream of nervous small talk, from which he could gather only that she had been doing some heavy thinking and had a lot to say, but didn't know how to say it. Whatever it was, it did not seem to be particularly explosive or melancholy; when the nurse came to tell her it was time to be back in bed, he ignored the girl's hopeful look, and said he would see her next day.

He started off up the corridor, knowing what he was heading for and hoping something or someone would stop him. Nothing and nobody did. He stepped through the wide door at the far end of the hall, and waited while the student nurse encased him in sterile visitors' coveralls. Inside, he wandered up and down the rows of tanks, stopping occasionally to stare through a glassed top as if he could see through the membrane and the liquids, or even perhaps through pale flesh and cartilage and embryonic organs, to some secret centre of the soul, to the small groupings of undeveloped cells that would some day spell *mind* and *psyche* in the walking, living, growing, feeling, thinking bodies of these flat-faced fetal prisoners.

Charlie, the Kaydet, had said to him wistfully, 'I wish the kid could have my name.' To carry to the stars, he meant. But not right now, not here on Earth, oh no, that would be too embarrassing. . . .

On the tanks there were no names: just numbers. And in the office down the hall, a locked file case contained a numbered folder full of names and further numbers and reports and charts and graphs of growth and in every folder of the 37, one name at least appeared. His own.

They're not my *babies,* he thought angrily, and with reluctance: *Yes they are.*

You need to get married, he told himself clinically. *Have one of your own.*

That would be an answer, one kind of answer. But *not* an answer to the problem now at hand. It was an answer for girls like Ceil, and later for boys like Charlie—for the people who had listened to his promises and pledges, and walked away, and left their babies here.

They walked out. So can I. . . . The job the Generals wanted done was not a job that he could do. *So quit!* It could be done. The typed-out request for a transfer was in his pocket now. Quit now, and let them find him a job that wasn't too big for a merely human being. Get married, have some kids. Let somebody else . . .

He couldn't.

If he knew *which* somebody, if there were a Colonel Edgerly to talk to him and reassure him and promise him, so he'd *believe* it, that his babies would be cared for . . .

He laughed, and the vapour forming on the face-plate of the sterile suit made him aware that he was uncomfortably warm and had been in there too long. He went out and stripped off the coveralls. His uniform was wet with sweat, and he smelled of it. Through empty halls he went upstairs, avoiding even the elevator, grateful to meet no one on the way. In his own office, he stood and stared out of the window at the faint edge of sunset behind the mountains, no more than a glow of red shaping the ridges against a dark sky.

He took the wilted sheet of paper from his pocket and would have torn it up, but instead he opened the bottom desk drawer and filed it with all the other unfulfilled acts of rebellion.

The parents of these children could walk out, and had done so. But the man who had eased the responsibility from their shoulders, who had used his knowledge of human beings and his trained skill in dealing with them to effect the transfer of a living human embryo from its natural mother to a tank of surrogate nutrient, the man who had dared to determine that one particular infant, as yet technically unborn, would be one of the thousand who would grow up not-quite-Earthmen, to become the representatives

of Earth over as yet-uncoverable distances—the man who
had done all this could not then, calmly, doff his Godhead,
hand it to another man, and say, 'I quit,' and walk away.

He changed his clothes and got his car from the near-
empty parking lot and drove. Not home. Anywhere else.
He drove towards the mountains, off the highway, on to
winding dirt roads that needed his full attention in the
dark. He kept the window down and let the night wind
beat him and when, much later, he got home, he was tired
enough to sleep.

The blessing of the Army, he thought, as he slid from
wakefulness, was that there was always someone over you.
Whatever authority you assumed, whatever responsibility
came with it, there was always some higher authority that
could relieve you of a Godhead you could not surrender.

IX

IN THE MORNING, he felt calm and almost cheerful. His
own personal decision was made, and the consequences
were clear to him, but the career that had mattered very
much at one time seemed comparatively unimportant at
this juncture.

He checked off the list of appointments for the day—
Kellogg, Barton, Mackintosh, two new names, FP applicants; he read the mail, and read the typed orders and
schedule that came down from the General's office; he went
efficiently through the day's routine, and whenever there
was ten minutes to spare, he worked on the report the
General required for Monday morning.

Saturday was an easier day. He talked to Ceil in the
morning, and signed her release, and told her to come see
him any time she felt she wanted to. Then he went upstairs, and finished the report. Read it through, and tore it
up, half-angry and half-amused at the obvious intent of
his defiance. Making sure you get fired is not at all different
from quitting.

He went carefully through the card-file of rejects and
selected half a dozen names, then started the report again.

Along towards mid-afternoon, he buzzed the Sergeant to order a belated lunch sent up, and not till after he had hung up did he stop to wonder what she was doing at her desk. She was supposed to go off duty at noon on Saturdays. He picked up the phone again.

'Hey, Sarge—didn't you hear the noon whistle?'

'Noon . . . ? Oh. Yes, sir.'

'You don't have to stick around just because I do, you know. They don't pay overtime in this man's Army any more.'

'I . . . don't mind, sir. There's nothing special I have to do today. I thought if I stayed to answer the phone, you could . . . you'll want that report typed when you're finished, won't you, sir?'

Well, I'll be damned! He was surprisingly touched by her thoughtfulness. 'It was good of you to think of it, Helen.' As soon as the words were out, he realized how wrong they were. Too formal, and then her first name— it didn't sound like what he meant. 'I appreciate it,' he added, even more stiffly.

'That's all right, Colonel. I really don't mind. I didn't have anything special to do, and I just thought . . .'

He put the receiver down, got up quickly, and opened the connecting door. She was sitting there, still holding her phone, looking slightly baffled and faintly embarrassed. He grinned, as the click of the door-latch startled her. 'You're a good kid, Sarge, but there's no sense hanging on to a phone with nobody on the other end.'

She flushed, and replaced the receiver on its hook. Apparently anything he said was going to be wrong—but this was hardly surprising when, after four months of almost daily association, he suddenly found a person instead of a uniform sitting at the outside desk.

'Tongue-tied schoolboy, that's me,' he said defiantly. 'I just never learned how to say *Thank You* politely. Even when I mean it. I think it was damned decent of you to stay, and I appreciate what you've done so far, but I'm not going to let you toss away the whole weekend just because *I'm* stuck in the mud. Look . . . did you order that stuff yet?'

'No . . . no, sir.'

'Could you stand to drink a cup of coffee?' He grinned. 'With a superior officer, I mean?'

Almost, she smiled. *The* Almost *Perfect Lady Soldier,* he thought with relief.

'Yes, sir, I think I could.'

'All right. Pick up your marbles and let's get out of here. I could use a break myself. After that,' he finished, 'you're going home. I'll tell the switchboard I've gone myself, and let them take any calls. And as far as the typing goes, I don't know when I'm going to have this thing finished. It could be three o'clock in the morning . . . and I can always get one of the kids from the pool to type it up to-morrow, if I'm too lazy to do it myself.'

She frowned faintly; then her face smoothed out again into its customary unruffled surface of competence. 'You're the boss.' She smiled and shrugged almost imperceptibly. 'Let's go!'

He had thought he wanted company. A short break would be good. Generalized conversation—enforced re-focusing of attention—sandwich and coffee—twenty minutes of non-concentration. Fine. But all the way to the commissary he walked in silence, and when they found a table and sat down, it took only the simplest query— 'How's it coming?'—to set him off.

He talked.

For an hour and a half, while successive cups of coffee cooled in front of him, he talked out all he meant to say. Then when he finally looked at the clock and found it read almost five, he said, abashed, 'Hey—didn't I tell you to go home?'

'I'm glad I didn't,' she said.

There was a note of intensity in the saying of it that made him look more closely. She meant it! It wasn't a proper secretarial remark.

'So am I,' he told her with equal seriousness. 'I got more done yakking at you here than I would have in five hours crumpling up sheets at my desk. Thanks.'

He smiled, and for an instant he thought the uniform would slip away entirely, but the answering smile was only in her eyes. At least, he thought, she'd refrained from giving him her standard Receptionist's Special. . . .

He didn't do any more that day. Sunday morning, he went into the office early, and started all over again, this time knowing clearly what he meant to say, and how. When the phone rang at eleven, he had almost completed a final draft.

'This is Helen Gregory, sir. I thought I'd call, and find out if you wanted that report typed up today . . . ?'

Bless you, gal! 'As a matter of fact, I'm just about done with it now,' he started, and then realized he had almost been betrayed by her matter-of-fact tone into accepting the sacrifice of the rest of her weekend. 'It's not very long,' he finished, not as he'd planned. 'I'll have plenty of time to type it up myself. Take yourself a day off, Sarge. You earned it yesterday, even if you didn't have it coming anyway.'

'I . . . really don't mind.' Her voice had lost its easy certainty. 'I'd *like* to come in, if I can help.'

Ohmigod! He should have known better than to crack a surface as smooth as hers. Yesterday afternoon had been a big help, but if she was going to start playing mama now . . .

'That's very kind of you, Helen,' he said. 'But there's really no need for it.'

'Whatever you say . . .' She sounded more herself again —or her familiar self—but she left it hanging, clearly not content. He pretended not to notice.

'Have a good day,' he said cheerfully. 'Tomorrow we maybe die. And thanks again.'

'That's all right, sir. I really— I suppose I'm just curious to see how it came out, really.'

'Pretty good, I think. I hope. I'll leave a copy on your desk to read in the morning. Like to know what you think — Hey! where do you keep those report forms?'

'Middle drawer on the left. The pale green ones. They're quadruplicate, you know—and onionskin for our file copy is in the top drawer on that side.'

'It's a good thing you called. I'd have had the place upside down trying to figure that out. Thanks, Sarge—and take it easy.'

He hung up thoughtfully; then shook his head and dismissed the Sergeant, and whatever problems she might represent, from his immediate universe. He spent another half-hour changing and rewording the final paragraph of the report, and when he was satisfied that he at least could not improve it further, found the forms and carbon sheets neatly stacked where she'd said. A hell of a good secretary, anyhow. Nothing wrong in her wanting to mother-hen a little bit. *He* was the one who was over-reacting. . . .

The father-pot calling the mother-kettle neurotic, he thought bitterly. And *that* was natural enough too. Who could possibly resent it more?

He stacked a pile of sheets and inserted them in the type-writer, wishing now he'd been rational enough to trade on the girl's better nature, instead of rejecting so hard. It would take him a couple of hours to turn out a decent-looking copy. She could have done it in thirty minutes. . . .

The phone jangled at his elbow; he hit two keys simultaneously on the machine, jamming it, and reached for the receiver.

'Colonel Edgerly . . . ?'

Excited young female type. *Not* the Lady Soldier.

'Speaking.'

'Oh . . . *Tom.* Hello. This is Ceil.' She didn't have to tell him; he knew from the breathless way she said his first name. 'I tried to call you at home, but you weren't there. . . . I hope I'm not busting into something *important?*'

'Well, as a matter of fact—' Whatever it was she wanted, this wasn't his day to give it out. 'Look, kid, will it keep till tomorrow? I've got a piece of work here I'm trying to finish up—' Maybe *she* could type, he thought, and reluctantly abandoned the idea.

'. . . really what I wanted anyhow,' she was saying. He had missed something and, backtracking, missed more. '. . . only time we're both free, and I wanted to check with you ahead of time . . .' Who was *both?* Charlie maybe? Coming to ask for his blessing?

I'm getting hysterical, he decided, and managed to say good-bye as calmly as if he knew what the call had been about. Tomorrow. She'd come in tomorrow, and then he'd find out.

One isolated phrase jumped out of the lost pieces: '. . . called yesterday . . .' The Sergeant had been turning away calls all day, and he hadn't looked at the slips when he left, because he thought he was coming back.

He found them on her desk, neatly stacked. Ceil had called twice: no message. A Mrs. Pinckney of the local Child Placement Bureau wanted to speak with him about a matter of importance; he dimly remembered meeting her at the Lazarus' party. Two candidates for FP had made appointments for next week. The rest were interdepartmental calls, and the Sarge had handled them all.

His hands hesitated briefly over the phone as he considered calling Sergeant Gregory and giving them both the gratification of allowing her to do the typing for him. Then he took himself firmly in hand, and headed back to the inner office and the typewriter. No need to pile up future grief just to avoid a couple of hours of tedium.

He settled down, unjammed the stuck keys, and started again with a fresh stack of paper.

In the morning, over his breakfast coffee, he read again through the carbon copy he had brought home, and decided it would do. He had managed to give the General what he'd asked for, and at the same time state his own position, with a minimum of wordage and—he hoped—a maximum of clarity.

The report began by complying with the specific request of the General. It listed the names of six rejected candidates who might be reconsidered. The first three, all of whom he recommended, included Mrs. Leahy, the madam; Mrs. Buonaventura, who had failed to be sent through for further testing because she had only one arm; and a Mr. George Fitzpatrick, whose application had been deferred, rather than rejected, since they planned to start sending men later.

He pointed out that in the first two cases the particular disabilities of the ladies would not, in practice, make any difference to their effectiveness; and in the case of the man —if the programme were to be accelerated other ways, why not this way too?

There followed a list of three names, conscientiously selected as the least offensive of those in his file who might be expected to qualify on Medic and Security checks; in these three cases he undertook, as Psychological Officer, to qualify any or all for emergency appointments of two months, but added that he could not, in his professional capacity, sign his name to full-term contracts for any one of them.

The next section was a single page of figures and statistics, carefully checked, recommending a general slow-down for the Project, based on the percentage of acceptable FP candidates encountered so far. A semi-final paragraph proposed an alternate plan: that if the total number of applicants for FP positions could be increased, by means of an intelligently directed publicity programme, the number of acceptable candidates might be expected to be large enough to get the Project back to its original schedule in three months.

And then the final paragraph:

'It should be remembered, in reviewing this situation, that on this Project we are dealing with human beings, rather than inanimate objects, and that rigid specifications of requirements must in each individual case be interpreted by the judgment of another human being. As an Officer of the Space Service, whose duty it is to make such judgments, I cannot, in all conscience, bring myself to believe that I should include in my considerations any extraneous factors, no matter of what degree of importance. My official approval or rejection of any individual can be based only on the qualifications of that individual.'

He read it through, and drove to work, wondering what the chances were that anyone besides the General would ever see it.

The day was routine, if you discounted the charged air of suspense that circulated through the building from the time the three star-studded Washingtonians drove into the parking lot and disappeared into the General's office. The Colonel conducted the usual number of interviews, made minor decisions, emptied a box of Kleenex, and replaced it.

For the Colonel, there was a feeling of farce in every appointment made for the future and every piece of information carefully elicited and faithfully recorded. But the Sergeant, at least, seemed to have come back to normal, and played the role of Lady Soldier with such conviction that the whole absurd melodrama seemed, at times, almost real. She complimented him gravely on the report when she handed him his list of appointments; thereafter, the weekend and its stresses seemed forgotten entirely in the familiar routine of a Monday morning.

At 10:30, Mrs. Pinckney called again. It seemed she was going to a social welfare convention in Montreal next month; would the Colonel like to work with her on part of a paper she meant to present there, in which she could 'plug' the Project?

He couldn't tell her, through the office switchboard, that the boss had rapped his knuckles and threatened to wash his mouth with soap if he kept talking about indelicate matters outside the office. He suggested that they get together during the week; he'd call her when he saw some free time. She hung up, obviously chagrined at the coolness of his tone, and immediately the phone buzzed again.

This time it was the Sergeant. 'I just remembered, sir, there were some phone slips from Saturday that you didn't see.'

'Thanks. I picked 'em up yesterday.'

'Oh. Then you know Mrs. Barton called? She seemed very eager—'

'Yuh. She called again yesterday. That's what made me check the slips. Oh, yes. She's coming in today, sometime.'

'She didn't say when, sir?'

'No. Or I'm not sure. If she did, I don't remember.' And what difference did it make?

'Shall I call her back and check, sir?'

'I don't see why.' It was getting irritating now. Apparently, the Sergeant was going to remain slightly off keel about anything connected with the weekend. Well, he thought, one could be grateful at least for small aberrations —if they stayed small. 'She'd be in class now, anyhow,' he added sharply.

'Yes, sir. It's just that I understand you'll probably be going up to the Conference right after lunch. So if it was important . . .'

'It wasn't,' he said with finality. 'If I'm busy when she comes in, she can wait.'

'Yes, sir.'

He hung up, wondered briefly about the exact nature of the rumour channels through which the secretaries of the Depot seemed always to know before the decisions were actually made just what was going to happen where and when, gave it up as one of the great insoluble mysteries, and went back to the ridiculous business of carrying on the normal day's work.

At noon, the General's secretary informed Sergeant Gregory that the General and his visitors were going out to lunch and that the Colonel's presence was requested when they returned, at 1330 hours. The Sergeant reported the information to her superior. He thanked her, but she didn't go away. She stood there, looking uncomfortable.

'Something else?'

'Yes, sir, there is. It's . . . not official.'

There was an urgency in her tone that drove away his first quick irritation. He focused on her more fully, and decided that if this was more of the mothering act, it was bothering her even more than it did him. 'Sit down, Sergeant,' he said gently. 'What's on your mind?'

'No, thanks. I . . . all right.' She sat down. 'I . . . just wanted to tell you, sir . . . just wanted to tell you, sir . . . I mean I thought I ought to let you know before you go up . . .'

'Yes?' he prompted. *And where has my little Lady Soldier gone?*

'It's about your report. I can't tell you how I know, sir, but I understand the General turned it over to the other officers. Maybe I should have . . .'

'Excuse me.' He was beginning to feel a burst of excitement. His first reaction to the idea of being included in the Conference at all had been a sinking certainty that Edgerly was going to play Goat after all. But if they'd seen his report . . . 'I won't ask you how you know, but I do want to find out just how reliable your source is,' he said eagerly. It was possible, just *barely* possible, that his ideas might be given some serious consideration by the Investigating Committee!

'It's reliable,' she said tightly and paused, then went on with quick-worded determination: 'Perhaps I should have said something before, when I read it, but it was too late by then to make any changes, so I . . . I mean, if you'd agreed with me, sir. But the way you wrote the report, it does—excuse me, sir, but it makes such a perfect out for the General! *I* know you've been co-operating with him, and *he* knows it, but anyone who just read the report . . .'

She stood up, not looking at him, and said rapidly, 'I just thought I ought to let you know before you go up, the way it looks to me, and how it might look to them. I'm sorry if I should have spoken up sooner.'

She turned and almost ran for the door.

'That's all right, Sarge,' he said, almost automatically. 'It wouldn't have done any good to tell me this morning. I should have let you come in yesterday. . . .'

Just before the door closed, he had a glimpse of a shy smile in which gratitude, apology, and sympathy merged to warm friendliness. But the marvel of this, coming from the Sergeant, was lost entirely in the hollowness of his realization that he was going to get what he wanted. He was going to get fired. The General had passed the buck with expert ease, and Tom Edgerly would be quietly relieved of a post that was too big for him, and—

He felt very very sick.

X

THE TWO GIRLS walked in through the open door, just how much later he didn't know. He'd been sitting with his back to the desk, staring out of the window, remembering the care he had taken to write that report in such a way as to defeat his own acknowledged weakness, and marvelling bitterly at the subconscious skill with which he had composed the final document.

He heard the noise behind him, a hesitant cough-and-shuffle of intrusion, and turned, realizing that Helen would have gone out for lunch and left the doors open.

It was Ceil; the other girl with her was the last PN before her. They had met in the Infirmary, he supposed; Janice had gone home last Tuesday; Ceil came in Monday. Yeah.

They both looked very intense. *Not today, kids. Some other time.* He stood up, and smiled, and began rehearsing the words to get rid of them.

Ceil stepped forward hesitantly. 'Was this a bad time to come? If you're busy, we could make it tomorrow instead. It's just lunch hour is the only time we're both free, and we wanted to come together. Jannie works late. . . .'

She was chattering, but only because she had sensed something wrong.

'It's not a good day,' he said slowly, and glanced at his watch and back at the girls, and knew defeat again. Whatever it was, it was *important*—to them.

'Well, we can come in tomor—'

'You're here now,' he pointed out, and formed his face into a smile. 'I have some time now, anyhow.' The time didn't matter to him. He had more than half an hour yet before he had to go upstairs and get put to sleep in the mess of a bed he had made. 'Sit down,' he said, and pulled the extra chair away from the wall over to the desk.

They sat on the edge of their seats, leaning forward, eager, and both of them started talking at once, and then both stopped.

'You tell him,' Ceil said. 'It was your idea first.'

'You can say it better,' the other one said.

For God's sake, one of you get to it! 'Spit it out,' he said brusquely.

They looked at each other, and Ceil took a deep breath, and said evenly, 'We want to apply for Foster Parent positions.'

He smiled tolerantly. Then he stopped smiling. It was impossible, obviously. A couple of kids—

'Why?' he asked, and as a jumble of answers poured out, he thought, with mounting elation, *Why not?*

'My mother acts like I committed a sin. . . .' That was Janice.

'In two years, Charlie can get married. . . .'

'. . . maybe I did, but if I helped to take care of some of them . . .'

'. . . I'd know more about how to manage in a place like that, in case we did . . .' Ceil.

'. . . even if it wasn't my own . . .'

That was the catch, of course. They'd play favourites. They'd—if they didn't *know*—Mrs. Mackintosh had said, *if you weren't so obviously oriented in the opposite direction. . . .*

Janice—she was the one who'd had an affair with her boss. He was going to marry her of course, but when she found out she was pregnant, it turned out he already had a wife. No job, no man. He would pay for her to get rid of it—but she wouldn't. She couldn't. And she couldn't stay home and have it; it would *kill* her mother, she said. . . .

Ceil—Ceil came in as a child, not knowing, not understanding, and downstairs, in a hospital bed, she grew up.

A couple of kids, sure. But *women,* too. Grown women, with good reason for wanting to do a particular job.

He heard the Sergeant come in, and flew into a whirlwind of activity. It was 1:15. By 1:27, they had both applications neatly filled out and the already-completed Medical and Security checks out of the folders. The psych tests for FP's were more comprehensive than the ones they'd had, but he knew enough to figure he was safe.

He took another twenty seconds to run a comb through his hair and straighten his tie. Then he went upstairs.

The Colonel sat at his desk, and filled in an application form neatly and quickly. He signed his name at the bottom and stood up and looked out of the big window and laughed without noise, till he realized there was a tear rolling down his cheek.

It was all over now, but it would all begin again tomorrow morning, and the next day, and the next. The visiting Generals had accomplished their purpose, which was to goose Nursemaid into action, and had gone back home. The resident General had come through without a blot on his record, because it was all the Colonel's fault. The Colonel had come through with a number of new entries in his record, and whether they shaped up to a blot or a star he could not yet tell.

The interview had been dramatic, but now the drama was done with and the last piddling compromise had been agreed on: the two new candidates; plus the man, Fitzpatrick; plus consideration for men from now on; plus reviewing the backfiles of PN's to see how many more were willing; plus the trickle that could be expected from this source in the future; plus an over-all 20 per cent slowdown in the original schedule; plus policy conferences in Washington on the delicate matter of publicity; plus a reprimand to the Colonel for his attitude, and a commendation to the Colonel for his work. . . .

He pushed the buzzer, and the Sergeant came in.

'Sit down,' he told her.

She sat.

'It just occurred to me,' he said, 'that the—uh—dramatic statements on those applications you typed up were . . . extraordinarily well put.' He kept the smile back, with a great effort.

'What statements did you mean, sir?' The Perfect Lady Soldier had her perfect deadpan back.

'The last questions, Sergeant. *You* know—"Why do you desire to . . ." The answers that were all about how Colonel Edgerly had inspired the applicants with understanding, patriotism, maternal emotion, and—similar admirable qualities.'

'I—' There was a faint, but not quite repressed, glint in the Sergeant's eye. 'I'm afraid, sir, I suggested that they let me fill that in; it would be quicker, I thought, than trying to take down everything they wanted to say.'

'Sergeant,' he said, 'are you aware that those applications become a part of the permanent file?'

'Yes, sir.' Now she was having trouble not looking smug.

'And are you also aware that it is desirable to have truthful replies in those records?'

'Yes, sir.' She didn't feel smug now, and for a moment he was afraid he'd carried the joke too far. He meant to thank her, but . . . 'Yes, sir,' she said, and looked directly at him, not hiding anything at all. 'I wrote the truth as I saw it, sir.'

The Colonel didn't answer right away. Finally he said, 'Thanks. Thanks a lot, Sergeant.'

'There's nothing to thank me for.' She stood up. 'I hope it—helped?'

'I'm sure it did.'

She took a step, and stopped. 'I'm glad. I think—if you don't mind my saying so, sir, I think they'd have a hard time finding anybody else to do the job you're doing. I mean, to do it as well.'

He looked at her sharply, and then at the filled out form on his desk.

'I guess I have to say *Thank You* again.' He smiled, and realized her embarrassment was even greater than his own.

'I'll—is there anything else you want, sir? I was just going to leave when you buzzed—' Her eyes were fixed one foot to the right of his face, and her cheeks were red.

'Yes,' he said. 'There is something else—unless you're in a hurry. It can wait till tomorrow, if you have a date or anything.'

'No, sir. I'm free.'

'All right, then. What do you like to drink, and where would you prefer to eat? I have lousy taste in perfume, and I owe you something, God knows—besides which, it's about time we got acquainted; we may be working together for a while after all.'

She was still embarrassed, but she was also pleased. And his quick glimpse before had not fully prepared him for how sweet her smile was, when she wasn't doing it professionally.

There was just one more thing he had to do before he left. He took the application for a Foster Parent position from the top of his desk—the one with his own name signed to it—and filed it in the bottom desk drawer. There was a job to be done here—a job he couldn't possibly do right. The requirements were too big, and the limitations were too narrow. It was the kind of job you could never be sure was done right—or even done. But the Sergeant— who was in a position to know—thought he could do it better than anyone else.

Time enough to go traipsing off to the Moon when he finished as much of the job as they'd *let* him do, here.

DAUGHTERS OF EARTH

I

MARTHA BEGAT JOAN, and Joan begat Ariadne. Ariadne lived and died at home on Pluto, but her daughter, Emma, took the long trip out to a distant planet of an alien sun.

Emma begat Leah, and Leah begat Carla, who was the first to make her bridal voyage through sub-space, a long journey faster than the speed of light itself.

Six women in direct descent—some brave, some beautiful, some brilliant: smug or simple, wilful or compliant, all different, all daughters of Earth, though half of them never set foot on the Old Planet.

This story could have started anywhere. It began with unspoken prayer, before there were words, when an un-named man and woman looked upward to a point of distant light, and wondered. Started again with a pointing pyramid; once more with the naming of a constellation; and once again with the casting of a horoscope.

One of its beginnings was in the squalid centuries of churchly darkness, when Brahe and Bruno, Kepler, Coper-nicus, and Galileo ripped off the veils of godly ignorance so men could see the stars again. Then in another age of madness, a scant two centuries ago, it began with the pioneer cranks, Goddard and Tsiolkovsky, and the com-pulsive evangelism of Ley and Gernsback and Clarke. It is beginning again now, here on Uller. But in this narrative, it starts with Martha:

Martha was born on Earth, in the worst of the black decades of the 20th century, in the year 1941. She lived out her time, and died of miserable old age at less than eighty years at home on Earth. Once in her life, she went to the Moon.

She had two children. Her son, Richard, was a good and dutiful young man, a loving son, and a sober husband when he married. He watched his mother age and weaken with worry and fear after the Pluto expedition left, and could never bring himself to hurt her again as his sister had done.

Joan was the one who got away.

II

. . . centure easegone manlookttuthe stahzanprade eeee maythem hizgozzenn izz gahahdenno thawthen izzgole . . .
'It's—beautiful!'

Martha nodded automatically, but she heard the catch in the boy's voice, the sudden sharp inhalation of awe and envy, and she shivered and reached for his hand.

Beautiful, yes: beautiful, brazen, deadly, and triumphant. Martha stared at the wickedly gleaming flanks of the great rocket resting majestically on its bed of steel, and hated it with all the stored and unspent venom of her life.

She had not planned to come. She had produced a headache, claimed illness, ignored the amused understanding in her husband's eyes.

Even more, she dreaded having Richard go. But his father voiced one rarely-used impatient word, and she knew there was no arguing about the boy.

In the end she had to do it too: go and be witness at disaster for herself. The three of them took their places in the Moon rocket—suddenly safe-seeming and familiar—and now they stood together in the shadow of that rocket's monstrous spawn, under the clear plastic skin of Moondome.

. . . rodwee havetrav uldsoslo lee beyewere eeyanway stfulmen zzz . . .

The silvery span of runway that would send it off *today* stretched out of sight up the crater wall, the diminishing curve beyond the bloated belly already lost in the distance, it was made to rule. Cameras ground steadily; TV commentators, perched on platforms stilted high like lifeguard chairs, filled in a chattering counterpoint against the drone from the loudspeakers of the well-worn words that had launched the first Moondome expedition, how long back? Sixteen years? Impossible. Much longer. How many children had painfully memorized those tired words since? But here was George, listening as though he'd never heard a word of it before, and Richard between them, his face shimmering with reflections of some private glory, and the adolescent fervour of his voice—'It's *beautiful!'*—drawing a baritone-to-tremolo screech across the hypnosoporific of the loudspeakers' drone.

She shivered. 'Yes, dear, it is,' and took his hand, held it too tightly and had to feel him pull away. A camera pointed at them and she tried to fix her face to look the way the commentator would be saying all these mothers here today were feeling.

She looked for the first time at the woman next to her and caught an echo of her own effort at transformation. All around her, she saw with gratitude and dismay, were the faint strained lines at lips and eyes, the same tensed fingers grasping for a hand, or just at air.

Back on Earth, perhaps among the millions crowded around TV sets, there could be honest pride and pleasure at this spectacle. But here—?

The cameras stopped roaming, and a man stood up on the raised central dais.

'The President of United Earth,' the speakers boomed sepulchrally.

An instant's hush, then:

'Today we are sending forth two hundred of our sons and daughters to the last outpost of the solar world—the far room from which we hope they may open an exit to the vistas of space itself. Before they go, it is proper that we pause . . .'

She stopped listening. The words were different, but it was still the same. No doubt the children would have to memorize this one too.

Did they *feel this way?*

It was a frightening, and then a cooling thought. There was no other way they could have felt, the other mothers who watched that first Moondome rocket leaving Earth.

'. . . for their children's children, who will reach to the

unknown stars.' Silence. That was the end, then.

The silence was broken by the rolling syllables of the two hundred names, as each straight neat white uniform went up to take the hand of the President, and complete the ritual. Then it was over and Joan was standing before her: her daughter, a stranger behind a mask of glory. Seven months ago—seven short and stormy months—a schoolgirl still. Now—what did the President say?—an 'emissary to the farthest new frontiers.'

Martha reached out a hand, but George was before her, folding the slender girl in a wide embrace, laughing proudly into her eyes, chucking her inanely under the chin. Then Richard, still too young not to spurn sentimentality, shaking Joan's hand, suffering her kiss on his forehead, saying thickly: 'You show 'em, sis!'

It was her turn now. Martha leaned forward, coolly kissed the smiling face above the white jacket, and felt the untamed tears press up behind her eyes.

'Joan,' she cried wildly. 'Joan, baby, aren't you *afraid?*'

What a *stupid* thing to say! She wiped hastily at her eyes, and saw that the shine in Joan's eyes was moisture, too.

Joan took her mother's hands, and held them tight.

'I'm petrified,' she said, slowly, gravely, and very low. No one else heard it. Then she turned with her brave smile to Alex, standing at her side.

'Pluto or bust!' she giggled.

Martha kissed Alex, and George shook his hand. Then the two of them went off, in their white uniforms, to join the other couples, all in line.

Martha felt proud.

(Parenthesis to Carla: i)

Josetown, Uller, 3/9/52

Dear Carla . . .

Forgive me my somewhat dramatic opening. Both the sections that preceded this were written years ago, at rather widely separated times and of course the one about Martha's farewell to Joan involved a good bit of imaginative assumption—though less of it than you may think at this point.

Frankly, I hesitated for some time before I decided it was proper to include such bits in what is primarily intended to be an informational account. But information is not to be confused with statistics, and when I found myself uncertain, later, whether it was all right to include these explanatory asides, I made up my mind that if I were to write the story at all, it would have to be done my own way, with whatever idiosyncratic eccentricities, or godlike presumptions of comprehension might be involved.

As you already know if you are reading this, I am putting this together for you as a sort of good-bye present for your trip. There is little you will be able to take with you, and when you leave, there will be no way to foresee the likelihood of our ever meeting again: even if your trip is entirely successful and you return from it safely, we both know how uncertain the time-transformation equations are. You may be back, twenty years older, five minutes after you leave; more probably, it may be many years after my own death that you return—perhaps only a year or two older than you are now.

But however we learn to juggle our bodies through space *or* time, we live our lives on a subjective time scale. Thus, though I was born in 2026, and the *Newhope* landed on Uller in 2091, *I* was then, roughly, 27 years old—including two subjective years, overall, for the trip. And although the sixty-one years I have lived here would be counted as closer to sixty-seven on Earth, or on Pluto, I think that the body —and I *know* the mind—pays more attention to the rhythm of planetary seasons, the alternations of heat and cold and radiation intensities, than to the ticking of some cosmic metronome counting off whatever Absolute Time might be. So I call myself 88 years old—and I digress, but not as far as it may seem.

I said, for instance, that Martha died 'of miserable old age' at less than eighty, and this would seem to contradict my talk of seasons-and-subjectivity here. I am not exactly senile, and can look forward to another forty years, in all likelihood, of moderately useful life. We do learn something as we go along: a hundred years before Martha's time (indeed, even at her time, on some parts of Earth) few people lived to see sixty. (You, at twenty-eight, would have been entering middle-age.) Yet the essential *rhythms* of their lives were remarkably similar to our own. The advances of biophysics have enlarged our scope: we have more time for learning and living both; but we have correspondingly more to learn and live. We still progress through adolescence and education (which once ended at 14, then 18, 21, 25 . . .) to youth, marriage, procreation, maturity, middle age, senescence and death. And in a similar way, I think, there are certain rhythms of human history which recur in (widening, perhaps enriched, but increasingly discernible) moderately predictable patterns of motion and emotion both.

A recognition of this sort of rhythm is implicit, I think, in the joke that would not go away, which finally made the official name of the—ship?—in which you will depart *The Ark* (for *Archaic?*). In any case, this story is, on its most basic levels, an exposition of such rhythms: among them is the curious business of the generations, and their alternations: at least it was that thought (or rationale) that finally permitted me to indulge myself with my dramatic opening.

On an equally important, though more superficial, level, my purpose in putting this together is to provide you with —this is embarrassing—a 'heritage'. I had something of this sort from Joan Thurman, and found it valuable; whether this will be equally so for you, I do not know. I do know I have only two months left in which to put this together and that is little enough for an inexperienced story-teller like myself. (And glory-be! there *is* something I am inexperienced at. Many things, actually—but the writing of this is the first reminder I have had in a while. It feels *good* to be doing something new and difficult.)

My parenthesis seems to be full of parentheses. Well, I never was what you'd call a straight-line thinker: the side-trails are often more productive, anyhow . . .

And there I go again. What I set out to tell you here, Carla, is that this story was lived over many years, and written over a shorter period, but still a long one. There are the odd bits (like the one about Martha preceding this) which I did a long time ago, as a sort of 'therapy-writing' and kept, till now, to myself. Other parts, like what follows here, are adapted from Joan Thurman's papers. Some parts are new. And then there is this matter of rhythms again—

Some things in life remain vivid in minute detail till the day you die; others are of interest only as background. Some things are very personal and immediate, no matter how remote in time; others seem almost to be happening to another person, even as they occur. Thus, you will find this narrative full of sudden changes of pace and style. I find, for instance, that it is almost impossible in some sections to write about myself as 'Emma' in the third person; and other places equally difficult to say 'I' and 'me', but I do not think you will have too much trouble following.

III

I WAS BORN on Pluto, in the Earth-year 2026, and I grew up there. I was twenty-two years old when we boarded the *Newhope* to come to Uller. But that was such a long time ago, and so much has happened since, that the words themselves have lost all personal meaning to me. They are statistics. I am Emma Tarbell now, and have been for many years. My home is on Uller. A little girl named Emma Malook grew up on Pluto. Her mother's name was Ariadne, and her father's name was Bob. Her grandmother, Joan Thurman, was a famous pioneer, one of the first-ship colonists.

In the normal course of events, Joan would have taken her degree that spring, and gone to work as a biophysicist until she found a husband. The prospect appalled her. Nineteen months earlier she'd started the accelerated studies, without mentioning it at home; her mother thought she was busy with the usual run of extra-curricular self-expression at school. She'd had a year of avid learning before she passed the prelims, and was ready for advanced special training. That meant a different school, and the beginning of the psych conferences and background inquiries. She had to tell her family then.

The school was too near home for her to live in the already crowded dorms. She had to stick it out at home for six months of battle and persuasion, sleepless nights and stormy mornings. And all the time studying to be done.

She wasn't the only one. Even the dorm residents got it; letters and telegrams and phone calls, and frantic unannounced visitations. Two thousand of them entered final training together; less than seven hundred lasted the full six months, and most of those who left did so of their own accord.

Joan stuck it out, and she met Alex, and added to her fears and doubts: if one of them was chosen, and not the other . . . ?

Cautiously, they held back from commitments till the end. And then, in spite of any heaven or earth Martha could move, the decision was made. Joan had her one last month on Earth of joy and triumph: graduation, marriage, four weeks of honeymoon and fame; the planning, the packing, the round of farewells.

Now with her hand in Alex's, she followed the others, all in their gleaming white uniforms, up the ramp to the airlock, and into the third of a waiting line of moonbuggies. Ten buggies, ten passengers to each, two trips apiece, and the gaping hole in the side of the giant rocket had swallowed them all.

The rocket was not really large, not from the inside. So much fuel, so much freight, so many passengers; the proportions were flexible only within narrow limits. Each couple passed through the airlock hand in hand, and edged along the corridor, crabwise, to their own cubicle.

Inside, they stripped off the white snowy uniforms, folded them neatly, and piled them in the doorway for collection. Stripped to the skin, they checked their equipment for the last time, and settled themselves side by side, in the grooves and contours carefully moulded to their bodies.

In perfect drilled co-ordination, almost ritualistically, they closed down the compartmented upper sections, starting at the feet, and leaned across each other to latch the complex fastenings. When they were enclosed up to the armpits, they laid their heads into the fitted hollow facing each other at one-quarter-view, and strapped down the forehead bands and chin pads. Alex pushed the button that brought down the glassine air-dome over their upper bodies, and both of them set to work testing the supplier tubes and nozzles inside, making certain for one last extra time, that everything reached as far as it should. Then, in perfect unison, as if this too were part of the ritual they had learned, each one extended a hand for a last touch; grasped and held tight, and let loose in haste.

Someone came down the hall—they could still see through the open doorway—collecting the uniforms to be dumped before takeoff.

They wriggled their arms down into the cushioned spaces along their sides; later, the arms could be freed again, to manipulate the supplier tubes, but during acceleration, every part of the body was enwombed, protected from shock and pressure, cold and heat, nauseous fear and killing radiations.

A gong went off inside the head-dome; that meant they were sealed in now. The loudspeaker began to tick off seconds. Frantically, foolishly, Joan tried to move her hips, suddenly certain that a necessary opening in the nest had been misplaced. She never remembered to feel glorious. There was a blasting of soundless vibration, and a pushing, squeezing pain within the flesh, and brief relief about the placing of the opening, before the blackout came.

IV

PLUTO, PLANET OF MYSTERY

'. . . frozen dark wastes, forever uninhabitable to man? Or will our pioneering sons and daughters find a new world to live upon? No one can foretell what they will find. Our best astronomers are in dispute. Our largest and most piercing telescopes give us daily—or nightly —new information, which only contradicts the hypotheses of the night before . . .

'We literally do not know, even today—and it is now three quarters of a century since Clyde Tombaugh confirmed the existence of the planet—what the size, the mass, or the true temperature of Pluto are . . . whether it has a frozen atmosphere or none . . . what composes its dark surface . . . or whether it is a native of our solar system at all!'

The newspapers and broadcasters of the time speculated loudly on the likelihood that the bright remote planet was a visitor from the stars, a wandering planet caught at the very fringe of the sun's gravitation, or even a watchful outpost of some alien race, a conscious visitant, swinging in distant orbit around this star against the day when men propelled themselves beyond the boundaries of their own system.

They even mentioned, but less often, the great likelihood that the confusing data on the planet merely meant it was composed entirely of very heavy metals. Uranium, for instance . . .

But for the far-sighted, for the world planners, the politicians and promoters who had made the trip possible, the near-certainty of heavy metals was second only to one other goal: a starship.

The basic design of the *Newhope* was even then under government lock and key, a full forty years before the first step was taken in its construction. The fuel was in development. Astronomers, sociologists, metallurgists, psychologists, thousands of technicians and researchers on Earth and Mars and the Moon were tackling the thousand and one problems of development. And the entire line of work hinged on one combination: there had to be a source of heavy metals near the building site: and the building site had to be at the outer edges of the System.

But Pluto was on the way *out:* a step to the stars.

They lived in the rocket at first; it was specially designed for that. The fuel tanks had been built for conversion to living quarters, because nobody knew for sure when they set out whether they'd ever be able to live on the surface. So they swung the ship into a steady orbit around the planet, and got to work on conversion. The designs were good; it was only a short time before the living quarters were set up, and they could turn their attention to their new world.

What they found is by now so obvious and so familiar it is hard to conceive of the excitement of the discovery to *them*. But the simple discoveries of that first month could never have been made from Earth, or from Mars. For years astronomers had puzzled over the discrepancy between Pluto's reflective powers and its otherwise extrapolated size and mass. There had never been a valid planetary theory to account for its unique inclination to the ecliptic or the eccentricities of its orbit. Two years of observation by the Ganymede Expedition had added barely enough to what was already known to weigh the balance in favour of the completion of Project Pluto.

But from the vantage point of an orbit around the planet itself, the facts became self-evident. A whole new theory of planetary formation came into being almost overnight— and with it the final justification for the construction of the *Newhope*. There was no longer any doubt that other planetary systems existed; and in a surprisingly short time, the techniques for determining the nature of such planets were worked out as well.

Three months after arrival, the Pluto colonists began ferrying down the material for construction of a dome. Altogether, they lived in the rocket for thirteen Earth-months, before their surface settlement was habitable. But long before that, every one of them had at one time or another been down to the planet, and mining operations had begun.

Message rockets carried the progress reports back to Earth, and financial gears shifted everywhere. The government of the world poured all its power into the energizing of space-travel industries. A new ship was built in a tenth the time the first had taken, and a crew of three piloted urgently-needed supplies to the colonists.

Still, it was a one-way trip. Still, and for years to come, the supply rockets were designed for dismantling on arrival. Every part of a rocket-ship, after all, has an equivalent use on the ground; by building the ships themselves out of needed materials, the effective cargo space could be quadrupled.

From the beginning, every plan was made with one objective in view: the starhop. Nobody knew at first where the ship would go; no one understood *why* it had to go. But go it must, and Pluto was a waystation.

Joan Thurman died young; she was barely sixty-seven when the accumulated strains of the early Pluto years wore her out: at that, she outlasted all but three of her fellow-passengers on that first Pluto rocket; and she outlived her husband, Alex, by 28 years.

Alex Thurman died in '06 in the Dome Collapse at what was to have been Threetown. Joan had been working before that on the theory for open-air cities; but it was after the crash that she turned her whole being to a concentrated effort. The result was TAP: the Thurman Atmosphere Process. Or that was *one* of the results.

When Alex died, Joan had three small children: Ariadne was ten years old, one of the very first Pluto babies; just exactly old enough to be able to take on most of the care of Thomas and John who were four and three respectively.

Adne was born into pioneer hardship and pioneer cheerfulness. Then at the age of ten, the cheerfulness abruptly departed. Her father's seemingly indestructible strength betrayed her; her mother's watchful care was turned elsewhere. From the premature beginnings of her adolescence through its duration, she was effectively mother and housekeeper and wielder of authority to two growing vigorous boys.

When she was nineteen the first 'passenger ships' were established between Pluto and Earth—round-trip transports —and a new kind of colonist began to arrive. The Malooks, who landed in '17, were typical and Robert, their son-and-heir, was Ariadne's romantic ideal. When she was twenty they were married, despite everything that was done in either family to avert the expected disaster. For her, it was paradise . . . for a while. She read Bob's Earth-microfilms, and learned to imitate his Earth-accent. She never had to do a day's hard work from that time on, and still she had the handling of a charming irresponsible boy-child—as well as his money—until he grew up.

Bob was a year younger, you see . . . and till he did grow up, he loved having Adne's sweetly feminine domination exerted on his behalf. She showed him how to spend his money, how to live comfortably under dome conditions, how to adapt his Earth-education to Pluto's circumstances.

The disaster Joan and the Malooks had anticipated did not occur. Adne and Bob simply drifted apart, eventually after a few assertive acts on his part and several unpleasant quarrels. My birth may have precipitated things somewhat:

they had managed well enough for ten years before colonial social pressures pushed Ariadne into pregnancy. Perhaps, once I was born, she found an infant daughter more interesting than a full-grown son. I don't know. I knew surprisingly little about either of them at the time; it is only in retrospect—in parallel perhaps I should say—that I understand Ariadne at all. (If there had been any relatives on hand when Leah was growing up, I expect they'd have said she 'took after' her grandmother.)

As for Bob, I hardly knew him at all until after they separated, when I was five or six; after that, he took me out on holidays and excursions, and he was beyond a doubt the most charming, exciting, fascinating man who ever lived—until I got old enough to be awkward for him. I never knew for sure, but I think he was some sort of professional gambler, or high-class con man, later on.

One way and another, I can see why Joe Prell looked good to Ariadne after Bob. I was nine, then.

V

JOE PRELL was a brash newcomer, as social standing went on Pluto: a passenger, not a pioneer. But he was energetic and smart. Two years after he landed, he and Ariadne were married.

It made very little difference to Em at first. If anything she was happier after the divorce, because when she saw Bob, she had him all to herself. Anyhow, Joan was still alive then; her death, a year later, was a more serious matter.

By that time, though, Emma had begun to find a life of her own. She already knew that she wanted to be a doctor. She had learned chemistry and biology from her grandmother as easily and inevitably as she'd learned to eat with a spoon or later, to do a picture puzzle. She was still too young to start specializing in school, but she had Joan's library to work with. Joan's personal effects came to Emma, too, but the box of papers and letter-tapes didn't begin to interest her till much later. She spent most of her time, the next few years, bent over a micro-reader unrolling reel after reel of fascinating fact and speculation, absorbing all of it, and understanding little; just letting it accumulate in her mind for later use.

Adne disapproved. She thought Emma should play more, and spend more time with other children. But Adne was too busy to disapprove very forcibly. Joe Prell was not a tyrannical man; he was a demanding one. And somewhere in there the twins came along: two baby sisters called Teenie and Tess. Emma was briefly interested in the phenomena of birth and baby-care, but her 'coldblooded' and 'unnatural' experimental attitudes succeeded in horrifying Ariadne so thoroughly that she returned without much regret, and no further restraint, to the library.

By that time, too, Pluto was becoming a pleasant place to live. The first open-air city, built on the TAP principles, was completed when Emma was fourteen. Of course, only the richest people could afford it. The Prells could. Joe was a man who knew how to make the most out of a growing planet.

His financial operations were typical of his personality: he had a finger in real estate, and a finger in transport, but of course the big thing on Pluto was mining, and he had the other eight fingers firmly clamped into that.

Until they started building the *Newhope*. Or really, when they started talking seriously about it. Prell wised up fast. He let the real estate go and cut down on mining, and wound up with Pluto Transport neatly tied up in a bundle just right for his left hand. From that time on, Prell's right hand sold his left everything that was needed to build the starship Prell was publicly promoting.

It was a really big deal to him. To Emma it was a dream, a goal, the meaning of everything. Joe didn't understand any part of the significance of that ship . . . but with his uncanny feel for such things, he was right in the middle of all the important projects. He was in on the actual construction job; he knew about the new designs, and the fuel specs . . . knew at least as much as Emma did, or most of the others actually in the expedition. But he and Emma had very different notions of what that fuel meant, and they argued about it right up to the last minute.

Or, rather, she argued. Joe Prell never argued with

anybody. If he couldn't find a basis for agreement, he just turned the discussion into a joke.

Nothing could have been better calculated to infuriate Emma. She was twenty-four then, and very intense. Life was exciting, but more than that, life was terribly *important*. (As indeed it is, Carla; though I think you now see—or feel—the importance more clearly than I.) Prell wouldn't—couldn't—understand that; he never understood why anyone was willing to make the trip at all . . . to take a dangerous voyage to a distant unknown star!

Oh, he *could* see part of it: the challenge, the adventure. These are common enough stimuli, and the response to them not so different in nature from his own kind of adventurousness. It wasn't just wealth and power Joe was after; it was the getting of them, and he played the game as an artist. Patiently, over and over again (quite clearly feeling his responsibility *in loco*) he explained to Emma, and later to Ken, how little chance there was that the ship would ever reach Uller . . . how the voyagers were almost certainly doomed from the start . . . and how many other ways there were for restless, bright young people to satisfy their craving for excitement.

Emma sputtered and stammered trying to make him understand, but she succeeded only in making herself ludicrous. Actually, she didn't believe any more than he did that the ship had much chance of getting here. There were so *many* hazards, so many unknown factors; it was almost certain that somewhere in the plans some vital defence, some basic need, had been overlooked.

But the Project itself was important, whatever happened to those who were engaged in it. Just *building* the starship was what mattered: new problems to conquer, new knowledge to gain, new skills to acquire. And beyond that, the dream itself: 'Centuries gone, man looked to the stars and prayed . . . He made them his gods, then his garden of thought, then his goals . . .'

Emma quoted the speech of a long-dead man, and thought Joe Prell would understand. She even brought him, hesitantly, Joan Thurman's diary to read; that, if anything, should have made him understand.

Prell was amazed, but unconvinced. He expressed at some length, and with considerable wit, his astonishment that the girl who wrote that diary could later have done the painstaking practical work that developed TAP. He couldn't see that all of it was part of the same dream.

He listened a little more respectfully when Ken tried to explain. Curiously enough, the two men got along. Prell liked Tarbell, and Ken at least could understand the other man. (I think, too, Joe was much impressed by Ken's audacity in marrying me; it had been firmly concluded at home some time before that I was doomed to single bliss. Too direct, too determined, too intellectual, too *strong*; no man would feel up to it, said Ariadne, and her husband agreed.) Ken spoke more calmly than Emma had, with fewer words, and much less argument, but what he said amounted to the same thing, and Joe Prell couldn't see it. He was too busy making money.

And he made it. He made enough, among other things, to fulfil Ariadne's greatest dream: before she died, she had her trip to Earth; she saw the sights and institutions and museums, made all the tourist stops, brought home souvenirs enough to keep her content for her remaining years.

But before that, she saw her daughter Emma off for Uller.

Ariadne was present when the tender took off from Pluto Port to deliver the lambs to the slaughter, carry them off to the starship that had hovered for months like a giant moon around the planet.

'It's . . . beautiful,' someone standing beside her said, looking up, and Ariadne nodded automatically. It *was* beautiful; the most beautiful, most dangerous, most triumphant enemy she'd ever known, and she hated it with all the stored-up passion of her life.

'Emma!' she cried involuntarily in her farewell, 'Emmy, aren't you *afraid?*'

I tried to look at her, to let her look *into* me, but there was an unexpected veil of moisture on my eyes.

'I'm scared stiff,' I said, and it was true, and then I smiled to let her know it didn't matter.

Then Ken had come up from somewhere, and was right beside me. He hadn't heard; at least I hoped he hadn't. I flashed the same smile up at him, and looked away quickly, blinking the tear-mist out of my eyes, and trying to send a wordless warning to my mother. If she said anything now . . .

She didn't have a chance.

'Come on, kid,' Ken said. 'They're waiting.' He took my hand in one of his while he was still shaking hands with Joe Prell, and I blew a last kiss each to Tess and Teenie; then we turned and ran to the tender. I can remember being very conscious of our importance at the moment, how we must look to all the people there: two tall slim citizens of the universe, shining symbols of glamour and excitement.

Then we were in the tender, the whole bunch of us on our way up to the giant ship. All the familiar faces looked just a bit more formal and self-conscious than usual, in spite of being jammed into the inadequate space, and doubled up on the seats.

Somewhere in a corner, a group started singing, but no one else took it up, and it faded out. There wasn't much talk. We just sat there two by two . . . men and women, boys and girls really—and tried to visualize what lay ahead.

Somewhere out there, beyond the spatial comprehension of a system-bound being, was a star. They called it Beta Hydri; and a group of strange men in a learned university said it had a planet. They called the planet Uller, and credited it with mass and gravity and atmosphere tolerable to humans.

They could be wrong, of course. In thirty years of star-searching from the Pluto Observatory, it was the only one so credited. The professors weren't sure, but . . .

But someone had to go find out, and we were lucky. Out of the thousands upon thousands who applied for the privilege, we had been chosen. And even before we knew we were both to go, we'd found and chosen each other. We weren't cautious and careful the way Joan and Alex had been . . . the way most of the others in training were. The first time we met, we knew how it *had* to be for us. And though we worried, sometimes, that one of us would be picked, and the other left behind, it never seemed very likely; it just wouldn't *happen* that way.

But now we had chosen and been chosen in turn, and we had come to the end of the choosing.

When we left the tender, we knew what to do. We'd all done it dozens of times before in practice drill. We fled behind the couple in front to the ice trays, and took our places, lying down. We got our shots. When the crane lowered us into the hold, we still had our hands firmly intertwined. I know I shivered once, and thought I felt a tremor in Ken's hand and . . .

VI

AND WOKE UP slowly, still shivering, tingling in her toes and fingertips and nose and ears, as her body warmed. Her hand was still in Ken's, and he was grinning at her.

'We made it, kid.'

'So far,' she said.

Somebody handed her a bowl of soup. That seemed outlandish, for some reason, and then she realized why. They weren't back on Pluto now; they were in space . . . far out . . . how far? Her hand shook, and the spoon with it, spilling hot soup on her leg, and there was no reason after all why they shouldn't have soup on a spaceship. *How* far?

She managed to get a spoonful to her mouth, and became curious. Somebody had given it to her; who? She looked up.

Thad Levine was leaning over her, slipping a tray under the bowl for balance. He looked anxious. Em remembered him, and now consciously remembered everything.

'Where's Sally?' she asked, and found her voice sounded normal.

'Instrument check,' Thad said. The phrase was meaningful within seconds after she heard it, and then, as if a key had been turned in her mind, a whole set of meaning and concepts fell into place, and she was oriented.

Thad was looking down at her, smiling. 'Feels funny, doesn't it?' he said. 'Coming out, I mean.' Of course; he'd been through it all already.

'A lot better than it felt going down!' Ken said explosively.

Em nodded. 'Only I didn't really feel anything then,' she said, 'Did you? I was just . . .'

'*Scared!*' Ken picked up promptly on her hesitation. 'You and me, and all the rest of 'em too, baby.'

'The freeze is too fast for you to feel . . .' Thad started mechanically, and grinned and let it drop. They'd all heard it over and over, said it to each other again and again, during the months of training. They'd had their practice-freeze periods, and come out to reassure each other once more. 'It's too fast to feel anything.' The phrase was drummed into all of them before they went aboard for the last time. They all knew it.

But *cold* was not the only way it might make you feel; they all knew that by now. *Scared* was a feeling, too.

In training, you went into a room, and lay down in the tray, and you came to again in the same room, with the same people standing around, just a few hours, or even minutes, later. This time . . .

This time, they'd all gone under *not knowing:* not knowing whether they'd ever come out of it alive . . . whether their bodies could withstand year after year of frozen suspension, instead of the brief testing period . . . whether they'd wake up in the ship, or wind up as floating particles in space, or smashed on the surface of some unknown planet.

The Tarbells, Em and Ken, were just about half-way down the list, their shift of duty was timed for the twenty-fourth year of the voyage. And no one knew for sure that day they left whether the ship would really still be on its way in a quarter of a century.

Sally came in, bustling a little, as always. She was so familiar, she made Em realize for the first time how long it was. *On Pluto we'd be past forty now!*

'Em!' Sally rushed over to kiss her, and Ken must have realized at the same time Emma did that they'd hardly touched each other.

'Hey, she's *mine,*' he said. And with his arms around her, everything was perfectly normal again.

(Parenthesis to Carla: ii)

27/9/52

It is a curious phenomenon of the human mind—or at

least of mine—that past pain is painless in recall, but pleasure past and lost is excruciating to remember. I have found that for the purposes of telling this story I can readily undergo Recall Process for almost any desired period. The 'Pluto Planet of Mystery' article came up intact from a batch of Joan Thurman's papers that I looked at more than a hundred years ago. And I went back to remember what Joe Prell looked like, and how he laughed at me. That didn't hurt in memory: it made me angry, both at his stupidity and his unkindness, but it didn't hurt.

Carla, I tried to do Recall on the eighteen months I spent in space with Ken, and with the four other couples who at one time or other were shift-partners. I know it was the *happiest* time I ever spent, but the one little part I remembered in detail, the section you have already read, was so packed with poignant pleasure that it almost stopped this work entirely.

I shall not attempt again to recall my days and nights with Ken. As much as I remember, through a rosy blur, is all I feel competent to talk of. It took years after his death to adjust to the loss. I do not know that I could make that adjustment again, and will not subject myself to it.

As for the details of the trip . . . they are interesting, but I'm afraid they're all laid over with the sentimental mist that emanates from my happiness. It must have been vastly uncomfortable in the tiny cubicle we had as home. Certainly, we fought claustrophobia every minute of the time. We worked very hard, I know, and we were never quite without fear.

The starship *Newhope* had accommodation for five hundred passengers in the deep freeze, but only six in the living quarters. Three tiny cubicles surrounded three beds, and the walls were lined with overarm storage space.

The ship had been carefully designed to be run in routine circumstances by a crew of six, and a cautious and foresighted psychologist had arranged for overlapping shifts. When we woke up, the Levines were ending their shift: it was their last night out. We shared the first six months with Ray and Veda Toglio, and the Gorevitches. Six months later, another couple replaced the Toglios and six months after that it rotated again. Shift-change nights were big events. Later, the new couple would read the Log, and catch up on everything, but that first night everything would come out in a jumble of incident and anecdote, gossip and laughter: the no-doubt grossly exaggerated story of the error Jommy Bacon made three shifts back, before the Levines came out . . . a joke written into the log by Tom Kielty, fourteen years ago, but still fresh and funny . . . the harrowing account of a meeting with a comet in the third year out.

It is difficult to picture the situation. Next month you are going to a planet infinitely farther away than Uller was from Earth, and yet you know with great exactness what you will find there. We had no such instruments in our day as now exist. All we knew when we set out was that this star appeared to have planets composed of terrestrial elements in quantities and proportions similar to those of the habitable solar planets.

We did not know whether we would find a place with breathable atmosphere, or bearable gravity, or water, or . . . or whether we'd find a planet at all. When our shift ended, and we went back into the freeze, it would be with almost as much uncertainty as the first time.

There was nothing to be certain of except the difficulties we had yet to face: if everything else worked out, if we completed the trip, and found a suitable planet, we would still be presented with almost insuperable obstacles. It was atomic fuel, after all, that made the starhop possible; it also made unthinkable any such doubling in space as had been designed for the Pluto ship. Our fuel tanks would be too hot for human habitation twenty years after we landed.

We weren't going to be able to live in an orbit; we were going to have to land and establish ourselves—wherever we were going—as quickly as we could.

VII

I DIDN'T GET out of the ship at all in the first thirty-six hours. There were twelve of us medics specially trained for the job of defrosting, and we had equipment to do only three couples at a time. Three medics to a unit, we worked over the humming machinery and the still bodies, testing, checking, adjusting, and checking again. You don't save seconds when the use of a limb or the functioning of an organ is involved.

Every delicate part of the human beings we worked over had to receive the same minute attentions: quick-thaw, circulator, oiler, hydrator . . . and then, when they began to come out of it, some familiar face to watch over them, to say the right things, to bring food at the right time.

But that part wasn't our job. Jose Cabrini was in charge in the awakening room. They came into our section frozen and motionless; they went out thawed, still motionless. It was weird and unreal and disheartening. We kept doing it because it was the thing to do, six hours on, three hours off to catnap in one of the cubicles, and back again to the waxen-stiff shapes of human bodies.

Ken was outside all that time. He was in the first batch of defrosts: a construction expert, he was also a third-generation Marsman. He was born in Taptown on Mars—the first TAP settlement—and had grown up under primitive open-air frontier conditions: a big-chested hawk-nosed man, wiry-muscled, steel-boned and almost literally leather-skinned. All the Marsmen we had were sent out in the first groups.

There were fifteen men altogether in his construction gang. In haste and near-total silence, still orienting to consciousness, they ate their bowls of fortified soup, drew their tools from Supply, and filed into the air space between the flimsy backwall of the tanks and the alumalloy sheets of the inner hull.

There was just space enough to stand and work while they pried the first plates loose. After that, they had more space: another twelve inches to the mid-plates.

Here they could begin to see space damage, the dents and warps of imploding matter from outside—even an occasional rent in the metal fabric.

Five of the big plates to make a shelter. Each one went a little more quickly. In twenty minutes they were ready to go Outside.

They knew it was safe. Other people were Out there already. But each of them had lived through eighteen months of that voyage, consciously: eighteen months of smooth plates underfoot and glowing indirect lighting, of cramped quarters enclosed by walls, and cutting corners to save space—eighteen months closed in *from* Space . . .

They stood in the lock, and hesitated. Eyes met, and looked away.

Then somebody said:

'What the hell are we waiting for?'

'Sure, let's go out and take a walk.'

'Come on out, the air is fine,' someone else said shrilly.

Ken was Mars-born, and tough; he couldn't remember ever feeling this way before. He noticed it was an Earther who finally laid hand on the lever to open the door.

They left the plates in the lock while they got their footing on the terrain, and blinked back the light of the sun.

Some of the others were cold, but Ken had chased sand devils on Mars at 10 below. He let the strange sun hit his head, drew the strange breath into his lungs, and exultation exploded inside him.

He wanted to shout; he wanted to run; he wanted to kiss the ground beneath his feet, embrace the man next to him. He wanted to get Emma and pull her out of the ship. He turned to the others.

'Come on!' he shouted. 'Let's go!'

They dragged the heavy plates over the ground to a spot already marked out, and started building.

It was almost too easy.

Everything went according to schedule. The plans for re-use of the inner plates turned out to be sound. The temporary shelters were up and ready for use before the sun went down, and by the next day they were even moderately comfortable inside. Every bit of material that had gone into the construction of the starship, save the fuel areas and the outer hull, had been designed to serve a double purpose, and almost every design was satisfactory and practicable.

Oh, it wasn't easy in terms of work. Every man and woman of the five hundred worked till they dropped, those first two days. It wasn't just construction and renovation. There was an infinite amount of testing and retesting to be done, checking and rechecking. Round-the-clock shifts were

stationed in the labs and at the instruments, for the ac-
cumulation of data about the new planet, its star and system, its chemistry and geology and biology.

And through all the furious activity, data continued to
accumulate. Almost-continuous broadcasts over the loudspeaker system relayed information to workers in and out
of ship.

We heard the story of the landing: how the crew had
tested the planets, one by one, with routine spectroscopy
and boomer-rocket samplers: the tenth at a distance vastly
greater than Pluto's from the sun; the eighth, fifth, fourth
(the missing ones were on the other side of the sun); and
each time found rock-ribbed wastes, without air, without
warmth, without hope of hospitality.

The third could have been made habitable, if necessary.
To create an atmosphere is possible, when you have a
base from which to work. But to have moved out of our
ship into domes would have been difficult. We didn't have
to. The second planet was Uller.

To those of us who were still in ship, the reports were
probably more impressive than to those outside. If you
could *see* the earth and feel it underfoot, if you were
actually *breathing* the air, and lifting and carrying against
the pull of gravity, the facts and figures wouldn't mean so
much.

To me, each new item of information was overwhelming.

Atmosphere almost Earth-normal (closer than Mars';
as good as the best open-air city on Pluto).

Gravity almost Earth-normal (closer than any other
solar planet).

Temperature outside, 8 degrees C. at the equator, where
we'd landed. (Warmer than Mars; infinitely warmer than
Pluto. *Liveable!*)

First chemical analyses showed a scarcity of calcium, a
scarcity of chlorine, an abundance of silicon.

Water: *drinkable!*

That floored me completely. To travel across the void,
to an unknown planet, and find good drinking water!
Well, not really *good;* the water here is actually a dilute
solution of what we used to call 'water glass' back on
Pluto. It didn't *taste* right, but it wasn't harmful. (And in
the early days in Josetown I got used to the taste, too. We

didn't take the trouble to Precipitate it half the time.)

Uller was simply, unbelievably, Earth-like. With the single exception of the silicon change in chemistry, it might almost have been Earth.

These things are easy to remember and record. Speeches and announcements, and the impact of thoughts and words . . . but I find it almost impossible to visualize again the way Uller looked to me when I first saw it. It all seems natural and familiar now; I know how strange and beautiful and frightening it was then, but I cannot quite place what was strange, or what was terrifying, or what seemed so lovely. What was a foreign place has become home.

And if I could remember clearly, how could I describe it to people who have grown here?

I can only describe it as it looked to Emma, who grew up on Pluto, when it was her turn at last to stand with a group of medics in the airlock, and hesitate.

Sound, sight, smell, sensation . . . a whole new world, a strange world, a fairyland fantasy world of gem-encrusted trees and opalescent plants, of granular smooth ground laid out in shimmering changeable striae of colour . . .

And all of it the stranger for the incredibly Earth-like sunset. She'd seen that sunset thirty times on Earth, and marvelled every time. Here it was again, the same in every way, except for the sparkling reflections it struck from the impossible tree-trunks and flowers.

Around it all the smell of growing things, subtly familiar, tangy, hard to identify, but undeniably the scent of life.

The double row of alumalloy structures looked dull and ugly in this stage-setting of iridescence.

And it was cool . . . cold even, but that didn't matter.

Where's Ken?

For thirty-six hours she had been awake, and she had not yet touched him or talked with him.

She stood there, feeling the gritty granular *earth* beneath her feet, through her boots, not really looking at things not trying to see or hear or taste or smell, but letting everything impinge on her, soak in as it would, while her eyes moved urgently, seeking one person in the weaving patterns around the street of houses, listening for just one voice in the murmuring welter of sound. Thirty-six hours one way, but literally *years,* in another sense . . .

'Em!'

He charged across the open space, big and bony and beautiful, grimy, unshaven, hollow-eyed, his coveralls flapping around his legs, his arms reaching out for her long before he got there.

'Em!'

His arms went around her, pulling her against him, lifting her clear off the ground. The bristly hair on his face scratched her cheek and the dirt of the new planet rubbed off his coveralls on to her spotless white jacket, and she smiled and opened her lips to his.

'You're cold,' he said, after a while.

'Cold?' They found each other again, with hands, with eyes, with lips, and they stood close in a warmth of their own while the wind went around them.

Cold?

She laughed against his shoulder, opened her eyes sidewise to a flash of brilliant colour, and backed off to look at *him* instead.

'Break it u-u-p!'

Someone was shouting at them, teasing, and someone else took her arm, and there was a whole crowd of people talking at once; she never remembered who they were, but friends, all of them, familiar faces. Hands to shake and cheeks to kiss, and excited words and gestures. And then more work to do.

Ten couples to a household; that was the plan for the temporary settlement. The outer walls and roofs were finished, but inside partitioning was still going on. Everyone helped; they all wanted their own rooms finished for the night.

Someone came around distributing mattress sacks, and Ken went off with Thad Levine to find an air pump. There was wild hilarity and a strange admixture of hysteria with relief, as one couple after another finished off their partitions, and joined the others in the central hall.

Ken and Em stood a little apart from the others, watching, very much aware of the special and extraordinary quality of their own happiness.

Out of a picked group of five hundred healthy eager young men and women it is not difficult to select two

hundred and fifty well-matched couples. Yet, when it is
necessary to couple off, and all five hundred know it, a
true marriage is the exception. Ken and Em were lucky,
and they knew it. Em, watching the others, with Ken's
arm around her, wanted somehow to share with all of them
the flood of emotion in which she herself was caught up.
They were all so impoverished by comparison . . .

The one unbearable thought ran fleeting across her mind,
and left with it a chill of envy for those other poor ones:

If anything happens to him . . .

Her hand tightened on his, and he looked down to her,
not smiling, knowing what she felt. Together, they moved
away from the group. They went into their empty room,
and closed the new-hung door behind them.

A body is a solitary thing. You live with it, live in it, use
its parts as best you can. But always it is alone, a thing
apart, your own unique and individual portion of space.

It stands alone while the mind flicks out to make contact
with the surrounding world; while the brain receives images
from the eyes, the nose, the ears; while the mouth tastes
and the fingers touch: and even while food is swallowed and
ingested. All this time the body, as a whole, is lonely.

At points in time, infinitely far apart from the viewpoint of the cell-components of this body, two people may
find unity, complete and perfect, with each other. In the
act of procreation confluence occurs—or more often in the
mimicry of the act.

Many bodies never know anything but solitude. The motions of procreation are gone through again and yet again,
without awareness. But Kenneth and Emma Tarbell were
fortunate in their bodies. Loneliness called to desperate
isolation, and they came together from the first with ease
and understanding.

They kissed. That was all, for the time being: mouth
to mouth, sealed together, while the breath sweetened between them, his hand on her shoulder, hers against his back,
merged to a single entity. They kissed, endlessly, and without reserve.

Then they lay back on the floor together, close and content, relaxed and knowledgeable in their unity with each
other.

After a while Ken moved. He lifted himself on an elbow, looked down on her peaceful face, and traced her smile with a fingertip. Her eyes opened, welcoming his touch, and she stretched luxuriously, with great contentment, then turned to meet his hunger with her own.

When Sally came banging on the door, yelling about dinner, they realized they were both starved. They went out and sat in a circle with the others, in the central hall, eating the landing meal of roast beef and corn and fruit that had left with them, and travelled with them in the freezer across the years. And with it they drank, most ceremoniously, coffee made from Uller-water. The vinegar-precipitation gave it an odd taste, but from that day on the taste of vinegar was good to all of them.

Little by little, the realization was sinking in. They were, thus, easily, and without obstacles, established on a planet twenty-one light years from home!

None of them stayed long after dinner. Two by two, they went off to their small separate cubicles, dragging their mattresses with them.

Leah Tarbell was not the only baby conceived that night.

VIII

THEY WOKE UP to brilliant sunlight, chill still air, and a hubbub of human activity. The big project now was exploration. The observations made by the landing crew indicated that the near-equatorial spot where they had landed was probably the most favourable location for a settlement. But we wanted closer ground observation before any further effort was made to establish the colony on a permanent basis.

Conditions over the surface of the planet varied widely— or *wildly* would be a better word, from the point of view of a solar meteorologist. This was the first human contact with a planet whose axis of rotation lay in the plane of its orbit of revolution. All the solar planets have axes more or less perpendicular to their orbits. On Earth, for instance, there is a short winter-night and corresponding summer-day at either pole: but only at the poles. It took a good deal of readjustment in thinking habits to calculate Uller conditions with any degree of realistic accuracy.

The most obvious activity that day was the beginning of the construction of light aircraft for exploratory trips. Ken, of course, stayed on construction work, salvaging parts from the bowels of the big ship to build the smaller ones.

Meantime, scouting parties were being briefed and trained for their work, absorbing new information about what they were likely to find just as fast as it came out of the labs, still operating in ship around the clock. And everyone not directly concerned with the big project, or working in the labs, was assigned to one of the local scouting groups or specimen-collecting squads. Em found herself safety-monitoring a batch of wide-eyed collectors under the direction of a botanist, Eric Karga.

There were seven of them in the party, the others loaded down with sample cases and preservatives, Emma with a battery of micro-instruments strapped about her waist, a radiophone suspended in front of her face; and a kit of testing tongs and chemical reactors flapping against her leg. Nothing was to be touched bare-handed, smelled, or sampled, until the monitors' instruments had analysed it, and a verbal report on procedure had been made to the ship. With these provisions, it became evident almost as soon as they entered the forest that there were too many collectors, and not enough instruments. Karga himself would have thrown all discretion to the winds . . . if there had been any wind, that is.

That was the first thing Emma became aware of, when they were out of range of the bustling activity of the settlement: the literally unearthly silence. Emma had grown up in this kind of background-silence, under domes. Later, she'd lived in a TAP open-air city filled with 'natural' noises: leaves rustling in a made-breeze; birds singing; small animals squeaking and creeping; an uninterrupted and infinitely inventive symphony of sound, behind and around the machines and voices and activities of men.

Here, in a *natural* open-air world, there was nothing to hear but the excited busy-ness of the small group of people: Karga rushing recklessly from horny-tipped plants to opalescent trees; the monitor-instruments clicking off their messages; the steady murmur of my own voice into the radiphone; and the awed exclamation of the collectors as novelty after unexpected novelty was uncovered in the fairyland fantasy of a forest.

The first two-hour period went by almost before they realized it. None of them wanted to go back, and the pre-arranged return for a complete checkup in medicentre seemed foolish even to Em, considering how careful on-the-spot precautions had been. But they really needed another monitor, or at least, another phone. And even more to the point: the rule had been established; therefore it must be obeyed. Regularity and conformity are the materials of which caution is formed, and caution was the order of the day.

Five hundred people seemed like a lot when they were all crowded into the tender that took them up to the *Newhope* orbit around Pluto; or when they were being processed through defrost, the first two days on Uller; or when shelter had to be provided, and fast, for all of them. Now, looking outward from a double row of thin metal-walled huts at an unknown planet, five hundred humans seemed very few indeed. One death would leave a hole that could not be filled.

They griped about the unnecessary precautions all the way back but back they went, and through the careful psychophysical that Jose Cabrini and Basil Dooley had worked out together.

Over a quick cup of coffee, they picked up some fresh data on the morning's discoveries. Evidence so far showed no signs of a dominant civilized, or even intelligent, natural species. Some small carapaced insect-like creatures had been found, one or two varieties in abundance. And the river from which they had drawn and purified their water was teeming with microscopic life. But nothing larger than a healthy Earth-type cockroach had turned up yet, and nothing any more dangerous either.

The small fauna, like the plant life, appeared to be almost entirely constructed along the lines of the silicate exoskeleton, carbon metabolism variety. Some of the smallest amoebae lacked the skeleton, but everything larger had it, and it seemed doubtful, therefore, that any larger form of mobile life would exist. The beautiful brittle tree-trunks had rigidity against the weather, but little flexibility. The arrangement would hardly be suitable for a large-size animal of any kind. Jose still seemed to be determinedly hopeful of finding intelligent life—but in the total absence of any such indications emphasis was being placed temporarily on the investigation of plant life.

When they came back from the second shift, they found tables and benches set up in the street between the huts, with a defrosting selector at one end. Emma hurried through her checkup, and went out to look for Ken. He wasn't at any of the tables, or anywhere in sight. Finally she picked out a lunch, and walked down the row of tables to where a group of medics were gathered. Most of them had been out on monitor duty that morning; all of them were engaged in eager debate; and Cabrini and Dooley seemed to be the opposing centres.

Jose was talking as she sat down. 'Lab says all the fauna so far are vulnerable to vibration. Those quartz shells are brittle,' he expounded earnestly. 'So suppose there *was* an intelligent species? Wouldn't it stay the hell away from a spot where a rocket came down?'

'And then all the building and tramping around,' someone else put in thoughtfully.

It fitted with the silence of the forest. 'It's hard to imagine a civilization without any noise,' she put in. 'I know it could happen, but it just doesn't fit *my* conditioning about what constitutes intelligence.' She grinned, and waved an arm pointedly around the table. 'What good is it if you can't have three people talking at once?'

'They're too small, anyhow,' Basil Dooley insisted. 'They'd shake themselves to pieces if they got big enough to *do* anything.'

'You can have intelligence without artifacts,' Jo said stubbornly, 'and without noise, too. Even without vocal noise.' He gulped at some coffee, and went on before anyone else could get fairly started: 'Or suppose they're so small we just haven't noticed? Why do they have to be *big*? Maybe something we think is a plant is really a termite-tower, like the ones on Earth? Or a hill out there somewhere is full of things the size of ants that are just smart enough not to want to show their faces? On a planet this size, a *small* species could have a completely material civilization, if that's what you're looking for—they could even make noise, by their own standards—and we'd have a hell of a time finding out about it.'

'Well, they'd have some kind of effect on the ecology of the planet, wouldn't they?'

'We wouldn't know that yet, either,' Emma said slowly. She was excited now, turning over the possibilities Jo was suggesting, but she knew better than to display her excitement in the discussion. People always seemed to mistrust enthusiasm. 'TAP is honest ecology,' she pointed out. 'An alien coming to Pluto would have a rough time finding out that the open-air cities are all artificial.'

Intelligent life! Non-human, non-solar intelligent life! And it was possible! This world had every prerequisite for it.

'Well, if they're that small, you're going to have some trouble talking to them.'

'Might *never* find out,' someone else suggested, 'if they didn't find some way to communicate with humans. That's your real problem, Jo. Suppose you find these critters? How are you going to talk to them? And turn it around: if they live in what looks like natural circumstances to us, how will we know which ones to try and talk to?'

'Which sums up neatly,' Jo answered him, 'the problems to which I shall probably devote the rest of my life.'

There was an intensity in his tone that silenced the table for a moment.

'Then whatever they are, let's hope you don't find 'em. We can't afford to lose your services, Jo.' It was Ken. He slid his long legs over the bench next to Emma, and squeezed her hand. 'What goes on?'

Everybody began talking at once again; everyone except Emma, who was surprised at the irritation she felt. He had no business stepping on Jo that way, she thought; and she didn't want to talk about it any more.

'Aren't you eating?' she asked.

'Ate before; they said you were getting a checkup, so I had lunch and left my coffee to have with you.'

He smiled at her, and reached for her hand again, and the irritation vanished. Even when the argument resumed, and she found that the two of them were tending to opposite extremes of attitude, she wasn't annoyed any more.

They didn't have to agree about everything, after all. They had disagreed before. But this was such an *important* thing—the way you'd feel about an alien creature.

Still, she could understand it better in Ken than in Basil. Ken was a constructions man. His work was in materials; in parts and pieces to fit together. He didn't think in terms of the living organism, or the subtle and marvellous interplay of functions between organs, organism, individuals, species. Basil was a medic, and a good one; he should have understood.

Karga was at her shoulder, politely restraining himself from urging her, but too anxious to keep himself from a silent display of impatience. She stood up, and threw off the whole foolish mood. Ken would understand when they had more time to talk. And there would be plenty of time later . . .

IX

IT MIGHT HAVE been a segment of petrified log. But it had legs, and the tapered bulbous end was a head. It might have been a cross between a pig and a dachshund, painted in streaky silver, and speckled with sequins. But it had *six* legs, and the head was too shapeless; there was no visible mouth and there were no ears at all.

And when you looked more closely, it wasn't actually walking. It was skating; six-legged tandem skating, with the sharp-runnered feet never lifting out of the ground, leaving an even double row of lines incised in the granular ground behind it. And the squat barrel body glided forward with unexpected grace.

It moved into the street of huts, its head set rigidly right in front of its body, while the bulging dull black eyes darted and danced in all directions.

The first man who saw it shouted, and it froze in mid-glide. Then the man's comrade silenced him, and the creature started forward again. A crowd began to gather and after the manner of a crowd, a murmuring noise grew from it. The creature froze once more, and veered off in another direction.

Someone in the crowd had a gun. He raised it, and took careful aim, but someone else reached out to lower the barrel before the fool could shoot.

'It hasn't hurt anything!'

'Why wait till it does?'

'How do you know . . .?'

'Here's Jose.'

'Hey, Jo, here's your native. Look smart to you?'

Laughter. Comments and wonder and more and more uncontrollable laughter, while the creature skated directly away from the crowd and edged up against an alumalloy hut.

'Think we can catch it?'

'The projector . . . are they getting it?'

Jose sent a whisper running back, and it only increased the volume of the sound. Better one noise than the hub-bub, he thought, and spoke sharply above the crowd.

'Quiet!' Then in the momentary silence spoke more softly. 'I don't think it likes noise.'

After that, he left the group, and stepped forward stead-ily, slowly, towards the shadow of the hut where the crea-ture stood.

He tried to curb his own eagerness, and make his ad-vance without hurry and without menace. He tried, too, to ignore the slowly swelling hum of the crowd behind him. All his thoughts were on the animal, all his attention focused.

If it had intelligence, there had to be a way, *some* way, to make contact with it.

He was close enough now to touch it if he would, but he held back. It was looking at him, and from that moment on, he never once doubted that the animal was rational, impressionable, capable of communication. It was there in the eyes, in the way the eyes studied him, in something he *felt* in his own mind, hazily and without comprehension, examination-and-greeting was exchanged between them.

The creature turned to the hut, and there was a ques-tioning feeling in Jose's mind. He did not want to speak aloud. Telepathy? Something of the sort. He thought the idea of a dwelling place, a shelter; all animals understood the concept. He thought it hard as he could, and knew he had failed, because the animal's next act was one of deliberate destruction.

Jose was the only one close enough to see exactly what was happening, but by that time they had cameras running from three different angles. Everybody saw the details, blown up, later: the people in the crowd, and those who, like Ken, were in ship, or like Em, out of the settlement.

It glided forward smoothly once again, edging towards the house, and gradually its body tilted sideways at an angle to the ground, without bending except at a concealed joint between the barrel-trunk and the right-hand set of legs.

The left-hand set described a perfect clean curve up the side of the building and down to the ground again. Then it reversed, and moving backwards, once more standing upright, edged the left-hand front runner slightly sideways and sheared a neat chord out of the wall.

The crowd saw the piece of metal fall away, and gasped, in unison, and then, for the first time, fell completely silent. What had just happened was virtually impossible. Alumalloy was *tough*. An oxy torch would cut it . . . in a matter of hours. This creature had sliced it like a piece of meat.

The man with the gun took aim again, and nobody stopped him, but he couldn't fire. Jose was too close to the beast.

'Jo!' he called, and then a woman's voice said loudly, 'Shhh!' as the animal froze again. Jose looked around and smiled and waved another silencing motion at them.

He looked back just in time to see the tuskongs coming out. Two parallel needle-edged blades, curved like a set of parentheses, they descended slowly from underneath the head, and went through the metal like tongues of fire through straw. The creature glided forward, and a long thin strip was sliced from the centre of the chord. The blades were hinged, somehow, and they seemed to be sticky inside. The needle edges met under the strip of metal, and the strip was carried up inside the tusks—or tongs—as they retracted slowly into whatever opening (a mouth?) they came from.

'Jo, get outa there! I'm gonna shoot!'

There was no doubting that tone of voice. Jose held up

a pleading hand, and stepping softly, walked backwards towards the crowd. Until he turned around, he knew, the man would hold fire. He waited till he was too close for his turned back to matter any more, then asked quietly, with all the command he could put into a low tone. 'Wait.'

'Why?' The man whispered in reply; then he would wait to shoot.

'We might as well see what it's going to do.'

'Ruined a wall already. Why wait for more?'

The words were passed back through the crowd, and the murmuring swelled again. The creature seemed to have adjusted to the noise. Calmly, it sliced another strip of the virtually impregnable alloy, and drew the metal into its interior.

Then, while they watched, it turned again to the wall, and, folding its front legs under it, slanted forward to edge its snub-ended snout inside.

The gun came up once more, and Jose knew he couldn't stop it: the beast had poked its head inside a sacrosanct human habitation. But: 'Higher!' he whispered piercingly, 'Over its head!' The barrel jerked upward imperceptibly just as the gun fired.

It couldn't have hit; Jose was sure of that. But a sunburst of cracks appeared on the surface of the animal's hide, for all the world like the impact of a projectile on bullet-proof glass. And at the same instant a jagged lightning-streak arced from the centre of the 'wound' to the side of the hut.

The gunner drew his breath in sharply. 'It's a goddam walkin' dynamo!'

And the crowd-talk started up once more.

'Quartz . . . crystals . . . piezo-electric . . . *generates!*'

It's scared, Jose thought—but now the animal had shown what power it had, so was the man. The gun came up again.

'*Stop!*' Jose shouted. 'Can't you see it's scared?'

It worked: not on the man, but as Jose had hoped, on the beast, and the man hesitated. The creature backed away from the wall, and started forward past the hut, away from the crowd and the street. It was leaning to one side, the good side, and lurching a little, going very slowly. Now its trail was a deep indentation on one side, and a barely marked line on the other, and in between a greyish ooze of something that didn't seem to be coming from the injured side. Perhaps from the 'mouth' or whatever those tusks went into? It was hard to tell.

The gunner still stood with his weapon half-raised.

'The field projector,' Jose whispered to him, and the man handed his gun to his neighbour, and ran for the rocket.

The Ullern animal had progressed perhaps fifty metres when he came out of the airlock again, a dozen others tumbling after him, with bulky pieces of equipment that took rapid shape on the ground.

There was grim speed in the way they worked. Jose, watching them, understood their fear, and could not share it; felt the pain of the hurt animal and grieved for it; fervently hoped the creature's piezo-electric properties would not make it unduly vulnerable to the projector.

There was a crackling, blinding flash of electricity as the field hit it.

Ken Tarbell answered the alarm bell reflexively, absorbed the data, and fell into drilled pattern responses with the projector team, getting it out of the airlock, setting it up, aiming, firing.

It should have trapped the animal in an invisible miniature dome through which no physical object could pass. Instead there was a small-scale electric storm over the creature, and when the glare was gone, it was lurching along just as slowly as before, with an odd look of urgency, but apparently none the worse for wear.

There was total silence in the camp, and then a shot shattered the quiet. Ken saw it hit; he saw the bullet *bounce* off the creature's hide, and saw the ragged black cracks radiate from the point of impact on the glittering surface of the skin. And he saw the *thing* keep moving, a little slower maybe, but still making progress. It was heading out of the camp, in the direction Karga's team had taken. It was heading towards the forest where Emma was.

Had anyone warned them?

Em had a radiophone; Ken turned and raced back to the ship, fear moving his feet while completely separate thoughts went through his head. The thing could fight off an electromagnetic field, but it was vulnerable to shock; he knew how to stop it.

In ship, he clambered up the ladder to Supply, grabbed the two things he needed, and leaped down again ignoring the footholds. Outside, he realized the others were on the same track; but their weapon was not strong enough. The crowd had separated into three groups, surrounding the thing, and they were shouting at it, screaming, singing, yelling, stomping, first from one side, then the other.

Each time it responded more feebly than before, moving away from the new source of noise. Someone ran past Ken, headed for the ship, and he caught from somewhere else a few words of questioning conversation. They thought they could head it into a trap; but what kind of trap would *hold* it?

Ken had the phone ready at his mouth, and his weapon in his hand. His eyes were on the beast, and he saw that each time the direction of the noises changed, it seemed a little less frightened, a little less anxious to change its path. Any animal learns what to fear and what is safe. The shouting wouldn't hold it long, he thought, and as he thought it, saw the creature head straight for the group that stood between it and the forest-edge, undeterred by stamping, screaming cacophony.

'Emma! Em!' He spoke urgently, low-voiced, into the phone. 'There's an animal here. Headed your way, *Watch out!*'

He didn't realize for the first instant what had happened. The Ullern wasn't limping out towards the forest any more. It was moving fast now, as if something had galvanized it into action, somehow summoned its last resources of strength and speed. It was gliding fast and smooth and with a purpose in its direction . . . back into camp, back towards the rocket, *straight at Ken.*

It was coming too fast to stop or fight or escape. There was only one thing to do, and Ken did it. He threw the hand grenade he'd brought from the ship.

Let me through now, everybody out of the way, I'm a doctor, let me get through. There's a man hurt in there, I'm a doctor.

Ken, oh Ken . . .

Come on now, everybody out of the way, this door is in the way. Oh, Ken!

'I'm sorry, Emma. You know we can't let you in. We're doing everything we can . . .'

'Oh, Basil, don't be silly. I have a *right* to help.'

'Em, I think we can manage better than you could. He's . . . he's pretty badly cut up. You'd be bound to . . .'

'What do you think I am, Dooley? Somebody's snivelling wife? I'm *a doctor!' And this is how they feel when we tell them they have to wait, now I'm not a doctor, he's right, I'm a snivelling wife, I'm even snivelling, I can hear it. But I'm a doctor, if I act like one they'll have to let me in . . .* 'What . . . what do you . . . What are his chances, Doctor?'

'They'll be better if we let Basil get back in there, Em.'

'Oh, it's you, is it? The nice careful semantic psychologist, the happy little word-weigher, the fellow who wanted to see some native life!' 'Leave me alone, Jose. Please, go away! Basil . . .'

Basil is gone, he went back to Ken, you can't go to Ken, they won't let you, they're going to let him die, and they won't let you help, they've got the door locked too, you tried that before, and they're all in there and they'll let him die.

'Em . . .'

'I said go away. Leave me *alone,* won't you?'

'Em . . . it's me, Thad.'

And she collapsed gratefully, childishly, in familiar, friendly arms, abandoning the effort to be calm, to be convincing, to be reasonable and professional. They weren't going to let her into that room, whatever she did, so she sobbed in Thad's arms, until he said:

'Go on, Emmy, cry all you want to.' And then she stopped.

The door opened and closed again, and she looked up at Thad, and saw the news there, and all the confused emotion was gone. Now she was calm enough, and tired.

'He's . . .'

'Dead,' Thad said the word out loud; one of them had to. 'They never let me say good-bye.'

'He wasn't conscious, Em.'
'He would have known!'
Thad didn't try to answer.

X

TWO DAYS LATER, the entire settlement was fenced in with a vibration-field. No other animals showed up in the time it took to get the fence operating; and the occasional creature that came in sight afterwards turned quickly away. We knew, from that first experience, that vibration was not necessarily fatal to the beasts, but that they could be frightened and/or hurt by anything along the line, in or out of the human sonic range.

I think now that most of us rather overestimated, at the time, the danger that vibration represented to them; it was natural enough, because we were all attributing the creature's obvious difficulty when it left the hut to the cracks the first shot had left on its surface. Actually, it took a shock as severe as the bomb that was finally exploded almost underneath it, to damage the brittle armour enough to stop it in its tracks.

It was interesting, too, that when they tested the bullets in the ballistics lab, it turned out the first hadn't touched the animal, and the second had hit squarely, been flattened by the impact of the super-hard hide, and *bounced* off. Yet the cracks from the second had been hardly more severe than from the first. It was difficult to visualize a living creature, a mobile animal, going about with a skin as brittle as glass, as easily shattered by shockwaves and vibration as by actual impact; yet that was obviously the case.

The bullet cracks, we decided during the autopsy, were just about as serious, and as painful, as whip-welts might be to a human. That is, there was no loss of 'blood' and no real impairment of function; there was, instead, a state of potential damage, in which any ill-considered motion might result in a serious tissue-break. However, if you cover a man's *entire* body with welts, no matter how carefully you place them so as not to break the skin, you can incapacitate him completely, and possibly even kill him, by reducing skin-function. This was, apparently, the net effect of the bomb: simply to destroy the animal's exterior mechanism for reacting to stimulus.

There was some doubt, too, as to whether the bomb had actually killed the thing. Possibly it wasn't entirely dead at first, but just immobilized. We didn't get close enough the first few hours to know for sure whether it was still breathing. We did, with instruments, check on temperature and response to various stimuli, and all the results, *in human terms,* indicated an absence of life. But it appears that the creature may have continued to ooze out that curious gel for some time after it fell. At least, when it was moved, there was a largish puddle underneath it; this might, of course, have been ejected at the time of the fall.

It took several days of fine and fancy improvisation at dissection (we had only the one sample, and we didn't want to spoil it) to find out just what that ooze was. Of course, we got a chemanalysis right away, but that only gave us an idea. The stuff was a mixture of alumalloy compounds and body fluids of a high Ph, containing shortchain silicones and some quartz. The analysis presented a variety of interesting possibilities, but it needed the completion of the dissection to be certain.

When we knew, it was funny, in a way. The visiting beastie had got itself a bellyache from eating our house. All we could figure was that it ordinarily subsisted on the native plant life, hard-shelled and soft-interiored, silicone outside the silicarb inside. It had identified, with whatever sense organs it used for the purpose, the discernible trace of silicate in the alumalloy, and the presence of carbon in the interior, and had mistaken the house for an extra-large new variety of plant life. The aluminum, in compound with more tidbits of this and that than I can now remember, had reacted to the additional jolt of silicones in the animal's stomach by turning into a mess of indigestible (even for *it*) gelatinous-metallic stuff. The oozing trail it left behind as it tried to leave the settlement was nothing more or less than the trickling regurgitation of an animal with an inflexible outer hide, and an extreme vulnerability to the shock of sudden motion.

This much we knew after we had traced the thing's alimentary canal, with an oxy-torch, a hacksaw, and (when we got inside) more ordinary surgical implements. The inner tissues were more familiar-looking than the outside, of about the same composition and consistency one would find in an earth-animal, differing only in the replacement of the carbon chain compounds by silicon chains. Perhaps the most curious and interesting phenomenon, from a medical viewpoint, was the way the soft inner tissues changed gradually to tough fibrous stuff, somewhat similar to silicon-rubber, and then, still gradually, so that it was almost impossible to determine at what point the actual 'skin' began, to the pure amorphous quartz of the hide-armour. The vicious-looking tuskongs were a natural enough adaptation for a creature that had to chomp up horn-hard surfaces with a minimum of vibration.

All this, and a good deal more of no especial interest except to a medic, we learned in the dissecting room and in reports from the chem lab during the two days it took to get the fence operating. Meantime, all exploration was stopped; a guard was maintained around the camp at all times until the field was in force, and a smaller lookout-guard afterwards. Work on the light aircraft went on, and construction of freight transport planes began immediately. We had already determined that we would move the settlement, if any habitable part of the planet could be found where these creatures did not exist. And all further investigation, as well as transport, would proceed by air.

The move was made exactly forty days after the Ullern came into the camp. If you've read the old Bible, there's a certain quaint symbolism in that figure. The date, of course, was 12/7—Firstown Day. And it is curious to note, in passing, the odd sentimentalities that were applied to this business of dates and calendars.

One of the most impressive similarities between Earth and Uller was in the matter of time. An Earth-hour is a few minutes shorter than an hour here; the Uller-day, according to the Earth-setting of the chronos when we arrived, was about 26 hours long. And the year on Earth—the actual period of revolution around the sun—is slightly more than 365 days, instead of our 400.

Logically, when we arrived, we should have established a

new metrical calendar and time-scale. Ten months of forty days, or forty weeks of ten days each—either one—would have been simple and efficient. A day divided into ten or twenty hours would have been sensible. But either one would have had the same effect: to make us stop and think when we spoke of time.

Humans—set apart from all other indigenous species of Earth by their ability to think—have a long-bred habit of avoiding mental strain. And the similarities to Earth-time were too noticeable and too tempting. We simply fixed our clocks and chronos to run slower and so saved ourselves from adjustment to the difference. The day here is still twenty-four hours, and the year has twelve months still. It didn't bother us to have 36 days each month; that part of the calendar had always been flexible. And the interim Fourday at year's end was an old Earth custom, too, I've since found out. Our only real departure was the six-day week.

(Parenthesis to Carla: iii)

2/10/52

I'm afraid I have been, in these last pages, rather drily concerned with facts as familiar to you as to anyone who has grown up side by side with the Ullerns. This was partly in an effort to get across to you some of the feeling we had then: how new all this information was to us and how difficult to assimilate. Also, the jump out of emotion into preoccupation with data was typical of my own reactions at the time.

I had one emotion that I was willing to identify, and that was hate. I worked in the dissection lab whenever I was awake, and took my meals there too, watching the work as it proceeded, and enjoying every slice and sliver that was carved out of that beast. That much I *felt;* for the rest I had ceased to be aware of any feelings at all. I had an overwhelming thirst for knowledge about the animal that had killed Ken; but Ken himself, and what his death meant to me . . . this I refused to think about at all.

When I realized I was pregnant, I was still sleepwalking as the true love of a dead man. I was gloriously happy, and terribly depressed. Ken's baby would be Ken-continuing, and so not-quite-dead. But Ken *was* dead! I had no husband, and my child would have no father to grow up with.

Most of the time, the first few months, I just forgot I was pregnant. I meant that, literally. Someone would say something about it, and I'd have to collect my wits and remember, consciously, what they were talking about. Maybe I didn't want to have the baby, and was trying to lose it by behaving as if I weren't pregnant, working long hours at tough jobs . . . but I don't think so. I think I was determined not to be happy about anything, and afraid of being depressed. I was, in short, determined not to *feel* anything.

You can't grow a child inside you without feeling it: feeling it physically, as your body changes, and feeling the subtle complex of emotions that accompanies the changes. But I tried, and for a short time I succeeded.

I remember that Jose fell into step with me one time, as I was going from my room to the lab, and tried to talk to me; it didn't occur to me that he was taking a professional interest. I thought I had myself completely under control, and was rather proud of the way I was behaving. I didn't even listen to what he said, but took for granted that he still considered me his ally in the stupid argument of the first day of exploration.

'How are you feeling, Emma?' I guess he said . . . some such thing, because it gave me an opening to turn on him and demand:

'How do *you* feel? Now you've got your *intelligent* life, how do you like it?'

I can remember thinking I'd said something witty as I stalked away. The unforgivable thing that Jose had done to me, you see, was not that he had convinced me of an erroneous attitude, but that he had convinced me of something about which I argued with Ken the last time I saw him . . . and that I had continued to question Ken, and to cling to Jo's attitude, right up to the moment Ken proved his point with his own death.

I do not now apologize for these reactions, or even comment on them, but simply state them here as honestly as possible. Perhaps it was healthy, after all, that I reacted as I did. Hate kept me going where grief would have, literally, prostrated me. And I did not mourn Ken, then; I just hated: everything and everyone that contributed in any way to his death.

It occurs to me only now that perhaps that curious business of our time-reckoning system, as well as many other apparently irrational things we did, were done in part to save our faculties of adaptation for necessities. I still don't know whether it was inherent weakness or instinctive wisdom. It doesn't matter, really, and I see I'm digressing again. I *am* getting older. But I can still remember being very scornful of the same sentimental clinging to a calendar, when I was a child on Pluto—and here they'd had more excuse. Pluto doesn't rotate at all; it has no natural day. And its year is hundreds of Earth-years long. So for a system of time-reckoning that applied to human values, the old one was as good as any other there, except in terms of arithmetical efficiency.

Here it was another matter altogether: we *forced* an old system to fit new circumstance; why? Because we were human, and each of us had grown up somewhere. Because we had been children back there, and some part of each of us was still a child *there*, and needed a safe familiar handle of some sort to cling to. In space, we were completely set apart from 'home'. Time was our handle.

XI

THE NIGHTS WERE already long when the colony moved south. Firstown was located just below the 47th parallel, close enough to the pole so that few of the Ullern animals cared to brave the scorching summers, or freezing winters; still far enough so that humans could hope to survive them.

They had just about nine weeks of steadily shortening days in which to prepare for the winter-night; and at that latitude, it would be fourteen weeks after the last sunset before it would rise again for a few minutes of semi-daylight. The temperature, in Fourmouth, was already below freezing, and Meteorology predicted cheerfully that the winter-night low would be somewhere about −50 deg.

To some of the others, the long stretch of cold and darkness was frightening. To the Plutonians and Marsmen the cold meant nothing, and for the former, artificial light was as natural as sun. Emma, had she stopped to think about it, would have been grateful for even the few months each year of Earth-normal temperate weather and sunlight.

She didn't think about it. She worked, with grim preoccupation, all through those early months. When she no longer had the body of the beast to cut up, she threw herself into the conquest of the *planet* that had killed Ken . . . which was, too, the fulfilment of their joint dream. She was alone now, but somehow if she worked twice as hard, she could still make the dream come true for *both* of them.

She was lucky, too, because throughout that fall and winter there was always more work to be done than there were hands to do it. When her own shift at Medicentre was done each day, she went out and found more work; filled in on the auxiliary power-plant construction when people were sick; helped build the nursery and furnish it; spent long hours in the library, as she had done in her youth. Now she was studying chemistry, silicon chemistry. *Organic* silicon chemistry, working it out where it didn't exist, from what little the films recorded of solar knowledge.

She worked alongside other people, but made little contact with any of them, and she was happiest in the hours she spent alone, studying. She did not join the others in the big social hall, when they met on 18/5 to spend the last full hour of sunlight under the U.V. glass dome; she barely noticed when the long night set in. Almost, she might have been Emma Malook again, living under the Pluto dome, moving through artificial light and air, such as she'd known since birth, between Joan Thurman's library and Joe Prell's home, living all the time, wherever she was, in a fantasy of being grown-up, and a doctor. Only now she *was* a doctor, and the fantasy was being Emma Malook. She was Emma Tarbell, and she was going to have a baby, by which she knew indisputably that she was full grown now.

The days went by, one like the last, and all of them almost painless, In her sleep, she would reach out across the bed to emptiness, and withdraw her hand before she woke to know her own loneliness. But once awake, she followed the pattern of work and study rigorously, tended her body and the new body growing inside it, and when she was tired enough not to lie awake, went back to bed again.

The single event that stirred her immediate interest that winter was the Ullern they caught. One of the regular weekly scouting parties brought it back, along with their charts and statistics on conditions outside. They'd thought it was dead at first, then they discovered it was living, but too weak to resist capture. In the lab, they found out quickly enough that the animal was simply half starved. They fed it on specimens of local flora, and it flourished.

Then why, outside, surrounded by the same plants in abundance, had it almost died of starvation? That took a little longer to find out. Cabrini tried a specimen from outside on it when the next scouting squad returned and found it refused the frozen food. After that, they tried a range of temperatures, and discovered it would eat nothing below the freezing point of carbon dioxide. That made sense, too, when you thought about the problem of eliminating solid CO_2.

Jo was tremendously excited. 'If they had fire, they could use the whole planet!' he pointed out, and met a circle of questioning eyes.

'Planning to teach this one?' Basil asked, too quietly. Jose joined the general laughter, and let the matter slide. It was encouraging to know that at least half the year the colony was completely safe from the beasts . . . and to have some kind of clue to a method of attack.

They kept the animal in a sort of one-man zoo, an island of Uller-earth and Uller plants surrounded by a five-foot moat of gluey fluid through which its runners could not penetrate. And Jo, apparently through sheer stubborn conviction that it was possible to do so, actually managed to make 'friends' with the creature, at least, he was the only one who could approach it when it regained its strength, without some display of hostility.

The first sun rose again on 6/8, and by the beginning of Nine-month, the days were already nine hours long. By then, too, Emma was far enough along to have to slow her pace; she had just twelve more weeks—two months—to term.

It was a sad and lovely springtime. In the last weeks of

waiting, Emma gave up everything except her regular work at Medicentre. Studying no longer interested her; instead she would go out and sit for hours in the crisp fresh air and Tenmonth sunshine, intensely conscious of the life within her, impatient for its birth, and yet somehow fearful of letting it loose. It would be a boy, of course, it had to be a boy, and she would name it Kenneth.

Leah was born on 36/10, right in the middle of Medicentre's first and biggest baby-room. There were twenty-three new infants in the colony in two weeks' time.

Inevitably, Emma spent much of her time the next month with the other young mothers, all of them learning and sharing the care of their babies. After the first—not disappointment, but surprise—she didn't mind Lee's being a girl; and she was surprised, too, to discover how much pleasure she could find in the simple routine of feeding and cleaning a tiny infant. Her own infant.

She was busy and useful again, because the other mothers came to her for advice and opinions at every turn. She was a medic, after all, and had *some* kind of previous experience with babies.

Under the best of circumstances, it is likely to be eight or ten weeks after birth before the mother is once again quite convinced of her own existence as a separate and individual person. Emma had little desire to return to that conviction. She was stirred by occasional questioning curiosities about the details of the refrigerating system, as the heat outside mounted through the summer-day. She began to pick up some of the chemistry films a little more often, and went, from time to time, to the zoo-in-a-lab where the Ullern was still kept, to find out what they had learned about it. But on the whole, she was more than content with the narrow slice of reality in which she found herself. Even her work at Medicentre, as she resumed it, somehow concerned itself primarily with babies: those already born, and those that were still expected.

The first New Year's Eve on Uller came in midsummer, just long enough after Lee's birth for Em to have gone to the celebration comfortably if she wished. She preferred to stay in the nursery, and let the other mothers go, with their husbands. Two months later, when the early fall nights were beginning to be long enough to cool the air a little, she found her first real pleasure in contact with the new environment.

In the hour before dawn, it was possible to go outside without frig-suits; and every day, from that time, Em adjusted her sleeping so that she would be awake at that time of day. First, when the nights were still short, she would leave the sleeping baby in the nursery; later, when dawn began to coincide with the chrono-morning, she would take Lee with her.

Alone, or with the baby at her side in a basket on the ground, she would sit by the edge of the dry river-bed, and watch the world wake up. The first sun's rays, felt before they were seen, brought a swarm of near microscopic life out of the moist earth of the river bed, and started an almost imperceptible stirring in the trees. Emma would sit and watch while the budded branches snaked up and out of the sparkling columns of their trunks, turned their tender new greenery up to the sun for a brief time, and then melted back into the safety of the cool trunk shells.

Day after day, she tried to remember why the flexible tree-trunks were so fondly familiar. It was *silly,* somehow; and then at last the memory came. A little ball of stuff that bounced, and broke off clean when you stretched it . . . that moulded to any shape, and dropped back slowly to a formless mass again when you left it alone . . . a childhood toy, that someone had called *silly putty.* Some kind of silicon compound, she supposed, and told little Lee, who did not understand: 'See? See the silly-putty tree?'

On another level of interest, the phenomenon of twice-yearly budding fascinated her, as well as the marvellous apparatus offered by the flexible branches to protect the leaves against too much sun as well as against the winter cold. Each day, too, as the sun rose farther in the north, the branches turned their budded sides to catch its rays aslant: like the sunflower on Earth, but these trees turned to face the source of life throughout the year, instead of by the day.

When the tree-trunks began to crawl back in their shells, it was time to go inside. Minutes later, the sun would be too hot to take. But for the hour before that, it was a cool and peaceful world on the river bank.

By the time Lee was six months old, the weather outside had passed its brief month of perfection, and was once again too cold for pleasure. By that time, too, the first epidemic of parenthood was dying down. Emma was back at general medic work; the world was achieving a sort of normalcy. She had her baby. She had her work. And she was beginning to be aware of the fact that she was terribly lonely.

By that time, too, there were some unattached men. A good many of those early marriages broke up in the first year. In spite of the growing emphasis on typically frontier-puritan monogamous family patterns, divorce was, of necessity, kept easy: simply a matter of mutual decision, and registration. For that matter, the morality in the early years was more that of the huddled commune than of the pioneer farmland.

Emma saw a lot of men that winter. Lee was a convenient age . . . old enough not to need hovering attention, young enough still to be asleep a large part of the time. Emma was a romantic figure, too, by virtue of her widowhood; her long grief for Ken established her as a better marriage risk than those who had made an error the first time, and had had to admit it. The dawning recognition of these facts provided for her at first with amusement, and later with a certain degree of satisfaction. She had been an intellectual adolescent, after all. Now, for the first time, she found out what it was like to be a popular girl. She discovered a new kind of pleasure in human relationships: the casual contact.

She found out that friends could be loved without being *the* beloved; that men could be friends without intensity; that affection came in varying degrees, and that she could have many different kinds of affection from many different people . . . even though Ken was dead.

Yes, she found out too that Ken *was* dead. Perhaps it was fortunate that Lee was a girl; a boy named Kenneth might have helped her keep the truth from herself a while longer. And the inescapable violence of the seasonal changes made a difference. Life was determined to continue, and to do so it was constantly in a state of change. Even the silly-putty trees told her that much.

There was an impulse towards gaiety throughout the

colony generally during the second winter-night. The first one had been too full of work and worry. Now, they felt established and moderately secure. They had survived a full year of what troubles the planet could offer, and Ken's death was still their only loss. A new science of chemistry and physics in the labs and a new technology beginning to appear. Perhaps a new biology as well: Jo now had two Ullerns in his zoo, and there was some reason to believe that the creatures were capable of mating.

There was a warm sense of security in the colony, and when they had to take to the underground corridors again to keep their warmth, it added a womb-like complacency. It was a winter of parties and celebrations and increasing complexities of human relations. It merged into a springtime of renewed activity and interest for everyone, and most of all for Emma.

Now, when she went to the river bank at dusk, instead of dawn, she had to watch the toddling one-year-old baby, and keep her from the rushing waters of the river. Everything, all around, was full of motion and excitement, even the intellectual life that was hesitantly picking up once more.

There was *so* much to learn: she started going to the library again, after Lee was in bed for the night, and scanning the recorded knowledge there for clues to the new facts of life. She spent hours, sometimes, in the zoo-lab, watching the two Ullerns, and in spite of her open amusement at Jo's undiminished belief in their intelligence as a species, she listened eagerly while he talked about their habits. He had been watching them for months. She did not have to accept his interpretation on the data he'd acquired, but the observations themselves were fascinating.

The zoo became something of a centre of debate throughout the colony. It was now firmly established that one of the creatures was, in human terms, female. Medicentre wanted the male for dissection now that a new generation was assured. Jose wouldn't hear of it. There was a good deal of humour at his expense, and an increasing amount of discussion and argument too, on both sides. Emma couldn't take it too seriously; the birth of her child had given her a new attitude towards time. There were years ahead of them. If Jo wanted his pet alive, why kill it? They'd catch more . . .

The days were constantly longer and fuller. Now sunset came too late to take Lee with her when she went down to the river bank, and the water was beginning to move more thinly and slowly, low between the sides. The half-hour out there before bed was the only part of the day now that was quiet and unoccupied. It was a time for feeling, in-stead of thinking or doing, for a renewal of the loneliness she refused, quite, to surrender.

Refused, that is, until the evening Bart Heimrich met her there, and in the cool of twilight, just as the sun went down, took her in his arms. It shouldn't have made that much difference; they were two grown people, and one kiss by the side of the slow moving water could hardly have mattered so much.

Emma was frightened. For two weeks after that, she stayed away from the river, and she wouldn't see Bart either. She'd been in love once, and once was enough. There were plenty of men around. This kind of thing was more than she wanted. As she had done a year ago, she threw herself into study and work.

There was still plenty to do. As unofficial specialist in obstetrics, she had been somehow selected to watch over the Ullern creature's pregnancy. She spent more time at the zoo, now, trying to weed out the facts and theories Jo threw at her. He was so sure of his conclusions about the Ullerns that it was almost impossible for him to separate observations from hypotheses, and Emma was alternately amused and infuriated by the problem of working with him. He was a first-rate psychologist, after all, and a careful semanticist . . . where other people's attitudes were con-cerned. Even about himself, she decided on reflection—ex-cept in this one area of most-intense belief.

Was that true for everyone? Was there, for each person, a space where one's own judgment *could not* be trusted? How about herself, and Bart?

Jo was a good psychologist, almost all the time. They were talking for the thousandth time, about the fate of the male Ullern. Jo had achieved a reprieve for the beast, till after the young ones were born, with the argument that they should at least wait and make sure they had another male to replace it. Emma approved the argument; it suited her tendency to temporize.

'Emmy,' Jo asked in a sudden silence: 'Has it occurred to you yet that *you* have a long time to live too?'

Her first impulse was to laugh. 'Never thought about it much,' she said lightly.

'Well, why don't you?'

'I don't know.' She was decidedly uncomfortable. 'What's that got to do with the price of baby Ullerns?'

'Nothing at all. I was just wondering, most intrusively, about you and Bart.'

'Me and . . . what are you talking about?'

'I told you I was being intrusive. It's none of my business. Would you rather not talk about it?'

'I'd much rather . . .' She changed her sentence half-way through: 'much rather talk about it, I guess.'

'All right then. What's the matter, Emmy? Don't you like him?'

'*Like* him? I . . .' Then she saw he was smiling, and grinned ruefully herself. 'All right, so I'm wild about him. But . . .' There was no way to explain it.

'But what?'

'Well . . . it's not the *same*. I can't feel the same way about him that I did about . . . Ken. I don't think I'll ever feel that way about anybody again. It wouldn't be fair . . .'

'Come off it, Emmy. What are you afraid of? If you're sure you'll never feel the same way, what's there to worry about?'

She looked up, startled, and waited a moment to answer, while she admitted to herself that it wasn't Bart she was afraid of hurting at all.

'I don't know. Look, things are all right the way they are. I don't need him; he doesn't need me. Why should we get all tangled up so we *do* need each other? What for? Oh, Jo, don't you see I can't take a chance on anything like that again? I . . . this is a crazy thing to say, but I think if he was married, I'd be more willing to . . . that's not very nice, is it?'

'Nice?' He shrugged. 'It's pretty normal. Understandable,

anyhow. And just what was I talking about. You've got a long time to live yet, Emmy. You going to stick it out alone?'

She nodded slowly. 'Yes,' she said. 'I am.' And with the words spoken aloud, the impossible loneliness of the future struck her for the first time fully. She hadn't cried since the day Ken died; now a slow tear came to one eye, and she didn't try to stop it. There was another, and another, and she was sobbing, great gasping sobs, against Jo's comforting shoulder.

He *was* a good psychologist. He didn't tell her it was all right to cry; he didn't tell her anything, except to murmur an occasional word of sympathy and affection. He stroked her hair and patted her shoulder, and waited till she was done. Then he grinned and said: 'You look like hell. Better wash up here before you go see him.'

For a year and more, Bart and Emma spent most of what free time they had together. They had fun, and they had tender happy moments. They understood and enjoyed each other. They might have married, but marriage was a sacred cow still; no matter how much she loved Bart, or liked being with him, Emma steadfastly refused to sign the vows. It wasn't the same as it had been with Ken; she was both relieved and disappointed to discover that. But if she married him, it might get to be the same—or it might not. Which prospect was the worse she hardly knew.

When, occasionally, she still felt frightened about caring as much as she did, there was always Jose to talk it over with, and talking to him always made her feel better. She might have resolved the ambivalence entirely through therapy. Jose hinted at the notion from time to time, but she didn't want to, and he knew better than to push it.

More and more, too, Emma and Jo were working so closely together in the zoo-lab that a therapy relationship between them would have been hard to establish. And Jo was the only really qualified therapist in the colony. The techniques were familiar to all the people in Medicentre, but psychotherapy is not a skill to be acquired in rapid training. Jo had a natural aptitude for it, that was all.

Jo was good to work with as Bart was to love. The important factor in each case was enthusiasm, the ability to

participate completely. Emma's interest in the Ullerns
differed from Jo's in all respects but one, and that was intensity. She listened to his theories both patiently and
painstakingly, believing little and using much to further
her own knowledge of the weird biology of the creatures.
She was quite content to discard the largest part of what
he said, and select the most workable of his ideas for
follow-up. By the end of that year, she had begun to recognize, reluctantly, that she was getting good results surprisingly often when she worked along the lines suggested by
his thinking. But it took a major incident to make her look
back and count the trials and errors, before she would admit how consistent the pattern of predictability had been.

The Ullern babies had been born in the fall of '92. There
were three of them, but it wasn't until early spring that it
was possible to determine with any degree of certainty that
two of them were female and one a male. Perhaps it could
have been determined a little sooner; Jose had managed to
get a postponement of the father-Ullern's death sentence
once again, until the sex of the young ones was known,
and there was some feeling that he, at least, knew for quite
a while before he told anyone.

Once the announcement was made, however, there was
no further question of delaying the opportunity for an
autopsy. The only question now was whether it might not
be best to take the older female, and gain some additional
information about the reproductive system.

Discussion and debate went round and about for some
ten days. It was terminated by the incredible information
that the adult male had escaped.

The talk stopped then, because nobody wanted to say
out loud what everybody was thinking. You see, it was
simply not possible for the creature to make his way un-
aided through that gluey moat.

If there was any doubt at all in the public mind about
what had happened, there was none in Emma's. She was
shocked and angry and she saw to it that she had no further
talks with Jo in which he might be tempted to confide anything she didn't want to know.

XII

The announcement, posted two days after the Ullern's escape, said simply:

LECTURE
In the Small Hall, 19/5/93, at 20.00 hours.
A report by Jose Cabrini on
the possibilities for direct communication
with the native inhabitants of Uller.

I read it, and couldn't help feeling relieved on Jo's behalf. I might have known he wouldn't risk anything so unpopular as letting that animal get away unless he had something else up his sleeve. What it was, I didn't know; Jose had never discussed with me any clues he had to the problem of direct communication.

He should have known the Small Hall wouldn't hold the crowd that turned out. Maybe he did know; if so, it was effective staging, when the early arrivals had to move to the Main Hall, and latecomers found a sign directing them there.

Jose began his speech very informally, joking about the size of his audience, with some hoary gags about being unaccustomed to such *very* public speaking. Then his tone changed.

'I'm afraid the news I have for you tonight is more dramatic than it is useful . . . so far. I think what has already been learned will eventually enable us to communicate directly with the natives of this planet, and perhaps—if my estimate of their capacities is accurate to live on a co-operative basis with them. For the present time, however, my information does little more than answer a question that has baffled a good many of us.'

I had no idea what was coming.

'If you will all think back to our first contact with an Ullern,' he said slowly and distinctly, 'You may recall that there was one particularly puzzling piece of behaviour on the part of the animal—one question that was never answered in the autopsy.'

Thinking back was still too vivid. I shuddered in the warm room, and missed the next few words.

'. . . attack Ken Tarbell? What gave it the renewed energy to make such a fierce charge, when it was already badly hurt, and was seeking nothing but escape? My own theory at the time was that the Ullern was reacting with what would be, in the human metabolism, an adrenal release, to the telepathically-received information that Tarbell had found a means of attacking it fatally.

'That theory was inadequate. If you think of telepathy as a mystic or metaphysical power, my analysis was *entirely* incorrect. But if you will try to think of it, for the moment as an emanation similar in nature to radio or electromagnetic waves, I was close to the truth.

'You are all familiar with the piezo-electric properties of the Ullern physiology. You can see it for yourselves in the zoo, even the babies react electrically to certain irritations. Analogizing pretty broadly, one might say that the electrical reaction to stimulus in an Ullern *is* similar to the adrenal reaction in humans: that is, it is produced by just such irritations as might reasonably be expected to provoke the emotion of fear or anger.

'Now: in a human, the application of such a stimulus can have differing results. An unkind word, the semi-serious threat of a blow, anything on that order, will produce enough of an adrenal release so that the person affected may express his reaction rapidly in expletive, or door-slamming, or some similarly mild expenditure of energy. A slightly greater threat will produce a cocked fist; a little more will make a man strike out. But a really strong stimulus, ordinarily, will not produce a direct counteraction. If a man threatens your life by holding a gun at your head . . . or if you are knocked over by a blow to the belly . . . you will conserve the extra energy of the resulting adrenal release for an all-out effort against the attacker.

'This is, essentially, what the Ullern did. The many irritations to which it was subjected produced a variety of reactions, most of them in the fear-spectrum. The first shot, which failed to hit it, but shattered a part of its armour with shock-vibrations, angered it only within the fast-reaction range, and it responded, without conscious "planning", by an emission of "lightning". Apparently it was unable to place the source of the shot, and believed the shock to have come from the building; so the electrical "punch" was aimed at the wall.

'Subsequent irritations made it aware of some consciousness on the part of large lumps of carbon which it had previously ignored as being, in all past experience, most likely inorganic, or at least inedible, entities. The idea was devastatingly new and at least as frightening as the actual vibrations the carbon creatures then commenced to "hit" it with . . .'

There was a murmur of noise through the hall; some laughter, some coughing, much shuffling.

'All right,' Jo said smiling, 'I'll get to the point now. So far it's all been theorizing and analogy. Briefly, my information is this: the Ullerns contain, in their quartz-hide armour, crystals capable of sending and receiving radio waves . . . by which I mean specifically that they can exchange information on the same frequency bands on which our radiphones operate.'

The sentence was delivered so quietly, it took a moment to penetrate. Then the hall was in an uproar. Jose couldn't go on with the speech until he had answered a hailstorm of questions from the audience.

'What's that got to do with Tarbell?' somebody wanted to know first.

'Emma,' Jo said from the stand, 'maybe you can explain that best?'

I was a little confused myself. I got to my feet, and said hesitantly, 'Ken tried to warn me . . . he phoned me about the Ullern heading our way . . . that's why we came back . . .'

'I suppose the gooks understand English!' somebody roared from the back of the room, and someone else added:

'Suppose they did? Wouldn't even an Uller-beast give a man the right to warn his wife?'

Laughter, and foot-stamping, and gradual quiet as I continued to stand in my place. 'Maybe it's funny to the rest of you,' I said, 'but *I'd* like to know just what Jo meant. So far, what he's said has made sense. If anybody who isn't interested will leave, perhaps the rest of us can learn something.'

I was just angry enough, and just intense enough, I guess, to get an effect. There was prompt and total silence. Jo went on.

There is no point in reproducing the rest of the speech here. It was, like most important discoveries, only very briefly incredible. After even the smallest amount of reflection, we could see how logical the explanation was. The wonder was that we hadn't thought of it before. The same explanation can be found, almost word for word, in the basic biology text on Ullerns. Cabrini said simply, that when Ken used the phone, on a frequency just a little off the personal-broadcast wave-length that particular Ullern was turned to, the heterodyning effect was the equivalent to it, in pain, of the belly-punch he'd mentioned earlier. It was immobilized momentarily, and the next immediate reaction was to utilize the energy thus generated in a life-and-death charge at the source of the intolerable pain. This time it had no trouble locating the source; a radio beam is easier to track than a bullet, if your senses happen to include a direction-finder.

I didn't listen to most of the discussion that followed the speech. I was busy readjusting, or admitting to readjustments. I had stopped hating the Ullerns a long time back, and now at last I had a rationale on which to hang what had seemed like a betrayal.

The attack on Ken was not irrational or unprovoked. In Ullern terms, Ken had attacked first. A silly difference, a piece of nonsense, really, but important to me at the time. It was no longer necessary to keep hating, even on a conscious verbal level.

As soon as I got that much clear in my mind, I wanted to leave.

'You stay if you want to,' I told Bart. 'I just want to get out of here and do some thinking.'

'Would you rather be alone?' He was a very sweet guy. I knew he meant just that; he'd let me go alone if I preferred it, or come along if I wanted him to.

I shook my head. 'No, I wouldn't. If you don't mind missing this, I'd like to have someone to talk to, a little bit.'

He took my arm, and saw to it that we got out without interference; stopped people who wanted to question me, and pushed through the knots of conversationalists who were too absorbed or excited to notice us.

Outside, it was hot. So close to summer-time it was always hot, but the sun was down when we left the hall, and it was possible to stay outdoors.

We walked down to the river bank in silence, and stood there and I looked around me and let myself know, for the first time, fully, how much I loved this place. It was mine; I had paid for it with the greatest loss I was ever likely to know. And now the loss was complete, because I understood it.

Bart saw the tears in my eyes.

'That son-of-a-bitch!' he said. 'Didn't he even *warn* you?'

'Who?' I didn't know what he was talking about.

'Cabrini. He had no business . . . look, darling, never mind about him. The big thing is, we've got the knowhow now. We've got a way to fight them! We can . . .'

'*What?*' I was sure I still didn't understand. 'What are you talking about Bart?'

'Don't you see, dear? Naturally, Cabrini didn't put it that way, but this thing is a weapon . . . a *real* weapon! We can live anyplace on the planet now. If radio waves hurt the things that much, they'll kill 'em too. We can . . .'

'Bart,' I begged. 'Don't you understand? Can't you see what it means? They're intelligent! We can learn to talk to them. We can make *friends* with them.'

I searched his face for some signs of comprehension, and found only indulgence there. 'Emma, you are just too good to be true,' he said. 'And you need some sleep. Come on, I'll take you back now, and we can talk about it tomorrow.' He put his arm around me.

He meant well. I have no doubt at all that he meant well.

'Will you please get the hell out of here?' I said, as quietly as possible. I would have said much more but he went.

When he was gone, I lay down on the river bank and pressed my face against the dirt of my planet and cried. That was the third time I cried, and now it was for the loss of Bart as well as Ken.

(Parenthesis to Carla: iv)

Josetown, Uller, 1/11/52

Dear Child:

I am, frankly, annoyed. This story was supposed to be about the generations of women who came before you, and about the early years on Uller. Looking back, I find it is almost entirely about one small portion of my own life.

I think I know what happened. Somewhat earlier in this narrative, I made a statement about the oddity of reversed pain and pleasure in Recall. I suspect that I enjoyed the reliving of those early months on Uller far more in the telling than I ever did in the experience. From the day Ken died till the day when I wept out my sorrows on the river bank, I was never entirely happy. There was much isolated pleasure during that period: delight in my baby, and fun with Bart, and satisfaction in my work . . . and certainly much more pleasure in knowing Jose than I realized. But all through those two years, life had no meaning beyond the moment. I did not, would not, believe in any kind of future, without Ken.

In the years that followed, there were many hardships and moments of unhappiness and despair, but from that time on, I had a growing purpose in existence. Apparently, I have less need to re-experience the productive years than the others. And of course, there is really very little more that I can tell you. Thad Levine wrote the story of the bitter three years' quarrel in the colony, and wrote it far better than I could. You have heard from me, and probably from a dozen others too, the woe-filled history of the establishment of Josetown. Jo himself wrote a painstaking account of the tortuous methodology by which the Ullern code was worked out, and I know you have read that too.

(I am sternly repressing the inclination to excuse my many omissions by pointing to the date above, and referring to the page number. Time is short now, and the story too long. But neither of these is an honest reason for my failure to do what I planned . . . no more than are my excuses in the paragraph immediately above.)

I had hoped, when I started this, to give you some clue

to my own mistakes, so that you might avoid them. There are such striking similarities, Carla dear, between Joan Thurman and myself, between me and you! And on the other side, there is such a pattern of identity between Martha and Adne and Lee. It seems to me there should be some way of braking the pendulum swing . . . of producing, sometime, a child who is neither rebelliously 'idealistic' nor possessively demanding of security in its most obvious forms.

It was at least partly in the hope that the history of those who went before you might teach you how to achieve this goal of impossible perfection with your children, when you have them, that I undertook this journal. I hope I have managed to include more helpful information in it than it now seems to me I have done.

In any case, I see little purpose in carrying the story further. I have mulled over it for weeks now, and have written several chapters about what came after the day of Jo's lecture, and have decided, each time, to leave them out.

There are many things I wanted to say that I've left out . . . little things, mostly, for which I could not find a proper spot in the narration. I could ramble on here, filling them in, but again there is no real purpose in it, except to satisfy myself.

But, reading what I have just written, I realize that there is still much unresolved conflict in my own attitudes. Yes (I tell myself), I should like to see you rear your children to be perfect little happy mediums—and yet I am so pleased, Carla, to see you playing out the rôle I know so well myself.

Perhaps the 'others'—Leah and Ariadne and Martha— perhaps they knew some happiness I never understood; but I am certain that they never knew the kind of total purpose in living that has been my great joy. I had a dream . . . I learned it from Joan Thurman. That dream is yours, too, and I'm quite irrationally pleased to think that you acquired it, in part, from me.

Tomorrow you will leave, Carla, and I will give you this film to take with you. When you leave, it will be as a part of the first great experiment with time . . . and like the fuel for the *Newhope,* which has made over the whole life of man, the mastery of time has come as an adjunct to a commercial venture. Joe Prell, if he were here today, would laugh at the implication I see in your voyage . . . but *not* at the possible profits. I . . . *I* think it is more risk than merited to go to Nifleheim for new and more uranium. But to go in profitable comradeship with the Ullerns—this is the fulfilment of my own life's dream. And to go as the advance guard of a whole new science—this is the beginning of yours.

If it takes uranium to make the Prells pay for a time machine (did you know that's what you have?—at least the beginnings of one), why let us have enough of the stuff to blow us all sky-high!

(Epilogue)

I have just come back from the ceremonies of the take-off, and I am more annoyed than ever. Now that I have handed over my imperfect gift, I have found out what it was lacking. There is no way of knowing, as I write, whether Carla has reached . . . will reach . . . her destination safely, or whether, if she does, she will arrive (has arrived?) there in a time-conjunction through which she can communicate with us. I can only wait, and hope there is some word.

But I shall assume, as I must, that she is safe, and that some time these words will reach her. The story is yet to be finished, and I found out today why I was unable to finish it before. (I suppose I thought I was too old and too objective to carry any more scars of hurt or hatred from Lee!)

Leah Tarbell was born on Uller, and grew up there. She was too young to understand the fury of the debate that preceded her mother's move from Firstown to Josetown; but she was not too young at all to resent the loss of her Uncle Bart's company a scant few weeks after she had learned to pronounce his name.

Over the next three years, she understood well enough that her mother was somehow in disrepute with the parents of most of her playmates. And at five years of age, she was quite old enough to blame her mother for the almost complete loss of those playmates. Only four other children ac-

companied the group of sixty-seven 'Josites' when they
betook themselves, their pet Ullerns, their special knowledge, and their apportioned share of the human colony's
possessions to the new location on the 20th parallel that
became known as Josetown.

Only one of the other children was near her own age;
that was Hannah Levine, and she was only four, really.
The two little girls, of necessity, became friends. They
played and ate and often slept together. At bedtime, they
were lonely together too, while their parents went off to
conferences and lab sessions. And late at night, sometimes,
they would wake up and be frightened together, remembering the stories they'd heard in the nursery at home about
the Ullerns who lived at the foot of the hill.

She tried to cry about leaving her mother when she was
sent back to Firstown a year and a half later, with Alice
Cabrini and the two Cabrini children, to go to school. But
she didn't really expect to miss Emma; Em was always
working, anyhow. Back home, the grown-ups had more
time to pay attention to kids.

From that time till she was fourteen, she lived with Alice
in Firstown, and she was happy there. When Alice decided it was safe to rejoin Jose in the smaller settlement,
Leah desperately did not want to go. She tried every device
an adolescent mind could contrive to keep Alice at home.
But when it came down to a choice of going with them,
or being left behind, she couldn't quite face the desertion
of the family she loved as her own.

She went along, and her adolescent imagination seized
on a whisper here and a word there to find real cause to
hate her mother. She was not blind, as the adults seemed
to be, to the fact that Emma and Jo had worked together
day after day through the years, while Alice endured long
nights of loneliness for the sake of the three children who
needed her care.

Lee watched the three grown-ups closely. She heard the
inflexion of every word they spoke to each other, and
noticed each small gesture that passed between them. In the
end, she satisfied herself that Emma and Jose were not
lovers (as indeed we had not been since Alice's return).
Then she felt something amounting almost to compassion
for her mother. She had not failed to observe the flush of

enthusiasm with which Emma listened to Jo's ideas, and poured out ideas of her own to command his attention. At the same time she saw how Alice, sitting quietly in the background, pretending interest in nothing but Jo himself, and his home and the children, succeeded in drawing his attention.

She did not understand how her mother could be so stupid as to try to attract a man by being *bright*. She did not even begin to understand the further fact that she could not help observing: Emma seemed to be perfectly happy sharing Jo's work, and letting Alice share his home and his bed. As long as it was true, however, Lee was willing to let Emma go her own strange way.

She was less willing to accept any of the belated affection her mother tried to give her. And Emma's ludicrous attempts to convince her of the importance of the work they were doing in Josetown did not succeed even in antagonizing her. Lee had lived long enough in Firstown to know how little it mattered whether the code was ever completed. She knew the plans the other colony had already laid down for an equatorial settlement—a settlement which was to follow the extinction of the Ullerns. The agreement between the larger group and the small one had given Jose ten years to make a go of his project. Eight of those years had passed now, and he could hardly claim that making friends with a local group of Ullerns constituted proof of their intelligence. Any animal may be domesticated by one means or another.

All these things Lee knew, and she was not interested in learning any part of the foolishness in which her mother was engaged. After a while, Emma stopped trying to interest her in the work at Josetown, and for a while they got along together.

Lee never thought of the Josetown period as anything more than an enforced hiatus in her life. If by some miracle the settlement continued after the ten years were up, she for one had no intention of remaining in it. When she was seventeen, she knew, she would have the right to live by herself if she chose and she had already chosen. She would live in Firstown, where her friends and loyalties were.

She stuck to her resolve, even after the message from

Earth. Not even the dramatic opening of subspace communication between Uller and the mother system disturbed her tight little plans. Nor did her private opinion of the foolishness of the Josetown project change when popular opinion shifted to favour it. Earth's problems were no concern of hers, and she saw no reason to give up her hopes or hatreds either one, just because Jose Cabrini had somehow turned out to be right.

Her strongest reaction to the news from Earth was irritation, because it meant that Josetown would continue beyond the ten-year period after all, and that she herself would have to spend a full year more there than she had expected.

She made use of the time. She started learning the code, and even studied a little Ullern biology. She helped Jo prepare his lab notes for printing in the form in which they are now available, and learned the history of the project while she did it. By the time she was old enough to go back to Firstown and take up residence in the single girls' dorm, she knew enough about the Josetown work to take a really intelligent part in discussions with the men back home.

As it turned out, Lee was our best ambassador. She had picked up, from Jo's notes, one item of information we had not intended to release just yet. Fortunately, as it turned out, she felt no ties of loyalty to us. That was how the news got out that Jose actually *had* taught Ullerns the use of fire, and it was that news that led to the Conference of 2108.

Fifteen of us went back to Firstown for the Conference, armed with notes and speeches and films to document our defence. We were somewhat taken aback to find that no defence was necessary; Firstown was way ahead of us in recognizing the implications of the Ullerns' use of fire. I suppose we had grown so accustomed to defensiveness by then, we simply couldn't see beyond the necessity of protecting next year's work. The people at Firstown were used to thinking in terms of expansion and utilization of knowledge; they had the engineering minds to put our research to use.

Lee was only seventeen, but her greatest ability, even

then, was the tactful manipulation of other people. It was her carefully developed friendship with Louis Dooley that made it possible for Basil and Jose to meet privately before the Conference started, and hash out their ideas. And it was in that private meeting that the mutual advantages of humans—Ullern co-operation in the Nifleheim venture were recognized.

When we went back to Josetown, it was with the long-range plan already worked out: the further development of the code to the point where we could communicate with Ullerns in the abstractions we were certain they were capable of understanding; they continued work on Ullern biochemistry to determine whether the quartz-to-teflon adaptation would actually take place, as we believed, in the atmosphere of Nifleheim; and the long, long process of persuading the Ullerns that other humans besides our own small group now wanted friendship with them.

That was our part of the job. Back in Firstown, they worked, in communication with Earth, on the other end of the problem: the improvement of sub-space transport to eliminate the mishaps, and make it safe for live freight.

(P.S. to Carla)

It is two weeks ·now since I went to the take-off of the Nifleheim *Ark* and stood beside my daughter Lee, watching the whole show through her eyes, gaining some of the understanding that made it possible for me to finish this story.

We were all together, Lee and Louis and the three youngsters. Carla, of course, was participating in the ceremonies.

Johnny, my youngest grandson, looked at the domed building in the centre of the field, and was disappointed.

'Just like any other building,' he grumbled.

Lee nodded automatically. 'Yes, dear, it is,' she said, but something made her shiver as she said it. It was ordinary-looking, far more like a house than a spaceship. Nothing frightening at all . . . to look at. Yet it stood there, triumphant and menacing, the most impregnable enemy she had ever met. She hadn't even been able to stay away from the take-off as she'd planned. She had to come: she was Louis Dooley's wife and Carla's mother, and Emma Tarbell's daughter, and they wouldn't let her stay home. She had to bring her other children, too, and any minute now, she'd have to watch the plain domed structure *disappear*.

'Centuries gone, man looked to the stars and prayed,' the worn tape intoned. 'He made them his gods, then his garden. . . .'

Leah shuddered, and reached for her young son's hand, but he never felt her touch. The magic of the old, old words was wrapping itself around him.

'. . . of thought, and at last his goal. We have not. . . .'

Inside the dome was all the equipment for separating and storing the uranium that could be had, for the simple extraction, from the atmosphere of Nifleheim. Inside, too, were quarters for humans and Ullerns to live side by side together. Inside was Carla's bridal home, and beyond the wall that held her bed was the dread machinery of sub-space itself.

'. . . reached that goal. This is not a beginning nor an end; neither the first step nor the last. . . .'

Lee looked around at all the others, the mothers who were supposed to be proud and pleased today, and saw the tense fists clenching, the tired eyes squinting, the hands reaching for a younger child's touch. She felt better then, knowing they shared the mockery of the moment.

She stood patiently, listening to Jo's speech, hearing him explain once more how Ullerns could venture forth on the surface of Nifleheim, and actually benefit by the change . . . how changing shifts of Ullern workers could spend an adaptation period on the alien planet, expose themselves to the fluorine that would change their brittle skins to flexible teflon hides, while human hands inside worked the machinery that would process the desperately-needed uranium for transport back to Earth. Lee stood and listened to it all, but it meant no more than it had meant last year, or forty years before, when they started work on it.

Then at last, Carla was standing before her, with all the speeches and display finished, and nothing left to do but say goodbye. She reached out a hand, but Louis was there first, folding the slender girl in a wide embrace, laughing proudly into her eyes. . . .

Then Johnny, and Avis and Tim, they all had to have

their turns. And finally Carla turned to her.

Lee leaned forward, kissed the smooth young cheek, and said, before she knew herself what words were coming:

'Carla . . . Carlie, darling, aren't you *afraid?*'

Carla took both her mother's hands and held them tight. 'I'm terrified!' she said. And turned and left.

HOMECALLING

I

THERE WAS NO warning. Deborah heard her mother shout, *'Dee! Grab the baby!'*

Petey's limbs hung loose; his pink young mouth fell open as he bounced off the foam-padded floor of the play-space, hit more foam on the side wall, at a neat ninety-degree angle, and bounced once more. The small ship finished upending itself, lost the last of its spin, and hurled itself surfaceward under constant acceleration. Wall turned to ceiling, ceiling to floor and Petey landed smack on his fat bottom against the foam-protected toy-bin. Unhurt but horrified, he added a lusty wail to the ever shriller scream-ing of the alien atmosphere, and the mighty reverberations of the rocket's thunder.

'. . . the bay-beeee . . . *Dee!'*

'I got him.' Deborah hooked a finger finally through her brother's overall strap, and demanded: 'What do I do now?'

'I don't know; hold on to him. Wait a minute.' Sarah Levin turned her head with difficulty towards her husband. 'John,' she whispered, 'what's going to happen?'

He gnawed at his lower lip, tried to quirk a smile out of the side of his mouth nearest her. 'Not good,' he said, very low.

'The children?'

'Dunno.' He struggled with levers, frantically trying to fire the tail rockets—now, after their sudden space-somer-sault became the forward jets. 'Don't know what's wrong,' he muttered fiercely.

'Mommy, it hurts . . .'

Petey was really crying now, low and steady sobbing, and Dee whimpered again, 'It hurts. I can't get up.'

166

'Daddy's trying to fix it,' Sarah said. 'Dee . . . listen . . .'
It was hard to talk. 'If you can, try to . . . kind of . . . wrap
yourself around Petey . . .'

'I *can't* . . .' Deborah too broke into sobs.

Seconds of waiting, slow eternal seconds; then incredibly,
a gout of flame burst out ahead of them.

The braking force of the forward rocket eased the
pressure inside, and Dee ricocheted off a foamed surface—
wall, floor, ceiling? She didn't know—her finger still stuck
tight through Petey's strap. The ground, strange orange-
red terrain with towering bluish trees, was close. Too close.
There was barely time before the crash for Sarah to shout
a last reminder.

'. . . *right around him!*' she yelled. Dee understood; she
pulled her baby brother close to her chest and wound her
arms and legs around his body. Then there was crashing
splintering jagged noise through all the world.

It was too warm. Dee didn't want to look, but she
opened an eye.

Nothing to see but foam-padded sides of the play-space,
with the toys scattered all over.

A bell jangled, and a mechanical voice began: 'Fire . . .
Fire . . . Fire . . . Fire . . . Fire . . .' Dee knew what to do.
She wondered about letting go of Petey, but she'd have to,
she couldn't ask her mother, because the safety door was
closed. Her mother and father were both on the other
side in front—that was where the fire would be. She
wondered if they'd get burned up, but let go of Petey, and
worked the escape lock the way she'd been taught. While
it was opening, she put on Petey's oxy mask and her own.
She didn't know for sure whether they would be needed
on this planet, but one place they'd been called Carteld,
you had to wear a mask all the time because there wasn't
enough oxygen in the air.

She couldn't remember the name of this planet. They'd
never been here before, she knew that much; but this
must be the one they were coming to, or Daddy wouldn't
have started to go down, and everything wouldn't have
happened.

That meant probably, at least the air wasn't poisonous.
They had space-suits and helmets on the ship, and Dee
had space-suit drill every week; but she was pretty sure

she didn't need anything more than the mask here. And there wasn't time for space-suits anyhow.

The lock was all the way open. Deborah went to the door and recoiled before the blast of heat; it was burning *outside*. Now she had to get away, quick.

She picked up Petey, looked around at all the toys, and at the closet where her clothes were; at the blackboard, the projector, and the tumbled pile of fruit and crackers on the floor. She bent down and stuffed the pockets of her jumper with the crumbly crackers and smashed sticky fruit. Then she looked around again, and felt the heat coming through the door, and had to leave everything else behind.

She climbed out, and there were flames in the back. She ran, with Petey in her arms, though she'd been told never to do that. She ran straight away from the flames, and kept going as long as she could; it was hard work, because her feet sank into the spongy soil at every step. And it was still hot, even when she got away from the rocket. She kept running until she was too tired, and began to stumble, then she slowed down and walked— until Petey began to be too heavy, and she couldn't carry him any more. She stopped, and put him down on the ground and looked him over. He was all right, only he was wet—very wet—and the whole front of her jumper was wet too, from him.

Deborah scowled, and the baby began to cry. She couldn't stand that, so she smiled and tried playing games with him. Petey wasn't very good at games yet, but he always laughed and stayed happy if she played with him. Sometimes she thought he liked her better than anybody else, even Mommy. He acted that way. Maybe it was because she was closer to his size—a medium size giant in a world full of giant-giants; that's how people would look to Petey.

When he was happy again, she gave him half a cracker from her pocket, and a piece of fruit for his other hand. He tumbled over backwards, and lay down, right on the muddy ground, smearing the food all over his face and looking sleepy.

Sooner or later, Dee knew, she was going to have to

turn around and look back, meanwhile, she sat on the ground, crosslegged, watching Peter fall asleep. She thought about her ancestors, who were pioneers on Pluto, and her father and how brave *he* was. She thought once, very quickly, about her mother, who was maybe all burned up now.

She had to be brave now—as brave and strong as she knew, in her own private self, she really was. Not silly-brave the way grownups expected you to be, about things like cuts and antiseptics, but deep-down *important brave.* She was an intrepid explorer on an alien planet, exposed to unknown dangers and trials, with a helpless infant under her wing to protect. She turned around and looked back.

Her own footsteps faced her, curving away out of sight between two tall distant trees. She looked harder in the direction they pointed to, if the fire was still burning, she ought to be able to see it. The trees were far enough apart, and the ground was clear between them—clearer than any ground she'd ever seen before. There were no bushes or branches near the ground, higher than a rocket-launch —tall yellow orange poles with whispering foliage at the top.

The overhead canopy was thick and dark, a changeable ceiling with grey and green and blue fronds stirring in the air. She couldn't see the sky through it all, or see beyond it to find out whether there was any smoke. But that made it dark here, underneath the trees, so Dee was sure she would be able to see the fire, if it was still going.

She got up and followed her own footsteps back, as far as she could go without losing sight of Petey, that was the spot where the trail curved away in a different direction. It curved again, she saw further on; that was strange, because she was sure she'd been going in a straight line when she ran away. The trees all looked so much alike, it would have been hard to tell. She'd heard a story once about a man who went around and around in circles in a forest till he starved to death. It was a good thing that the ground was so soft here, and she could see the footprints so clearly.

Petey was sound asleep. She decided she could leave him alone for a minute. She hadn't seen any wild beasts or animals, or heard anything that sounded dangerous. Deborah started back along her own trail, and at the next bend she saw it, framed between two far trees: the front part of the rocket, still glowing hot, bright orange red like the persimmons Daddy had sent out from Earth one time. That was why she hadn't been able to see it before, the colour was hardly different from the ground on which it stood: just barely redder.

Nothing was burning any more.

'Mommy!' Deborah screamed, and screamed it again at the top of her lungs.

Nothing happened.

She started to run towards the rocket, still calling; then she heard Petey yelling, too. He was awake again and she had to turn around and run back and pick him up. Then she started the trip all over again, much slower. Petey was dripping wet now, and still hollering. And heavy. Dee tried letting him crawl, but it was too slow. Every move he made, he sank into the soft ground an inch or so; then he'd get curious and try to eat the orange dirt off his fingers, so she had to pick him up again.

By the time they got back to the rocket, Dee was wet all over, plastered with the dirt that Petey had picked up, and too tired even to cry when nobody answered her call.

II

THE LADY OF the house sat fat with contentment on her couch, and watched the progress of the work. Four of her sons—precision masons all—performed deft manoeuvres with economy and dispatch; a new arch took place before her eyes, enlarged and redesigned to suit her needs.

They started at the floor, sealing the jagged edges a full foot farther back on either side than where the frame had been before. They worked in teams of two, one to stand by and tamp each chip in place with sensitive mandibles, smoothing and firming it into position as it set; the other stepping off to choose a matching piece from the diminishing pile of hard-wood chips, coating it evenly with liquid plastic from his snout and bringing it, ready for placement in the arch, just at the instant that his brother completed the setting of the preceding piece.

Then the exchange in roles: the static partner moving off to make his choice; the second brother setting his new chip in perfect pattern with the rest: Two teams, building the two sides of the arch in rhythmic concert with each other. It was a ritual dance of function and form, chips and plastic, workers and work, each in its way an apparently effortless inevitable detail of the whole. Daydanda gloried in it.

The arch grew taller than ever before, and the Lady's satisfaction grew enormous, while her consort's fluttering excitement mounted. 'But *why?*' he asked again, still querulous.

'It is pleasant to watch.'

'You will not use it?' He was absurdly hopeful.

'Of course I will!'

'But, Lady . . . Daydanda, my dearest, Mother of our children, this whole thing is unheard of. What sort of example . . . ?'

'Have you ever,' she demanded coldly, 'had cause to regret the example I set to my children?'

'No my dear, but . . .'

She withdrew her attention entirely, and gave herself over to the pure aesthetic delight of watching her sons—the two teams of masons—working overhead now on the final span of the arch, approaching each other with perfect timing and matched instantaneous motions, preparing to meet and place the ceremonial centre-piece together.

Soon she would rise, take her husband's arm and experience—for the first time since her initial Family came to growth—the infinite pleasure of walking erect through her own door into the next chamber.

Even the report, shortly afterwards, of a fire spreading on the eastern boundary, failed to diminish her pleasure. She assigned three fliers to investigate the trouble, and dismissed it from her mind.

III

FOR A LONG, long time Deborah sat still on the ground, hugging Petey on her lap, not caring how wet he was, nor even trying to stop his crying—except that she rocked gently back and forth in a tradition as ancient as it was instinctive. After a while, the baby was asleep; but the girl still sat crosslegged on the ground, her shoulders moving rhythmically, slower and slower, until the swaying was almost imperceptible.

The rocket—the shiny rocket that had been new and expensive a little while ago—lay helpless on its side. The nozzles in the tail, now quiet and cool, had spouted flame across a streak of surface that stretched farther back than Dee could see, leaving a Hallowe'en trail of scorched black across the orange ground. Up forward, where the fire in the ship had been, there was nothing to see but the still-red glow of the hull.

Deborah tried to figure out what flames she had seen when she left the ship with Petey; but it didn't make sense, and she hadn't looked long enough to be sure. She'd been taught what to do in case of fire: *get out!* She'd done it; and now . . . The lock was still open where she'd climbed out before. Very very carefully, not to wake him she laid her baby brother on the soft ground, and step by reluctant step she approached the ship. Near the lock, she could feel heat; but it was all coming from one direction—from the nose, and not from inside. She touched a yellow clay stained finger to the lock itself, and felt the wall inside, and found it cool. She took a deep breath, ignored the one tear that forced its way out of her right eye, and climbed up into the rocket.

It was quiet in there. Dee didn't know what kind of noise she'd expected, until she remembered the last voice she'd heard when she left, saying calmly, 'Fire . . . fire . . . fire . . .'

She thought that out and knew the fire had stopped;

then it was all right to open the safety door to the front part. Maybe . . . maybe they weren't hurt or anything; maybe they just couldn't hear her call. If there was just a *little* fire in there, it might have damaged the controls so they couldn't open the door for instance.

She knew where the controls on her side were, and how to work them. Her hand was on the knob when she had the thought, and then she was afraid. She knew from T.Z.'s how a burning body smelled; and she remembered how hot the *out*side of the hull was.

Her hand withdrew from the knob, returned, and then withdrew again, without consulting her at all.

That wasn't any *little* fire.

If they were all right, they'd find some way to open the door themselves: Daddy could always figure out something like that.

If people ask, she told herself, *I'll tell them I didn't know how.*

'Mommy,' she said out loud. 'Mommy, *please* . . .'

Then she remembered the tube. She ran to it and took the speaker off the hook, fumbling with impatience so that it fell from her hand and dangled on its cord, it buzzed the way it should; it was working!

She grabbed at it, and shouted into it. 'Mommy! Daddy! Where are you?' That was a silly thing to say. 'Please answer me. Please. *Please!*' I'll be good all the rest of my life, she promised silently and faithfully, all the rest of my life, if you answer me.

But no one answered.

She didn't think about the door controls again. After a while she found she could look around without really *seeing* the locked safety door. She had only to try a little, and she could make-believe it was a wall just like the sidewalls, that belonged there.

Eight and a half years is a short span of time to an adult; no one seriously expects very much of a child that age. But almost nine years is a long time when you're growing up, and more than time enough to learn a great many things.

Besides the sealed-off control room, and the bedroom-play-space, the family rocket has a third compartment, in the rear. Back there were the galley, bathroom facilities, and the repair equipment, with a tiny metals workshop. Only this last section held any mysteries for Deborah. She knew how to find and prepare the stored food supplies for herself and the baby; how to keep the water-reuser and air-fresher operating; where the oxy tanks were, and how to use them if she needed them.

She knew, too, how to let the bunks out of the wall in the play-space, and how to fasten Petey in so he wouldn't smother or strangle himself, or fall out, or even get uncovered in the night. And she knew where all the clean clothes were kept, and how to change the baby's diapers.

These things she knew as naturally and inevitably as a child back on Earth would have known how to select a meal on the push-panel, how to use the slide-walks, how to dial his lessons.

For five days, she played house with the baby in the rocket.

The first day it was fun; she made up bottles from the roll of plastic containers, and mixed milk in the blender from the dried supply. She ate her favourite foods, wore all her best clothes, dressed the baby and undressed him, and took him out for sun and air in the clearing blasted by the rocket jets. She discovered the uses of the spongy soil, and built fabulous mud castles while Petey played. Inside, when he was sleeping, she read films, and coloured pictures, and left the T.Z. running all the time.

The second day, and the third, she did all the same things, but it wasn't so much fun. Petey was always crying for something just when she got interested in what she was doing. And you couldn't say, 'Soon as I finish this chapter,' because he wouldn't understand.

Deborah got bored; then she began to get worried, too.

At first she had known that help would come; the people who lived on this planet would come looking for them. They'd rescue her and Petey; she'd be a heroine, and perhaps they'd never even ask if she knew how to open that door.

The third day, she began to think that perhaps there weren't any people on the planet at all—at least not on this part of it. There always had been a *few* people at least, whenever they went any place. The Government didn't send out survey engineers or geologists, like John and Sarah Levin, until after the first wildcat claims began to come in from a new territory. But this time maybe nobody knew they were coming. Or perhaps nobody had seen the crash. Or maybe this wasn't even the right planet.

She worried about that for a while, and then she remembered that her father always sent back a message-rocket when they arrived anyplace. He'd told her it was so the people on the last planet would know they were safe; if it didn't come at the right time, somebody would come out looking, to see what had happened to them.

Dee wondered how long it would take for the folks back on Starhope to get worried and come and rescue them. She couldn't even figure out how long they'd been in space on the way here. It was a long trip, but she wasn't sure if it had been a week, or a month, or more. Trips in space were always long.

The fourth day, she got tired of just waiting, and decided to explore.

She wasn't bothering with the masks any more. The dials still said *full* after the first three times they went out, and that meant air had enough oxygen in it so that the masks weren't working. So *that* was no problem.

And she could take along plenty of food. The only thing she wasn't sure about was Petey. She was afraid to leave him by himself, even in the play-space, and he was too heavy to carry for very long. She took his stroller out and tried it, but the ground was too soft to push it when he was inside.

The next morning, early, Deborah packed a giant lunch, and took the stroller out again. She found out that, though it wouldn't push, it could be *pulled,* so she tied a rope to the front, and loaded it up with bottles and diapers and her lunch and Petey. Then she set off up the broad black avenue of the rocket jets; that way she could always see the ship, and they wouldn't get lost.

IV

DAYDANDA WAS TIRED. Truthfully, all this walking back
and forth between chambers was a strain. Now she submitted gratefully to Kackot's fussing anxiety as he plumped
the top mat here and pulled it there, adjusting the big
new dais-couch to conform to her swollen body.

'I told you it was too much,' he fumed. 'I don't see
why you want to do it anyhow. Now you rest for a while.
You . . .'

'I have work to do,' she reminded him.

'It can wait; let them think for themselves for once!'

She giggled mentally at the notion. Kackot refused to
share her amusement.

'There's nothing that can't wait half an hour anyhow.'
He was almost firm with her; she loved to have him act
that way sometimes. Contentedly, she stretched out and
let her weight sink into the soft layers of cellulose mat.
Her body rested, but her mind and eye were as active as
ever. She studied the new shelves and drawers and files,
the big new desk at the head of the bed. Everything was at
hand; everything in place; it was wonderful. The old room
had been unbearably cluttered. Now she had only the active records near her. Everything connected with the departed was in the old room: easy to get at on the rare
occasions when she needed it; but not underhand every time
she turned around.

Daydanda examined the perfect arch her sons had built,
and exulted in the sight of it. When she wanted anything
on the other side, all she had to do was *walk right through*.

She was aware of Kackot's distress. Poor thing, he did
hate to have her do anything unconventional. But no one
had to know, no one who wasn't really *close* to them . . .

'Lady! Mother Daydanda!'

Kackot's image blanked out. This was a closed beam, an
urgent call from an older daughter, serving her turn in

training as relay-receptionist for messages from the many less articulate children of the Household.

'What's wrong?'

'Mother! The Stranger Lady has left her wings at last! She came out from *inside* them! And with a babe in arms! She . . . oh, Mother, I do not know how to tell it; I have never known the like. She is *not* of our people. The wings are not proper wings. She has no consort. A Family of *one!* I do not understand . . .'

'Be comforted, child. There is no need for *you* to understand.' With her own mind seething, Daydanda could still send a message of ease and understanding to her daughter. 'You have done well. She is *not* of our people, and we must expect many strange things. Now I want the scout.'

The daughter's mind promptly cleared away; in its place, Daydanda felt the nervous tingling excitement of the winged son who had been sent out to report on the fire in the east, and then to keep watch over the Strange Wings he had found there.

'Mother! I am frightened!'

The message was weak; the daughter through whom it came would be struggling with her curiosity. She was of the eighth family, almost mature, soon to depart from the Household and already showing signs of individualism and rebelliousness. She would be a good Mother, Daydanda thought with satisfaction, even as she closed the contact with the scout and shut the daughter out with a sharp reprimand for inefficiency.

'There is nothing to fear,' she told her son sharply; 'tell me what you have seen.'

'The Strange Lady has left her Wings. She has not enough limbs, and she uses a Strange litter to carry her babe. She . . .'

'She is a Stranger, son! And you have already quite adequately described her appearance. If you fear Strangeness for its own sake, you will never pierce the tree-tops, nor win yourself a Wife. You will remain in the Household till your wings drop off, and you are put to tending the corral . . .'

As she had expected, the familiar threat reassured him

as nothing else would have done. She listened closely to his detailed report of how the Stranger had left her Wings, and set off down the blackened fire-strip, pulling behind her a litter containing the Strange babe and some Strange, entirely unidentifiable, goods.

'She has not seen you?' the Mother asked at last.

'No.'

'Good; you have done well. Keep her in sight, and do not fear. I shall assign an elder brother to remain near the Wings, and to join you when the Stranger chooses her new site. Do not fear; your Mother watches over all.' But when the contact was broken, she turned at once in perturbation to her consort: 'Kackot, do you suppose . . . please, now, try to use a *little* imagination . . . do you suppose . . . ?' She caught his apprehensive agreement, even before the thought was fully articulated; clearly that was the case: 'The little one is no babe, but her consort!'

That put a different complexion on the whole matter. The flames of landing clearly could not be considered an act of deliberate hostility, if the Strange Lady's consort were so small and weak that he could not walk for himself, let alone assist in the clearing of a House-site. The fire thus assumed a ritual-functional aspect that made good sense.

If the explanation were correct, there need be no further fear of fire. And since the Strangers' march now was in a direction that would carry them towards the outer boundary of Daydanda's Houseland—or perhaps over it, into neighbouring territory—there was no need either for immediate conflict of any kind.

Daydanda wondered that she did not feel pleased. As long as one assumed the smaller creature to be a babe, it would have meant that a fully-developed Mother was capable of leaving her home, and walking abroad . . .

Kackot, pacing restlessly across the big room, sputtered with derision. 'A Mother,' he reminded her irritably, 'of a *very* Strange race!'

'Yes,' Daydanda agreed. In any case, they had been wrong in assuming the smaller one to be a babe, simply because of size. Still, as she lay back to rest and think, the Lady was bemused by a pervading and inexplicable sense of disappointment.

V

IT WAS VERY hot. After half an hour of sweat and glare, Deborah compromised with her first plan of staying out in the open, and began following a path just inside the forest edge. She kept one tree at a time—and only one—between herself and the 'road'. That way she had shade and orientation both.

Lunch time seemed to come quickly, judging from her own hunger. She stepped out from under the trees, and tried to look up at the sun to see how high it was. It was too bright; she couldn't look at it right. Then she realized she was fooling herself. You didn't need a clock if you had Petey. He would be wanting his bottle before it was time for her to eat. She trudged on, dragging the ever-heavier stroller behind her. Petey just sat there, quiet and content, gurgling his approval of the expedition, and refusing to show any interest in food at all.

Dee might have been less concerned with her insides if the exterior were any less monotonous. It didn't seem to matter where she was, or how far she walked: the forest went on endlessly, with no change in appearance except the random situation of the great trees.

After a while, she stepped out again and sighted back to the rocket; then off the other way. The end of the blasted road was in sight, now; but as far as Dee could see, there was nothing beyond it but more trees—exactly the same as the ones that stretched to left and right: tall straight dirty-yellow trunks, and a thin dense layer of grey-blue fronds high up on top.

At last Petey cried.

Dee was delighted. She tilted him back in his seat, and adjusted the plastic bottle in the holder, then fell ravenously on her own lunch.

When she was finished, she looked around again, more hopefully; at least they'd come this far in safety. Tomorrow, maybe she'd try another direction, through the woods, away from the road. While Petey napped, she raised a magnificent edifice of orange towers and turrets in the soft dirt; when he woke, she pulled him home again, content.

Maybe nobody lived here at all; maybe the planet had no aborigines. Then there was nothing to be afraid of, and she could wait safely with Petey till somebody came to rescue them. She was thinking that way right up to the time she stepped around the tail-jets of the rocket, and saw tracks.

There were two parallel sets of neat V-prints, perhaps two feet apart; they came from behind a tree near the ship, went almost to the open lock, and curved away to disappear behind another tree.

Two not-quite-parallel sets of tracks; nothing else.

Dee had courage. She looked to see what was behind the tree before she ran. But there was nothing.

That night was bad. Dee couldn't fall asleep, even in the foam bunk, even after the long walk and exercise. She twisted and turned, got up again and walked around and almost woke Petey, and got back in bed and tried to read. But when she got tired enough to sleep, and turned the light out, she'd be wide awake again, staring at the shadows, and she'd have to turn the light on and read some more.

After a while she just lay in her bunk, with the night light on, staring at the closed safety door to the control room, where her mother and father were. Then she cried; she buried her face in the pillow and cried wetly, fluently, hopelessly, until she fell asleep, still sobbing.

She dreamed, a nightmare dream with flaming V-shaped feet and a smell of burning flesh; and woke up screaming, and woke Petey too. Then she had to stay up to change and comfort him; by the time she got him back to sleep again, she was so tired and annoyed that she'd forgotten to be scared.

Next morning, she opened the lock cautiously, expecting to see . . . almost anything. But there were only giant trees and muddy orange ground: no mysterious tracks, no strange and horrifying beasts. And no glad crew of rescuers.

Maybe the V-tracks never existed, except in that nightmare. She spent most of the morning trying to decide

about that, then looked out again, and noticed one more
thing. Her own footsteps were also gone; the moist ground
had filled in overnight to erase all tracks. There was no
way to know for sure whether she had dreamed those tracks
or seen them.

The next two days, Dee stayed in the rocket. She was
keeping track of the days now. She'd looked at the chrono
right after they crashed, so she knew it was seven Starhope days since they came to the planet. She knew, too,
that the days here were different, shorter, because the
clock was getting ahead. The seventh day on the chrono
was the eighth Sunday here; and at high noon the dial
said only nine o'clock. She could still tell noon by Petey's
hunger, and she wondered about that: his hunger-clock
seemed to have set itself by the new sun already. Certainly,
he still got sleepy every night at dusk, though the clock
told three hours earlier each time.

Deborah spent most of one day working out the difference. She couldn't figure out any kind of arithmetic she'd
been taught to do it with, so she ended up by making little
marks for every hour and counting them. By evening, she
was sure she had it right. The day here was seventeen
hours instead of twenty. And then she realized she didn't
know how to set days on the chrono anyhow; all that work
was useless.

The next morning she went out again. Two days of
confinement had made Petey cranky and Dee brave.

Nothing happened; after that, they went out daily for
airings, as they had done at first. Dee made a calendar,
and marked the days on that; then she started checking
the food supplies.

They had enough of almost everything, too much to
figure out how long it would last. But she spent one
afternoon counting the plastic bottles on Petey's roll, and
figured out that they'd be gone in just three weeks, if he
kept on using four a day.

Someone would come for them before that; she was sure
of it. Just the same, she decided that baby was old enough
to learn to drink from a glass, and started teaching him.

Eight days became nine and ten, eleven and twelve;

still nothing happened. There was no sign of danger nor of help. Dee was sure now that she had dreamed those tracks, but somewhere on this planet she knew there were people. There *always* were; always had been, whenever they came to someplace new. And if the people didn't come to her, she'd have to find them. Deborah began to plan her second exploratory expedition.

There was no sense in covering the same ground again. She wanted to go the other way, into the woods. That meant she'd need to blaze a trail as she went; and it meant she couldn't use the stroller.

She added up the facts with careful logic, and realized that Petey would simply have to stay behind.

VI

THE BABY CRAWLED well now, and he could hold things; he could pick up a piece of cracker and get it to his mouth. He couldn't hold the bottle for himself, of course, but . . .

She tried it, closing her ears to the screams that issued steadily for an hour before he found his milk. But he did find it; her system worked. If she hung the bottle in the holder while his belly was still full, he ignored it; but when he was really hungry, he found it, and wriggled underneath to get at the down-tilted nipple. That gave her, really, a whole day to make her trip.

The night before, she packed her lunch, and for the first time, studied the contents of her father's workshop. There was a small blowtorch she had seen him use; and even in her present restless state Deborah was not so excessively brave that the thought of a weapon, as well as tree-marker, didn't tempt her. But when she found the torch, she was afraid to try it out indoors, and had to wait till morning.

At breakfast time, she stuffed Petey with food till he would eat no more. Then she clasped a bottle in the holder she'd rigged up, set the baby underneath to give him the idea once again, and went outside to try her skill with the torch. She came back, satisfied, to finish her preparations. When she left, a second bottle hung full and tempting in the play-space; Petey's toys were spread around the floor;

and a pile of the crackers in the corner would keep him happy, she decided, if all else failed. There was no way to solve the diaper-changing problem; he'd just have to wait for her return.

At first she tried to go in a straight line, marking every second tree along the way. After just a little while, she realized that it didn't matter which direction she took; she didn't know where she was going, anyway.

She walked on steadily, a very small girl under the distant canopy spread by the tall trees; very small, and insignificant, but erect and self-transporting on two overalled legs; a small girl with a large hump on her back.

The hump disappeared at noon, or somewhat earlier. She stuffed the remaining sandwich and a few pieces of dried fruit into her pockets, and tied the emptied makeshift knapsack more comfortably around her waist where it flopped rhythmically against her backside at every step.

Never did she forget to mark the trees, every second one along the way.

Nowhere did she see anything but more trees ahead, and bare ground underfoot.

She had no way of knowing how far she'd gone, or even what the hour was, when the silence ceased. Ever since she'd landed, the only noise she'd heard had been her own and Petey's. It was startling; it seemed impossible, by now, to hear anything else.

She stopped, with one foot set ahead of the other in midstep, and listened to the regular loud ticking of a giant clock.

It *was* impossible. She brought her feet into alignment and listened some more, while her heart thumped sympathetically in time to the forest's sound.

It was certainly impossible, but it came from the right, and it called to her; it promised warmth and haven. It was just an enormous alarm-clock, mechanically noisy, but it was somehow full of the same comfort-and-command she remembered in her mother's voice.

Deborah turned to the right and followed the call; but she didn't forget to mark the trees as she passed, every other one of them.

If it weren't for the trail-blazing, she might have missed

the garden entirely. It was off to one side, not directly on
her path to the ticking summons. She saw it only when she
turned to play the torch on one more tree: a riot of colours
and fantasy shapes in the near distance, between the upright trunks.

Not till then did the ticking frighten her: not till she
found how hard it was to move crosswise, or any way
except right towards it. She wanted to see it. Most likely
it was just wild, but there was always a chance . . .

And when she tried to walk that way, her legs didn't
want to go. Panic clutched at her, and failed to take hold.
She was an intrepid explorer on an alien planet, exposed
to unknown dangers. Also, she was a Space Girl.

'I pledge my honour to do everything in my power to
uphold the high standards of the human race,' she intoned,
not quite out loud, and immediately felt better. 'A Space
Girl is brave. A Space Girl is honest. A Space Girl is truthful. A Space Girl . . .'

She went clear down the list of virtues she had learned
in Gamma Troop on Starhope, and while she mumbled
them, her legs came under control. The ticking went
on, but it was just a noise—and not as loud as it had been,
either. She dodged scoutwise from behind one tree-trunk
to another, approaching the garden. If, indeed, it *was* a garden. Two trees away, she stopped and stared.

Every planet had strange new shapes and sights and
smells; the plants in each new place were always excitingly
different. But Dee was old enough to know that everywhere
chlorophyll was green, as blood was red. Oh, blood could
seem almost black, or blue, or pale pink, or even almost
white; and chlorophyll could shade to dark grey, and down
to faint cream-yellow. But growing gardens had green-
variant leaves or stems. And everywhere she'd been, the
plants, however strange, were unified. The trees here grew
blue-green-grey on top. The flowers should not grow, as
they seemed to do, in every random shade of colour.

There was no way to tell the leaves from seeds from
stems from buds. It was just . . . growth. A sort of arched
form sprouted bright magenta filaments from its ivory
mass. A bulbous something that tapered to the ground
showed baby blue beneath the many-coloured moss that

covered it. Between them on the ground, a series of concentric circles shaded from slate grey on the outside to oyster white in the centre, only it was so thin that a tinge of orange showed through from the soil below. Dee would not have thought it lived at all, until she noticed a slow rippling motion outward towards the edges.

Farther in, one form joined shapeless edges with another; one colour merged haphazard with the next. Deborah blinked, confused, and walked away, following the call of the great ticking clock, then mumbled to herself. 'I pledge my honour to do everything . . .' She turned back to the puzzling growths again, aware now that the calling power of the sound diminished when she said the words aloud.

The colours were too confusing. She had to concentrate, and couldn't think about the garden while she talked to herself. Maybe the Pledge wasn't the only thing that would do it. She said under her breath: 'That one is purple, and the other's like a pear . . .'

It worked. All she had to do was make her thoughts into words. It didn't matter what she said, or whether she whispered or shouted. As long as she kept talking, the summoning call would turn to a giant clock again, with no power over the movements of her legs. She went up closer to the baffling coloured shapes, and made out a fairy-delicate translucent spiral thing and then a large mauve mushroom in the centre.

Mushroom! At last she understood. They were so big, she hadn't thought of it at first: it was all fungus growth, and that made sense in the dim damp beneath the trees.

Strange it isn't every place, all over, she thought, and realized she was moving away from the garden again, and remembered this was one time it was all *right* to *talk* to herself out loud. 'There must be some people here. Some kind of people or natives. That noise is strange, too. It couldn't just *happen* that way; *some*body lives here . . .'

She didn't want to touch the fungus, but she went up close to it. 'Things *don't* just happen this way. That stuff would grow all over if it was wild; somebody planted it.' She peered through the arch-shape to the inside, and jumped back violently.

The thing was lying on its side, sucking a lower follicle

of the arch, its livid belly working as convulsively as its segmented mouth, its many limbs sprawled out in all directions.

Dee jumped away in horror, and crept back in fascination. 'It doesn't know I'm here,' she remembered to whisper. From around the other side of the bulbous growth she watched, and slowly understood.

'It's like some kind of insect.' It couldn't really be an insect, of course, because it was two feet long—much too large for an insect. An insect this size, on a planet as much like Earth as this was, wouldn't be able to breathe. They'd explained about why insects couldn't be any larger than the ones you found on Earth in Space Girl class. But men had found creatures on other planets that did look a lot like insects, and acted a lot like them, too. And even though people knew they weren't really insects, they still called such creatures 'bugs' . . .

Well, this thing was as close to an insect as a thing this size could be, Deborah decided. It was two feet long, and that made sense when you stopped to think about it, what with the tall trees and the giant mushrooms. She counted six legs, and then realized that the other two in front, resting quietly now, were feelers. The two front legs clutched at a clump of hairy shoots on the arched moss, almost like Petey holding his bottle. The back leg that was on top was longer than the front ones; it was braced against the arch for steadiness. The lower leg was tucked underneath the body; its lower middle leg also lay still on the ground, stretched straight out. The upper middle leg was busily scratching at a small red spot on the belly, acting absurdly independent of the rest of the feeding creature.

There was really, Dee decided, nothing frightening except the mouth. She looked for eyes, and couldn't see them, then remembered that some bugs on other planets had them on the backs of their heads. But that mouth . . .

It worked like Petey's on a nipple; but not like Petey's, because this one had *six* lips, all thick and round-looking instead of like people's lips, and all closing in towards each other at the same time. It was horrible to watch.

Dee backed off silently, and found herself walking the wrong way again. She tried the multiplication table while she made a circuit of the 'garden', examining it for size and shape, and looking for a clear part that would let her see into the centre.

She found, at last, a whole row of the jelly-like translucent things, lying flat and low, so she could look inside. The ground beneath them was scattered with flashing jewel-like stones . . .

No, black stones, with the bright part in the middle, she thought in words. *No, not the middle. At one end* . . . each stone was lying partly on an edge of the jelly-stuff . . . *about as big as my foot,* she thought, and saw the tiny feet around the edge of every stone.

Eyes on the backs of their heads, she thought, *and they have car . . . carpets? . . . carapaces!* These bugs were smaller than the first one, and not frightening at all. Bugs only looked bad from the bottom, she realized, and instantly corrected that impression.

Something walked into the garden, and picked up four of the little ones. Something as tall as Dee herself when it went in, and half again as high when it left. It entered on four legs, and walking upside-down, head carried towards the ground, and looking backwards . . . no, *facing* backwards, *looking* forward. It entered calmly, moving at a steady even pace; approached the edge of the garden where Deborah watched the infants feeding . . . and froze.

An instant's immobility, then the big bug erupted into a frenzy of activity: scooped up the four closest little ones—two of them with the long hairy jointed arms (or legs? back legs?), and two more hurriedly with two front legs (or arms?)—and almost *ran* out, now on just two legs, the centre ones, its body neatly balanced fore and aft, almost perfectly horizontal, the heavy hooded head in front, the spiny rounded abdomen at the back.

It scuttled off with its four tiny wriggling bundles, and as it left, Dee registered in full the terror of what she had seen.

She fled . . . and by some miracle, fled past a tree she'd marked, so paused in flight to find the next one, and the next, and followed her blazed trail safely back. The ticking of the forest followed for a while, then stopped abruptly. But while it lasted, it *pushed* away as hard as it had pulled before.

VII

DAYDANDA MADE THE last entry in her calendar of the day, and filed it with yesterday's and all the others. Things were going well. The youngest Family was thriving; the next-to-youngest—the Eleventh—was almost ready to start school-ing; ready, in any case, for weaning from the Garden. Soon there would be room in the nurseries for a new brood.

Kackot was restless. She hadn't meant the thought for him at all, but he was sensitive to such things now, and he moved slightly, eagerly, towards her from his place across the room—perhaps honestly mistaking his own desire for the summons.

She sent a thought of love and promise, and temporary firm refusal. The new Family would have to wait. Within the Household, things were going well; but there were other matters to consider.

There was the still-unsolved puzzle of the Strangers, for instance. For a few hours, that mystery had seemed quite satisfactorily solved. When the Strange Lady left her Wings with baby-or-consort—now it seemed less certain which it was—to travel the path the flames had cleared for her, the whole thing had assumed a ritual aspect that made it easier to understand. Whatever Strange reasons, motives, or tradi-tions were involved, it all seemed to fit into a pattern of some kind . . . until the next report informed Daydanda that the two Strangers had returned to their Wings—an act no less, and no more, unprecedented than their manner of arrival, or their strange appearance.

They had not since departed from the—

The house? she wondered suddenly. Could a House be somehow made to travel through the air?

She felt Kackot's impatient irritation with such fantasiz-ing, and had to agree. Surely the image of—*it*—relayed by the flier-scout who had approached most closely, resem-bled in no way any structure Daydanda had ever seen or heard of.

But neither was it similar in any way, she thought—and this time guarded the thought from her consort's limited imagination—to ordinary, Wings, except by virtue of the certain knowledge that it had descended from the sky above the trees.

Today there had been no report. The fliers were all busy on the northern boundary, where a more ordinary sort of nesting had been observed. When the trouble there was cleared up, she could afford to keep a closer watch on the apparently not-hostile Strangers.

Meantime, certainly, it was best to let a new Family wait. Laying was hard on her; always had been. And with possible action developing on two fronts now . . .

Kackot stirred again, but not with any real hope, and the Lady barely bothered to reply. It was time to bring the young ones in. Daydanda began the evening Homecalling, the message to return, loud and strong and clear for all to hear: a warning to unfriendly neighbours; a promise and renewal to all her children in the Household, young and old.

'Lady! oh, Mother!' Daydanda sustained the Homecalling at full strength, through a brief surge of stubborn irritation; then, suddenly worried—the daughter on relay knew enough not to interrupt at this time for anything less than urgent—she allowed enough of her concentration to be distracted so as to permit a clear reception.

'Lady! . . . nurse from east garden . . . very frightened, confused . . . message unclear . . . she wishes.'

'Send her in!' Daydanda cut off the semi-hysterical outburst, and terminated the Homecalling abruptly, with extra emphasis on the last few measures.

The nurse dashed through the archway, too distraught to make a ritual approach, almost forgetting to prostrate herself in the presence of the Lady, her Mother. She opened communication while still in motion, as soon as she was within range of her limited powers. Daydanda recognized her with the first contact: a daughter of the fifth Family— not very bright, even for a wingless one, but not given to emotional disturbance either, and a fine nurse, recently put in charge of the east garden.

'The Stranger, Mother Daydanda! The Strange Lady!

. . . she came to the *nursery* . . . she would have stolen . . .
killed . . . she would have . . .'

To the nursery!

The Mother had to quell an instant's panic of her own
before she could commence the careful questioning and
reiterated reassurance that were needed to obtain a coherent
picture from the nurse. When at last she had stripped away
the fearful imaginative projections that stemmed from the
daughter's well-conditioned protectiveness, it appeared that
the Strange Lady had visited the Garden, had spied on the
feeding babies, and then had departed with haste when the
Nurse came to fetch them home for the night.

'The babies are all safe?' the Mother asked sternly.

'Yes, Lady. I brought them to the House quick as I
could before I came to you. I would not have presumed
to come, my Lady, but I could not make the winged one
understand. Will my Mother forgive . . .'

'There is nothing to forgive; you have done well,' Daydanda dismissed her. 'You were right to come to me,
even during the Homecalling.'

Breathing easy again, and once more in full possession
of her faculties, the nurse offered thanks and farewell, and
wriggled backwards out of sight under the arch, quite
properly apologetic. The Lady barely noticed; she was already in contact with the flier-scout who had been reas-
signed from the North border by the daughter on relay, as
soon as the nurse's first wild message was connected with
the Strange Wings.

It was a son of the eighth Family, the same scout who
had approached the Wings before, a well-trained, conscientious, and devoted son, almost ready to undertake the
duties of a consortship. Daydanda could not have wished
for a better representative through whose sense to perceive the Strangers.

Yet, there was little she could learn through him. The
Strange Lady had returned to the Wings . . . *the House?*
More and more it seemed so . . . where the small Stranger
presumably awaited her. Now they were both inside, and
the remarkable barrier that could be raised or lowered in
a matter of seconds was blocking the entranceway.

Perception of any kind was difficult through the dense

stuff of which the . . . whatever-it-was: Wings? House? . . . was made. The scout was useless now. Daydanda instructed him to stay on watch, and abandoned the contact. Then she concentrated her whole mind in an effort to catch some impression—anything at all—from beyond the thick fabric of . . . whatever-it-was.

Eventually, there was a flash of something; then another. Not much, but the Lady waited patiently, and used each fleeting image to build a pattern she could grasp. One thought, and another thought, and . . .

To Kackot's astonishment, the Lady relaxed suddenly with an outpouring of amusement. She did not communicate to him what she knew, but abruptly confirmed all his worst fears of the past weeks with a single command: 'I will go to the Strange Wings, oh Consort. Prepare a litter for me.'

When she addressed him thus formally, he had no recourse but to obey. If she noticed his sputtering dismay at all, she gave no sign, but lay back on her couch, thoroughly fatigued, to rest through the night while her sons and daughters prepared a litter, and enlarged the outer arches sufficiently to accommodate its great size.

VIII

DEE WAS SCARED, and she didn't know what to do. She wanted her mother; it was no fun taking care of Petey now. She made him a bottle to keep him from screaming, but she didn't bother with his diaper or fixing up his bunk or anything like that. It didn't matter any more.

There were no people on this planet.

Nobody was going to rescue them; nobody at all.

It wasn't the right planet, at all. If anybody on Starhope got worried and went to look for them, it was some other planet they'd look on. It had to be, because there were no people here. Just *bugs!*

Petey fell asleep with the bottle still in his mouth, sprawled on the floor, all wet and dirty. Deborah didn't care; she sat on the floor herself and fell asleep and didn't even know she slept till she woke up, with nothing changed, except that the clock said it was morning.

And she was hungry after all.

She started back to the galley, but first she had to open the outer lock. She actually had her hand on the lever before she realized she didn't *want* to open it. She was hungry; the last thing in the world she wanted to do was look outside again. She went back and got a piece of cake and some milk.

Milk for Petey, too. If she got it fixed before he woke up, she wouldn't have to listen to him yelling his head off again. She started to fix a bottle, but first she had to open the lock.

This time, she stopped herself half-way there.

It was silly to think she had to look out; she didn't want to.

Petey was awake, but he wasn't hollering for once. She went back and got the bottle, and brought it into the play-space.

'Open it,' Petey said. 'Come out. Mother.'

'All right,' Dee told him. She gave him the bottle, went over to the lock, and then turned around and looked at him, terrified.

He was sucking on the bottle. 'Come on,' he said. 'Mother waiting.'

She was watching him while he said it. He didn't say it; he drank his milk.

She didn't think she was crazy, so she was still asleep, and this was a dream. It wasn't really happening at all, and it didn't matter.

She opened the lock.

IX

Once she had flown above the tree-tops, silver strong wings beating a rhythm of pride and joy in the high dry air above the canopy of fronds. Her eyes had gleamed under the white rays of the sun itself, and she had looked, with wild unspeakable elation, into the endless glaring brilliance of the heavens.

Now she was tired, and the blessed relief from sensation when they set her down on the soft ground—after the lurching motion of the forest march—was enough to make her momentarily regret her decision. A foolish notion this whole trip . . .

Kackot agreed enthusiastically.

The Lady closed her thoughts from his, and commanded the curtain at her side to be lifted. Supine in her litter, safely removed from the Strangers under a tree at the fringe of the clearing, her vast body embedded on layers of cellulose mat, Daydanda looked out across the ravaged black strip. And the sun, in all its strength, collected on the shining outer skin of the Strange Wings, gathered its light into a thousand fiery needles to sear the surface of her eye, and pierce her very soul with agony.

Once she had flown above the trees themselves . . .

Now her sons and daughters rushed to her side, in response to her uncontained anguish. They pulled close the curtain, and formed a tight protective wall of flesh and carapace around the litter. And from the distance, came a clamouring bloodlust eagerness: the Bigheads waking in answer to her silent shriek of pained surprise. She sent them prompt soothing, and firm command to be still; not till she was certain they understood, and would obey, did she dare turn any part of her mind to a consideration of her own difficulties. Even then she was troubled with the knowledge that her stern suppression of their rage to fight would leave the entire Bighead brood confused, and useless for the next emergency. It might be many days before their dull minds could be trained again to the fine edge of danger-awareness they had just displayed. If any trouble should arise in the meanwhile . . .

She sent instructions to an elder daughter in the House to start the tedious process of reconditioning at once, then felt herself free at last to devote all her attention to the scene at hand. Tomorrow's troubles would have to take care of themselves till tomorrow. For now, there was disturbance, anxiety, and mortification enough.

That she, who had flown above the trees, higher and further than any sibling of her brood, that *she* should suffer from the sunlight now . . .

'It was many years and many Families ago, my dear, my Lady.'

Daydanda felt her consort's comforting concern and thought a smile. 'Many years indeed . . .' And it was true; she had not been outside her chamber till this day—since the first Family they raised was old enough to tend the fungus gardens, and to carry the new babes back and forth. That was many years behind her now, and she had grown through many chambers since that time: each larger than the last, and now, most recently, the daring double chamber with the great arch to walk through.

The Household had prospered in those years, and the boundaries of its land were wide. The gardens grew in many places now, and the thirteenth Family would soon outgrow the nursery. The winged sons and daughters of Seven Families had already grown to full maturity, and departed to establish new Houses of their own . . . or to die in failure. And through the years, the numbers of the wingless ones who never left the Household grew great; masons and builders, growers and weavers, nurses and teachers—there were always more of them, working for the greater welfare of the House, and their Mother, its Lady.

Through all those building, growing, widening years, Daydanda had *forgotten* . . . forgotten the graceful wings and the soaring flight; the dazzling sunlight, and the fresh moist air just where the fronds stirred high above her now; the bright colours and half-remembered shapes of trees and nursery plants. Not once, in all that time, had she savoured the full sensory sharpness of *outside* . . .

She thought longingly of the nursery garden, the first one, that she and Kackot had planted together when they waited for the first Family to come. She thought of it, determined to see it again one day, then put aside all thoughts, hopes, and regrets of past or future.

Daydanda directed that her litter be moved so that the opening of the curtain would give her a view of the forest interior. Then, while her eye grew once again accustomed to their former function, she began to seek—with a more practised organ of perception—the mind-patterns of the Strangers inside that frighteningly bright structure in the clearing.

It was hard work. Whether there was something in the nature of the dense fabric of the Wings, or whether the difficulty lay only in the Strangeness of the beings inside, she could not tell, but at the beginning, the Lady found that proximity made small difference in her ability to perceive what was inside.

Strangers! One could hardly expect them, after all, to provide familiar friend-or-enemy patterns for perception. Yet that very knowledge made the brief flashes of contact that she got all the more confusing, for they contained a teasing familiarity that made the Strange elements even less comprehensible by contrast.

For just the instant's duration of a swift brush of minds, the Mother felt as though it were a daughter of her own inside the Strange structure; then the feeling was lost, and she had to strain every effort again simply to locate the image.

A series of slow moves, meantime, brought her litter gradually back round to where it had been at first; and though she found it was still painful to look for any length of time directly at the blazing light reflected from the Wings, the Lady discovered that by focusing on the trees diagonally across the clearing, she could include the too-bright object within her peripheral vision.

That much assured, she ceased to focus visually at all. Time enough for that when—*if*—the Strangers should come forth. Once more she managed to grasp, briefly, the mental image of the Strangers, or of one of them; and once again she felt the unexpected response within herself, as if she were in contact with a daughter of the Household . . .

She lost it then; but it fitted with her sudden surmise of the instant before.

Now, in the hopeful certainty that she had guessed correctly, she abandoned the effort at perception entirely; she gathered all her energies instead into one tight-beamed communication aimed at penetrating the thick skin of the Wings, and very little different in any way from the standard evening Homecalling.

It took some time. She was beginning to think she had failed: that the Strangers were not receptive to her call, or would respond only with fear and hostility. Then, without warning, the barrier at the entranceway was gone.

No . . . not actually *gone*. It was still there, and still somehow attached to the main body of the Wings, but turned round so it no longer barred the way. And the opening this uncovered turned out to be, truly, the double-arch she had seen—but not quite credited—through her son's eyes.

Two arches, resting on each other base-to-base, but open in the centre: the shape of a hollowed-eye. Such a shape might grow, but it could not be *built*. Half-convinced as she had been that the Wings or House, or whatever-it-was, was an artificial structure rather than a natural form, Daydanda had put the relayed image of the doorway down to distortion of communication the night before. Now she saw it for herself: that, and the device that moved like a living thing to barricade the entrance.

Like a living thing . . .

It could fly; it was therefore, by all precedent of knowledge, alive. Reluctantly, the Lady discarded the notion that the Wings had been built by Strange knowledge. But even then, she thought soberly, there was much to be learned from the Strangers.

And in the next moment, she ceased to think at all. The Stranger emerged—the bigger of the two Strangers—and at the first impact of full visual *and* mental perception, Daydanda's impossible theory was confirmed.

X

DEBORAH STOOD OUTSIDE, on the charred ground in front of the rocket, earnestly repeating the multiplication table: 'Two two's are four. Three two's are six. Four two's . . .'

She was just as big as any of these bugs. The only one that was bigger was the one inside the box that she could only see part of—but that one had something wrong with it. It just lay there stretched out flat all the time, as if it couldn't get up. The box had handles for carrying, too, so Dee didn't have to worry about how big that one was.

All the rest of them were just about her own size, or even smaller but there were too *many* of them. And when she thought about actually touching one, with its hairy, sticky legs, she remembered the sick crackling sound a beetle makes when you step on it.

She didn't want to fight them, or anything like that; and she didn't think they wanted to hurt her specially, either. She didn't have the knotted-up, tight kind of feeling you get when somebody wants to hurt you. They didn't *feel* like enemies, or act that way, either. They were just too . . .

'Four four's are sixteen. Five four's are twenty. Six four's are twenty-four. Seven . . .'

. . . too *interested!* And that was a silly thing, because how could *she* tell if they were interested? She couldn't even see their faces, because all the ones in front were bending backwards-upside-down, like the one she'd seen in the garden . . .

'. . . four's are twenty-eight. Eight four's are thirty-two. Nine four's are . . .'

. . . just standing there, the whole row of them, with their back legs or arms or whatever-they-were sticking up in the air, and their heads dipped down in front so they could stare at her out of the big glittery eye in the middle of each black head . . .

'. . . thirty-six. Ten four's are forty. Eleven . . .'

What did they want, anyhow? Why didn't they *do* something?

'. . . four's are forty-four. Twelve four's . . .'

The Space Girl oath was hard to remember if you were trying to think about other things at the same time; but Deborah knew the multiplication tables by heart, and she could keep talking while she was thinking.

Daydanda was fascinated. She had guessed at it, in her chamber the night before . . . more than guessed, really. She would have been *certain,* if the notion were not so flatly impossible in terms of knowledge and experience. It was precisely that conflict between perception and precedent that had determined her to make the trip out here.

And she was right! These two were neither Lady and consort, nor Mother and baby, but only two children: a half-grown daughter and a babe in arms. Two young wingless ones, alone, afraid, and . . . *Motherless?*

Eagerly, Daydanda poured out her questionings:

Where did they come from?

What sort of beings were they?

Where was their Mother?

'Twelve four's are forty-eight. One five is five. Two five's are ten. Three . . .'

The important thing was just to keep talking—Dee knew that from when she had so much trouble at the garden. As long as she was saying *some*thing at all, she could keep the crazy stuff out of her head.

'. . . five's are fifteen. Four five's are twenty. Five five's . . .'

It was harder this time, though. At the garden, with the drumbeat-heartbeat sound that felt like Mommy's voice, all she had to do was *think* words. But now, it was stuff like thinking Petey was saying things to her—or feeling like somebody else was asking her a lot of silly questions. And every time she stopped for breath at all, she'd start wanting to answer a lot of things inside her head that there wasn't even anybody around to have asked.

'. . . are twenty-five. Six five's are thirty.'

The aching soreness in her body from the jolting journey through the forest . . . the instant's agony when the sunlight seared her eye . . . the nagging worry over the disturbed Bigheads . . . all these were forgotten, or submerged, as the Lady experienced for the first time in her life the frustration of her curiosity.

Every answer she could get from the Strange child came in opposites. Each question brought a pair of contradictory replies . . . if it brought any reply at all. Half the time, at least, the Stranger was refusing reception entirely, and for some obscure reason, broadcasting great quantities of arithmetic—most of it quite accurate, but all of it irrelevant to the present situation.

Would they remain here? the Lady asked. Or would

they return to their own House? Had they come to build a House here? Or was the Wing-like structure on the blackened ground truly a House instead?

The answers were many and also various.

They would not stay, the Stranger seemed to say, nor would they leave. The structure from which she had emerged was a House, but it was also Wings: Unfamiliar concept in a single symbol—Wings-House? *Both!*

Their Mother was nearby—inside—but—dead? *No! Not dead!*

How could the child possibly answer a sensible question sensibly if she started broadcasting sets of numbers every time anyone tried to communicate with her? *Very rude,* Daydanda thought, and very *stupid.* Kackot eagerly confirmed her opinion, and moved a step closer to the litter, as if preparing to commence the long march home.

The Lady had no time to reprimand him. At just that moment, the Strange child also broke into motion—perhaps also feeling that the interview was over.

'. . . Thirty. Seven five's are thirty-fi . . .'

One of them moved!

Just a couple of steps, but Dee, panicked, forgot to keep talking and started a dash for the rocket; her head was full of questions again, and part of her mind was trying to answer them, without *her* wanting to at all, while another part decided *not* to go back inside, with a mixed-up kind of feeling, as if Petey didn't want her to.

And *that* was silly, because she could hear Petey crying now. He wanted her to come in, all right, or at least to come and get him. She couldn't tell for sure, the way he was yelling, whether he was scared and mad at being left alone—or just mad and wanting to get picked up. It sounded almost more like he thought he was being left out or something, and wanted to get in on the fun.

If he thinks this is fun . . . !

'We're lost, that's what we are,' she said out loud, as if she were answering real questions someone had asked, instead of crazy ones inside her own head. 'I don't *know* where we are. We came from Starhope. That's a different planet. A different *world.* I don't know where . . . One five is five,' she remembered. 'Two sixes are seven. I mean two seven's are twenty-one . . . I can't think *anything* right!'

It *really* didn't matter what she said; as long as she kept talking. If she answered the silly questions right out loud that was all right too, because they couldn't understand her anyhow. How would *they* know Earthish?

It was possible that the Stranger's sudden move to return to the Wings-House was simply a response to Kackot's gesture of readiness to depart. The Lady promised herself an opportunity to express her irritation with her consort— soon. For the moment, however, every bit of energy she could muster went into a plea-command-call-invitation to the Strange child to remain outside the shelter and continue to communicate.

The Stranger hesitated, paused—but even before that, she had begun, perversely, now that no questions were being asked, to release a whole new flood of semi-information.

More contradictions, of course!

These two, the Stranger children, were—something hard to comprehend—not-aware-of-where-they-were.

They were in need of help, but not helpless.

The elder of the two—the daughter who now stood wavering in her intentions, just beside the open barrier of the Wings-House—was obviously acting in the capacity of nurse. Yet her self-pattern of identity claimed reproductive status!

Certainly the girl's attitude towards her young sibling was an odd mixture of what one might expect to find in nurse or Mother. Possibly the relationship could be made clearer by contact with the babe himself. There was little enough in the way of general information to be expected from such a source, but here he might be helpful. Tentatively, with just a small part of her mind, Daydanda reached out to find the babe, still concentrating on her effort to keep the older one from departing . . .

'Food . . . mama . . . suck . . . oh, look!'

The Lady promptly turned her full attention to the babe.

After the obstructionist tactics, and confused content of the Strange girl's mind, the little one's response to a brushing contact was doubly startling. Now that she was fully

receptive to them, thoughts came crowding into the
Mother's mind, thoughts unformed and infantile, but
buoyantly eager and hopeful.

'Love . . . food . . . good . . . mama . . . suck . . . see
. . . see . . .'

'Three seven's are twenty one!' Dee remembered tri-
umphantly, and began feeling a lot better. They were all
standing still again, for one thing; and her head felt clearer,
too.

She moved a cautious step backwards, watching them as
she went, and not having any trouble now remembering
her multiplication.

'Four seven's are twenty-eight . . .'

Just a few more steps. If she could just get back inside,
and get the door closed, she wouldn't open it again for
*any*thing. She'd stay right there with Petey till some *people*
came . . .'

'. . . MAMA . . . SUCK . . . see . . . see . . . good
. . . love . . .'

It might have been one of her own latest brood, so easy
and familiar was the contact. Just about the same age-
level and emotional development, too. Daydanda was suddenly imperatively anxious to see the babe directly, to hold
it in her own arms, to feel what sort of strange shape and
texture could accommodate such warmly customary long-
ings and perceptions.

'The babe!' she commanded. 'I wish to have the babe
brought to me!' But the nurse to whom she had addressed
the order hung back miserably.

'The babe, I said!' The Lady released all her pent-up
irritation at the Stranger child, in one peremptory blast
of anger at her own daughter. '*Now!*'

'Lady, I cannot . . . the light . . . forgive me, my
Lady . . .'

With her own eye still burning in its socket, Daydanda
hastily blessed the nursing daughter, and excused her.
Even standing on the fringes of the bright-lit area must be
frightening to the wingless ones. But whom else could she
send? The fliers were unaccustomed to handling babes . . .

'Kackot!'

He was good with babes, really. She felt better about

sending him than she would have had she trusted the handling of the Stranger to a nurse. Kackot himself felt otherwise; but at the moment, the Lady's recognition of his
discomfiture was no deterrent to her purpose; she had not
forgotten his ill-advised move a little earlier.

The consort could not directly disobey. He went forward, doubtfully enough, and stood at the open entranceway, peering in.

'Oh, *look!* . . . love . . . look!'

The babe's welcoming thoughts were unmistakable;
Kackot must have felt them as Daydanda did. Stranger or
not, the near presence of a friendly protective entity made
it beg to be picked up, petted, fondled, loved—and hopefully, though not, the Mother thought, truly hungrily—
perhaps also to be fed.

Meantime, however, there was the older child to reckon
with. The babe was eager to come; the girl, Daydanda
sensed, was determined not to allow it. Once more, the
Mother tried to reach the Strange daughter with empathy
and affection and reassurance. Once again, she met with
only blankness and refusal. Then she sent a surge of loving
invitation to the babe, and got back snuggling eagerness
and warmth—and suddenly, from the elder one, a lessening
of fear and anger.

Daydanda smiled inside herself; she thought she knew
now how to penetrate the strange defences of the child.

XI

DEE STOOD STILL and watched it happen. She saw the
nervous fussy-bug—the one that had scared her when he
moved before—go right over to the rocket and *look inside.*
He passed right by her, close enough to touch; she was going to do something about it, until Petey started talking
again.

He said, 'Baby come to mama.'

At least, she *thought* he said it. Then she *almost* thought
she heard a Mother say, 'It's all right; don't worry. Baby
wants to come to mama.'

'Mother's *dead!*' Deborah screamed at them all, at Petey and the bugs, without ever even opening her mouth. 'Five seven's are thirty-five,' she said hurriedly. She'd been forgetting to keep talking, that's what the trouble was. 'Six seven's are forty-two. Seven . . .'

And still, she couldn't get the notion out of her head that it was her own mother's voice she'd heard. 'Seven seven's . . .' she said desperately, and couldn't keep from turning around to look at the part of the rocket where Mommy was—would be—had been when—

The smooth gleaming metal nose looked just the same as ever, now it was cool again. There was no way of knowing anything had ever happened in there. *If anything had happened . . .*

Deborah stared and stared, as if looking long enough and hard enough would let her see right through the triple hull into the burned-out inside: the wrecked control room, and the two charred bodies that had been Father and Mother.

'. . . seven seven's is forty—forty seven? . . . eight . . . ?'

She floundered, forgetting, she was too small, and she didn't know what to do about anything, and she wanted her mother.

'It's all right. Stand still. Don't worry. Baby *wants* to come to mama.'

It wasn't her own mother's voice, though; that wasn't the way Mommy talked. If it was these bugs that were making her hear crazy things and putting silly questions in her head . . . seven seven's . . . seven seven's is . . . just stand still . . . don't worry . . . everything will be all right . . . seven seven's . . . *I don't know* . . . don't worry, all right, stand still, seven's is . . .

'Forty-nine!' she shrieked. The fussy-bug was all the way inside, and she'd been standing there like any dumb kid, hearing thoughts and voices that weren't real, and not knowing what to do.

'Forty-nine, fifty, fifty-one, fifty-two,' she shouted. She could have been just counting like that all along, instead of trying to remember something like seven times seven. *Get out of there, you awful hairy horrible old thing!* 'Fifty-three, fifty-four. You leave my brother alone!'

The fussy-bug came crawling out of the airlock, with Petey—soft little pink-and-wet Petey—clutched in its sticky arms.

'Fifty-five,' she tried to shout, but it came out like a creak instead. *You leave him alone!* her whole body screamed; but her throat was too dry and felt as if somebody had glued it together, and she couldn't make any words come out at all. She started forward to grab the baby.

'Come to Mama,' Petey said. 'Nice Mama. Like. Good.'

She was looking right at him all the time, and she *knew* he wasn't *really* talking. Just drooling the way he always did, and making happy-baby gurgling noises. He certainly didn't act scared—he was cuddling up to the hairy-bug just as if it was a *person*.

'Come to Mama,' the baby crooned inside her head; she should have made a grab for him right then, but somehow she wasn't *sure* . . .

The fussy-bug walked straight across the clearing to the tree where the big box was, and handed Petey inside.

'Oo-oo-ooh, *Mama!*' Petey cried out with delight.

'Mommy's *dead!*' Deborah heard herself shouting, so she knew her voice was working again. 'Dead, she's dead, can't you understand that? Any dope could understand that much. She's *dead!*'

Nobody paid any attention to her. Petey was laughing out loud; and the sound got mixed up with some other kind of laughter in her head that was hard to not-listen to, because it felt *good*.

XII

HOLDING THE BABE tenderly, Daydanda petted and patted and stroked it, and made pleased laughter from them both. Cautiously, she experimented with balancing the intensities of the two contacts, trying to gauge the older child's reactions to each variation. Reluctantly, as she observed the results, she came to the conclusion that the Strange daughter had indeed been consciously attempting to block communication.

It was unheard-of; therefore impossible—but impossibilities were commonplace today. The Mother's own presence at this scene was a flat violation of tradition and natural law.

Nevertheless:

The child had emerged from the Wings-House, in response to a Homecalling pattern.

Therefore, she was not an enemy.

Therefore she could not possibly feel either fear or hostility towards Daydanda's Household.

These things being true, what reason could she have for desiring to prevent communication?

Answer: Obviously, despite the logic of the foregoing, the Strange child was *afraid*.

Why? There was no danger to her in this contact.

'Stupid,' Kackot grumbled; 'just plain stupid. As much brains as a Bighead. Lady, it is getting late; we have a long journey home . . .'

Daydanda let him rumble on. A child was likely to behave stupidly when frightened. She remembered, and sharply reminded her consort, of the time a young winged one of her own, a very bright boy normally—was it the fifth Family he was in? No, the sixth—had wandered into the Bigheads' corral, and been too petrified with fear to save himself, or even to call for help.

The boy had been afraid, she remembered now, that he would call the Bigheads' attention to himself, if he tried to communicate with anyone, so he closed off against the world. Of course, he knew in advance that the Bigheads were dangerous. If the Stranger here had somehow decided to be fearful *in advance*, perhaps her effort to block contact was motivated the same way . . .

'The Homecalling,' Kackot reminded her; 'she answered a Homecalling.'

'She is a Stranger,' Daydanda pointed out. 'Perhaps she responded to friendship without identifying it . . . I don't know . . .'

But she would find out. Once again she centred her attention on the babe, keeping only a loose contact with the older child.

Dee kept watching the box on the ground that had the big bug inside it. She couldn't see much of the bug, and she couldn't see Petey at all, after the other bug handed him in. But it wasn't just Petey she was watching for.

It was that big bug that was—talking to her. Well, anyhow, that was making it sound as if Petey talked to her and putting questions in her head and . . .

She didn't know how *it* did it, but she couldn't pretend any more that it wasn't really happening. Somebody was picking and poking at her inside her head, and she didn't know how they did it or why, or what to do about it. But she was sure by now that the big bug in the box was the one.

'Let's see now—seven seven's is forty-nine.' Just counting didn't seem to work so well. 'Seven eight's is . . . I mean, *eight seven's* is . . . I don't *know* I can't *remember* . . . We came for Daddy and Mommy to make reports. That's what they always do. Daddy's a Survey Engineer and Mommy's a Geologist. They work for the Planetary Survey Commiss . . . I mean they *did* . . .'

It was none of their business. And they did know Earthish!

If they didn't, how could *they* talk to *her?*

'Seven seven's is forty-nine. Seven seven's is forty-nine. Seven seven's . . .'

At the first exchange, the Lady had put it down to incompetence, but she could no longer entertain that excuse. The Strangers had no visible antennae, yet the ease of communication with the babe made it clear that they could receive as well as broadcast readily—if they wished.

The perception appeared to be associated with an organ Daydanda had at first mistaken for a mouth: small and flat, centred towards the bottom of the face, and enclosed by just two soft-looking mandibles.

In the babe, the mandibles were almost constantly in motion, and there was a steady flow of undirected, haphazard communication, such as was normal for the little one's apparent level of development. With the older child, it was apparent that the messages that came when the mandibles were moving were stronger, clearer, and more purposeful in meaning than the others. Unfortunately, the content of these messages was mostly nothing but arithmetic.

Yet even when the 'mouth' was at rest, Daydanda noticed that there was a continuous trickle of communication from the Strange daughter—a sort of reluctant release of thought, rather like the babe's in that it was undirected and largely involuntarily, but with two striking differences: the eagerness of the babe to be heard, and the fact that the content of the older one's thoughts were not at all infantile, but sometimes startlingly mature.

Daydanda repeated her questions, this time watching the mandibles as the answers came, and realized that the thin stream of involuntary communication went on even while mandible messages were being sent—and that the 'opposite' answers she'd been receiving were the results of the differences between the purposeful broadcasts and the background flow.

The Strangers' Mother and her consort, it appeared, (gradually, the Lady learned to put the two answers together so that they made sense) had come here to survey the land (to look for a House-site, one would assume), and they had techniques as well for determining before excavation what lay far underground. However, they were now dead . . . perhaps . . . and . . .

More arithmetic!

'What is it that you fear, child?' the Mother asked once more.

'I'm afraid of those (unfamiliar symbol—something small and scuttling and unpleasant), the daughter addressed her sibling, mandibling. 'Scared, scared, *scared!*' came the running edge of thought behind and around it.

'Don't be scared,' Petey told her.

'I'm not afraid of those old bugs!' she told him.

But it wasn't Petey, really; it was that big Mother-bug in the box. *Mother-bug?* What made her think that? That was what *Petey* thought. . . .

Deborah was all mixed up. And she *was* scared; she was scared for Petey, and scared because she didn't know how they put things in her mind, and scared . . .

Scared all the time except when that good-feeling laugh-

ing was in her head; and then, even though she knew the—
the *Mother-bug* must be doing that too, she *couldn't* be
scared.

Deborah stood still, trembling with the realization of the
awfulness of destruction she would somehow have to visit
upon this bunch of bugs, if anything bad happened to
Petey. She didn't understand how she had come to let them
get him out of the ship at all; and now that they had him,
she didn't know what to do about it. The first large tear
slid out of the corner of her eye and rolled down her
cheek.

'Make food for sibling?' the Mother inquired, as she
watched the clear liquid ooze out of the opening she had at
first thought to be twin eyes.

The Strange daughter was apparently receiving all communication as if from the babe, for her answer was addressed to him: a reassurance, a promise, 'I will prepare
(unfamiliar symbol) inside the . . .' Another unfamiliar
symbol there—*ship*—but with it came an image of an interior room of Strange appearance; and Daydanda safely
guessed the symbol to refer to the Wings-House. The first
symbol—*bottle,* she found now, in the babe's mind—was a
great white cylinder, warm and moist, and connected with
the sucking concept . . . but no time to classify it further,
because the older child was mandibling another message,
this time directly to the Mother.

'Return the babe to me, The babe is hungry. I must prepare his food.'

'You have food for the sibling now,' Daydanda pointed
out patiently. 'Come here to the litter and feed him.'

'Sure there's milk,' Dee said. 'There's lots of milk,
Petey. I'll give you a bottle soon as we get back inside,'
she promised, and warned the big bug hopefully: 'That
baby's hungry; he's awful hungry—you wait and see. He'll
start yelling in a minute, and then you'll see. You better
give him back to me right now, before he starts yelling.'

'There is much food inside the ship,' the child told the
babe, but all the while a background-message trickled out:

'There isn't; there really isn't. It won't last much longer.'
And even as the two conflicting thoughts came clear in her
own mind, Daydanda saw a large drop of the precious fluid
roll off the girl's face and be lost forever in the ground.

'Come quickly!' she commanded, *'Now!* Come to the
Mother, and give food to the babe. Quick!'

But the doltish child simply stood there rooted in her
fears.

Maybe if she just walked right over and lifted him out
of the big box, they wouldn't even try to stop her . . .
but there were too many of them, and she didn't dare get
much further away from the rocket.

'You better give him back to me,' she cried out hopelessly.

It took a while to sort out the sense from the nonsense.
Of course, the child believed the babe to be hungry because
the message about feeding came to her through him.
Actually, the little one was warm and happy and content,
with no more than normal infantile fantasies of nourishment in his mind. His belly was still half-full from earlier
feeding.

But half-full meant also half-empty. If the older child
was now producing food, and could not continue to do so
much longer—as seemed clear from the contradictory content of her messages—the babe should have it now, while it
was available. The daughter's reluctance to provide him
with it seemed somehow connected with the *bottle* symbol.
It was necessary to go into the Wings-House to get the
bottle . . .

Daydanda searched the babe's mind once again. *Bottle*
was food . . . ? No . . . a *mechanism* of some sort for
feeding. Perhaps the flat mandibles were even weaker
than they looked; perhaps some artificial aid in nourishment was needed . . .

And that thought brought with it an equally startling notion in explanation of the Wings-House . . . a Strange race
of people might possibly need artificial Wings to carry
out the nuptial flight . . .

That was beside the point for now. Think about it later. Meantime . . . she had to reject the idea of artificial aid in feeding; the babe's repeated sucking image was too clear and too familiar. He nursed as her own babes did; she was certain of it.

Then she recalled the Strange daughter's earlier crafty hope of finding some way to return to the Wings-House with the babe, and emerge no more. Add to that the child's threat that the babe, if not immediately returned to her, would start *yelling*—would attempt to block communication as the girl herself did. It all seemed to mean that *bottle* was not a necessity of feeding at all, but some pleasurable artifact inside the *ship*, somehow associated with the feeding process, with which the daughter was trying to entice the babe.

'You wish to feed?' Daydanda asked the little one, and made a picture in his mind's eye of the girl's face with liquid droplets of nourishment falling unused to the ground.

'Not food,' came the clear response. 'Not food. *Sad.*' Then there was an image once again of the tubular white container, but this time she realized the colour of it came from a cloudy fluid inside . . . *milk.* 'Milk-food, Tears-crying-*sad.*'

Tears-crying was for the face-liquid. It was useless, or rather useful only as emotional expression. It was a waste product . . . (and she had been right in the first guess about twin eyes!) . . . and then the further realization that the great size she had at first attributed to the *bottle* was relative only to the babe. The thing was a reasonably-sized, sensibly-shaped storage container for the nutrient fluid the babe and child called *milk;* and it was furthermore provided with a mechanism at one end designed to be sucked upon.

Out of the welter of freshly-evaluated information, one fact emerged to give the Lady an unanticipated hope.

There was food—*stored, portable* food inside the winged structure. The Strangers were *not biologically tied* to the Wings; there was no need to return the babe in order to satisfy its hunger. Babe and Strange daughter both could, if they would, return to Daydanda's House, there to communicate at leisure.

It remained only to convince the daughter . . . and Day-danda had not forgotten that the child was susceptible to the Homecalling and to laughter both.

XIII

DEBORAH WALKED BEHIND the litter where Petey rode in state with . . . with *the Mother* . . . and all around her walked a retinue of bugs; dozens of them. They walked on four front legs, heads carried down and facing backwards, eyes looking forward. The tallest of them was just about her own height when it stood up straight. Walking this way, none of them came above her waist; they weren't so awful if you didn't have to look at their faces.

Certainly they were smart—so smart it scared her some . . . but not as much as it would have scared her to keep on staying in the rocket. She was just beginning to realize that.

Dee still didn't know how they made her think things inside her head; or how they made Petey seem to talk to her; or how they knew what she was thinking half the time, even if she didn't say a word. She wasn't sure, either, what had made her decide to do what *the Mother* wanted, and packed up food to take along back to their house. She didn't even know what kind of a house it was, or where it was. But she was pretty sure she'd rather go along with them than just keep waiting in the rocket alone with Petey.

Wherever they were going, it was a long walk. Dee was tired, and the knapsack on her back was heavy. They'd started out right after lunch time, and now the dimness in the forest was turning darker, so it must be evening. It was hot, too. She hoped the milk she'd mixed would keep overnight; but she had crackers and fruit, too, in case it didn't. It wasn't the food that made the knapsack so heavy, though; it was the oxy torch she'd slipped into the bottom, underneath the clean diapers.

These bugs were smart, but they didn't know *everything*,

she thought with satisfaction. They never tried to stop her from taking along the torch.

It was hot and damp, and the torch in the knapsack made a knobby hard spot bouncing against her back. But the bugs never stopped to rest; and Dee walked on in their midst, remembering that she was a Space Girl, so she had to be brave and strong.

Then suddenly, right ahead, instead of more trees, there was a bare round hill of orange clay. Only when you looked closer, it wasn't just a hill, because it had an opening in it, like the mouth of a cave, because the edges of the arch were smooth. It was even on both sides, and perfectly round on top; it had little bits of rock or wood set in cement around the edges to make it keep its shape.

She couldn't tell what was inside. It was dark in there. *Too dark.* Deborah paused inside the entranceway, oppressed by shadows, aghast at far dim corridors. One of the bugs tried to take her hand to lead her forward. The touch was sticky. She shuddered back, and stood stock-still in the middle of the arch.

'*I hate you!*' she yelled at all of them.

'Not hate,' said Petey, laughing. 'Fear.'

'I'm not scared of anything,' she told him; 'you're the one who's scared, not me. Petey's afraid of the dark,' she said to the big bug. 'You give that baby back to me right now. That's not your baby. He's *my* brother, and I want him back.'

The rocket, lying helpless on its side in the bare black clearing, seemed very safe and very far away. Dee didn't understand how she could have thought—even for a little while—that this place would be better. Everything back there was safety: even the burned-out memory of the control room was sealed off behind a *safety* door. Everything here was strange and dark, and no doors to close on the shadows—just open arches leading to darker stretches beyond . . .

' 'Fraid of a *door!*' said Petey.

'I'm not afraid of any old door.' Deborah's voice was hoarse from pushing past the choke spot in her throat that was holding back the tears. 'You give me back my brother, that's all; we're not going into your house. He is, too, afraid of the dark; and he hates you too!' *A Space Girl is brave,* she thought, and then she said it out loud, and walked right over to the shadowy outline of the big bug's box, and reached in and grabbed for Petey.

Only he didn't want to come. He yelled and wriggled away; held on tight to the Mother-bug, and kicked at Dee.

She didn't know what to do about it, till she heard that good laughing in her head again. Petey stopped yelling, and Dee stopped pulling at him. She realized that she was very tired, and the laughing felt like home, like her own mother, like food and a warm room, and a bed with clean sheets—and maybe even a fuzzy doll tucked in next to her as if she were practically a baby again herself.

She was tired, and she didn't feel brave any more. She didn't want to go inside, but she didn't want to fight any more, either—especially if Petey was going to be against her, too. She sat down on the ground under the arch to figure out what to do.

'Light?' a voice like Mother's asked gently inside her head. 'You want a light inside?'

'I've got a light,' Dee said, before she stopped to think. 'I've got a light right here.'

She dragged the knapsack around in front of her and dug down into it. She was going to have to go in after all; there wasn't anything else to do. She got the torch out, and turned it on low, so it wouldn't get used up too fast. Then she started laughing, because this time it was the bugs who were scared. They all started running around like crazy, every which way, and half of them ran clear away, inside.

The child was certainly resourceful, Daydanda thought ruefully, as she issued rapid commands and reassurances, restoring order out of the sudden panic that the light had caused among the sensitive unpigmented wingless ones.

No daughter of mine, she thought angrily, with admiration, *no daughter of mine would even dare to act this way!*

'So you begin to see, my dear Lady . . .' Kackot was obviously irritated and *not* impressed . . . 'They have no place in the Household. Useless parasites . . . Why not admit . . . ?'

'*Quiet!*'

Useless parasites? No! *Dangerous* they might well be; *useless* only if you counted the acquisition of new knowledge as of no use. The child would certainly have to be watched closely. This last trick with the light was really quite insupportable behaviour: rudeness beyond belief or toleration. Yet the bravado of the Stranger's attitude was not too hard to understand. Still unequipped for Motherhood, she had already acquired the instincts for it; she was doing, in each case, her inadequate best to protect both sibling and self from any possible dangers. And each new display of unexpected—even uncomfortable—ingenuity left Daydanda more determined than before to make both Strangers a part of her Household.

There was much to be learned. And . . .

Daydanda was many things:

As a Mother, she felt a simple warm solitude for two unmothered creatures.

As the administrative Lady of her Household, it was her duty first to make certain that the Strangers were so established that they could do no harm; and then to learn as much as could be learned from their Strange origins and ways of life.

As a person—a person who had flown, long ago, above the treetops—a person who had only a short time ago walked through the enlarged archway in defiance of all precedent and tradition—a person who had just this day dared the impossible, and ventured forth from her own House to make this trip—Daydanda chuckled to herself, and wished she knew some way to make the Stranger understand the quite inexplicable affection that she felt.

The child said the babe feared darkness; this was manifestly untrue. The Mother still held the soft infant in her arms, and she *knew* there was no fear inside that body. As for the older one—it was not lack of light that *she* feared, either. Yet if the presence of accustomed light could comfort her—why, she should have her light!

'Come, child,' Daydanda coaxed the girl gently through the mind of the babe. 'Inside, there is a place to rest. You have done much, Strange daughter, and you have done well;

but you are tired now. Inside, there is safety and sleep
for the babe and for you. Come with us, and carry your
light if you will. But it is time now to sleep; tomorrow we
will plan.'

At the Lady's command, the litter-bearers picked up her
stretcher once more, and the lurching forward motion
recommenced. The child on the ground stood up slowly,
holding her light high, and followed after them. All down
the dim corridors, Daydanda's warning went ahead, to
spare those whom the little light might hurt from the shock
of exposure.

XIV

DEBORAH LAY ON her back on a thick mat on the floor. It
had looked uncomfortable, but now that she was stretched
out on it, it felt fine. She had no blanket, and no sheets,
and she'd forgotten to bring along pyjamas. At first she
tried sleeping in all her clothes, but then she decided they
were only bugs after all, and they didn't wear anything; so
she took off her overalls and shirt. The room was warm,
anyhow—almost too warm.

She got up and went across the room to the other mat,
where Petey was, and changed his diaper and took off the
rest of his clothes, too. She didn't know what to do with the
dirty things; there was no soil-remover here. Finally, she
folded them up and threw them in a far corner. The rest of
the things they'd have to wear again tomorrow, dirty or not.

Then she propped up Petey's almost empty bottle, and
went back to her own mat, lay down again, and turned the
oxy torch as low as she could, without letting it go out altogether. She could barely see Petey across the room, still
sucking on the nipple, though he was just about asleep.

They hadn't really been captured, she told herself. Nobody tried to hurt them at all. It was more like being
rescued. She didn't know what would happen tomorrow,
except one thing—and that was that she would have to go
back to the rocket to get some clothes at least. It was a long

walk, though. Right now, she felt warm and safe and sleepy.

These bugs were smart, but there were plenty of things they didn't know at all . . .

She was pretty sure they wouldn't understand anything about the safety door, for instance. Unless . . .

Maybe they could find out about it in her mind. But even if they did, they wouldn't *understand* . . .

And they couldn't even find out anything, if she just didn't *think* about it any more. . . .

That was the best way. *I'll just forgot all about it,* she decided.

She felt very brave. The Space Girl Troup Leader on Starhope would be proud of her now, she thought, as she reached out and turned the light all the way off before she fell asleep.

Petey was crying again. 'Shut up,' Dee said crossly; 'why don't you shut up a minute?'

Her eyes felt glued together. She didn't want to wake up. She was warm and comfortable and still very sleepy; and now that it was all over, why didn't Mommy come, and . . . ?

She opened one eye slowly, and couldn't see anything. It was pitch dark in the room; no lights or windows . . .

She reached out for the oxy torch, her hand scraping across the smooth clay floor, and it wasn't there. The bugs had taken it away. They had come in while she was sleeping and taken it . . .

Her hand found the torch, fumbled for the switch, and she had to close her eyes against the sudden bright flare of light. Petey, startled, stopped crying for a minute, then started in again just twice as loud.

The knapsack was in the corner, back of the light, and there was a bottle all ready for him inside it, but Dee still didn't want to get up. If she got up, it would be admitting once and for all that this was real, and the other part had been a dream—the part where she'd been waking up in a real bed, with Mommy in the next room ready to come and take care of them and give them breakfast.

It still felt that way a little bit, as long as she lay still with her eyes closed. *Mother in the next room* . . . Dee didn't want the feeling to stop, but she couldn't help it if the food was in this room. *Mother can't feed me* . . . That was a silly thing to think. She was a big girl; nobody had to *feed* her . . .

Dee got up and got the bottle for Petey, and some fruit and crackers for herself. She was wide awake now and she knew what to do. There was still some food left, but she wasn't really hungry. She knew she might need it later on, so she just sat around listening to Petey making sucking noises on his bottle, and wondering what was going to happen next.

XV

THE MORNING PATTERN of the Household was a familiar and punctilious ritual: a litany of order and affirmation. Each member of each Family knew his role and played it with conditioned ease; the sum of the parts, produced a choreography of timing and motion, such as had delighted the Mother on that day when she watched her mason sons construct the new arch in her double chamber.

Daydanda's great body rested now, as then, on the couch of mats from which she had once thought she would never rise again; but her perceptions spread out of the boundaries of her Household, and her commands and reprimands were heard wherever her children prepared for the day's labour.

Some of the pattern was set and unvarying: the nurses to care for the babes, and the babes to the gardens to feed; the growing sons and daughters to their classrooms, workrooms, and the training gardens; those whose wings are sprouting to instruction in the mysteries of flight and reproduction.

The winged ones whose nuptial flight time has not come as yet wait in their quarters for assignments to scouting positions for the day; the builders breakfast largely to prepare cement, and gather up clay and chips for work in some new structure of the House; the growers, gardeners, and harvesters spread out across the forest, clearing the fallen leaves and branches, sporing the fungi, damming or redirecting a flow of water to some more useful purpose, bringing back new stores of leaf and wood and brush to fill the storage vaults beneath the House.

It was never precisely the same. There was always some minor variation in the combination of elements: a boundary dispute today on this border, instead of the other; a new room to add to the nursery quarters, or an arch to repair in the vaults; a garden to replant into more fertile soil. And on this particular morning, two matters of special import claimed the Lady's attention.

The most urgent of these was the reconditioning of the disturbed Bigheads. Two of the eldest winged daughters—both almost ready for nuptial departures from the Household—had been assigned to work with the nurses who ordinarily tended to the needs of the corral. Under different circumstances, Daydanda would have considered the process worthy of her own direct supervision. Now, however, she contented herself with listening in semi-continuously on the work being done. The programme was proceeding slowly—too slowly—but as long as some progress was being made, she refrained from interfering, and concentrated her own efforts on a matter of far greater personal interest: the Strangers in the House.

Or, rather, the Strange daughter. The babe was no great puzzle; his wants were familiar, and easy to understand. Food and love he needed. The latter was easy; the former they would simply have to find some way to provide . . .

She pushed aside the train of thought that led to making these new arrivals permanent members of the Household. No telling how much longer their supply of their own foods would last; nor whether it would be desirable to keep them in the House. For the time being, Daydanda could indulge her curiosity, and concentrate on the unique components of the Strange daughter's personality.

The child was a conglomeration of contradictions such as the Mother would not previously have believed possible in a sane individual—in one who was capable of performing even the most routine of conditioned tasks, let alone initiating such original and independent actions as those of the Stranger.

And yet, the confusions that existed in the child's

thought patterns were so many, and so vital, it was a wonder she could even operate her own body without having to debate each breath or motion in her neurones first.

Fear! The child was full of fear. And something else for which there was no proper name at all: *I should-I shouldn't.*

Impossible confusion, resulting even more impossibly in better-than-adequate responses!

Hunger ... Mother ... hunger ... Mother? ...

The drifting thoughts merged with the Lady's reflections, and for a moment she was not certain of the source. Too clearly-formed in pattern to be the babe ... and then she realized it was the older one, just waking from sleep, and still stripped of defences.

'I cannot feed you, child,' she answered the Strange daughter's unthinking plea. 'Not yet. You brought food with you from your ... *ship*. Eat now, and feed the babe; then we will make plans for tomorrow.'

But in her own mind, Daydanda knew, there was no question of what plans to make. If there were any way to do so, she meant to have the Strangers stay within her House. She meant to have the secrets of the Strange Wings-House explored and uncovered and to learn the Strange customs and knowledge. It remained only to determine whether it was possible to feed them and care for them adequately within the Household ... and to convince the Strange daughter to stay.

The Mother opened her mind once more to her sons and daughters, at their tasks, and found that all was well throughout the Families. Then she waited patiently till the Strangers were done feeding.

Petey was sleeping. All he ever did was drink milk and go to sleep and yell and act silly. Dee got up and walked around the room, but there was nothing to see and nothing to do.

She didn't even remember which way they had come to get to this room last night, and she didn't know whether they'd let her go out if she wanted to. There was no door closing the room off from the corridor—just another open archway. But outside there was only dimness and darkness.

Abruptly, she picked up the torch and walked to the doorway, flared brilliance out into the hall, and peered up and down. After that she felt better, at least they weren't being *guarded*. She had seen half a dozen other open arches along the corridor, but not even a single bug anywhere.

When Petey woke up, she decided they'd just start walking around until they found some way to get out. She'd have to wait for him to get up, though, because she couldn't carry the lighted torch and the baby both; and even if she didn't need it to see with, she had to have the torch turned up real bright, because that's what they were afraid of. They wouldn't bother her . . .

They're not all scared of the light, she thought. *Just the white-coloured ones are.* She wondered how she knew that, and then forgot about it, because she was thinking: *If we get out of here, I don't know how we could get back to the rocket.*

It was a long way, and she'd have to carry Petey most of the time; and she didn't know *which* way it was, and . . .

I'm going to find the Mother-bug! she decided. For just an instant after that she hesitated, wondering about leaving Petey, but somehow she felt it was all right. He was asleep, and she figured if he woke up and started yelling, she could hear him; any place in here she'd be able to hear him because there weren't any doors to close in between.

She picked up the torch again, and turned it down low, so there was just enough light to see her way. *Don't scare them,* she thought. *They're friends.* But it was comforting to know, anyhow, that she *could* scare them just by turning it up. The white ones were the only ones who couldn't *stand* it, but none of them were used to bright light.

She wondered again how she knew that, and tried to remember something from last night that would have let her know it, but that time she was too busy trying to figure out which corridors and archways would take her to the Mother-bug's room.

XVI

A TREMENDOUS EXCITEMENT was building up inside Daydanda's vast and feeble bulk, while she guided the Strange
child through the labyrinth of the House from the visitor's
chamber near the outer walls to her own central domain.

Yesterday, for the first time in many years of Motherhood, she had experienced once more—with increasing
ease and pleasure through the day—the thousand subtly
different sensations and perceptions of direct vision.
Through all the years between, she had known the *look* of
things outside her chamber—and of beings outside her own
Families—only through the distortions and dilutions of the
minds of her sons and daughters, travelling abroad on mis-
sions of her choosing, and reporting as faithfully as they
could, all that they saw and touched and felt for her ap-
praisal.

But no image filtered through another's brain emerges
quite the same as when it entered . . . and no two beings,
not even those as close as Mother and daughter, can ever
see quite the same image of an object. Certainly, Daydanda
had perceived both more and less of the winged object in
the clearing when she viewed it with her own eye, than
when she had watched it through the mind of her own
scouting son.

And now she was to have the Strange child here before
her eyes again, to watch and study! The thought was so
far-removed from precedent and past experience, it would
not have occurred to her at all to have the girl come to her
chamber. But when she tried to make the child aware of
her desire to converse, to exchange information, the prompt
and positive response had come clearly: *I want to see the
Mother. I want to try and talk to her.*

And behind the response was a pattern Daydanda dimly
perceived, in which two-way communication was *com-
monly* associated with visual sensation. The girl seemed to
assume that an exchange of information would occur only
where an exchange of visimages was also possible!

DAYDANDA

And now the child was standing in the entrance to the new chamber, and the background patter of her mind was a complaint about the difficulty of seeing clearly.

'You may have more light, child, if you wish to see me more clearly,' the Mother assured her. 'I told you before, it is only the ones unpigmented who are harmed by the brightness, and only the wingless who fear it at all.'

An instant later, she realized she had been boasting. The flaring-up of the light caused her no agony, such as she had experienced the day before; but it was quite sufficient to cause her to turn her face abruptly towards the stranger, so as to shield her eye.

And then there was a far worse pain than anything her eye could feel. The Mother's vanity was almost as carefully fed, and quite as much enlarged, as her great abdomen; certainly it was far more vulnerable to attack.

Nobody had ever thought her anything but beautiful before. The Stranger child,

DEBORAH

Deborah stood in the open archway between the two big rooms, and peered intently at the great bulk of the Mother-bug on the couch of mats against the far wall. Then she decided it was all right now to turn the torch up high, so she could see something more than her own feet ahead of her.

The shadows jumped back, and the gently heaving mass on the cot sprang suddenly into full view. Deborah stood still, and gawked at ugliness beyond belief.

The big bug's enormous belly was a mound of grey-white creases and folds and bulges under the sharp light, reflecting pin-points of brightness from oily drops of moisture that stood out all over the dead-looking mass.

And up above the incredible belly, a cone-shaped bulbous lump of the same whitish grey that must have been a face despite its eyeless lack of any expression, tapered into six full thick lips just like the ones of the baby bugs in the fungus garden.

at the first clear look, thought she was . . .

Ugly and awful and frightening and fat!

It was the clearest, sharpest message she had had at any time from the Strange daughter . . . that she was hideous!

Shame and disappointment both receded before a sudden access of fury. Reflexively, Daydanda shot out a spanking thought; and in the very next instant, regretted it.

'I am sorry, child. I should not have punished you for what you could not help thinking, but . . . I am not used to such thoughts.'

'You did that?' the child demanded, and angrily: 'You meant to do it?'

'I did not plan to do it; but it was done with volition, yes.'

The Stranger, Daydanda felt, had no clear concept in her mind to understand that distinction. A thing was done either—on purpose was the child's symbol, or else involuntarily. Nothing in between. Well, it was a common enough childish confusion, but not one the Mother would have expected in this uncommon child.

'It was a punishment,'

It was a good thing, Dee thought, that she hadn't seen the Mother-bug this close the day before. She never could have made herself believe that anything that looked . . . that looked like that . . . could possibly be friendly.

She tried now to believe it was true, tried to remember that good-feeling laughter that she was certain had come from the big bug; but the inside of her head had begun to prickle, just as if somebody was sandpapering in back of her eyes. She shook her head, rubbed at her stinging eyes, sniffled, and the feeling went away as suddenly as it had come.

Then she got mad. 'You did that on purpose!' she gasped. And then a moment later, she had a crazy thought come through her head that the Mother-bug wanted her to feel better, like sometimes Mom . . . the way a mother, maybe, would feel bad after she'd spanked a child. The idea of being a big fat bug's little girl was too silly, and she couldn't help laughing. Then she felt the same kind of panting inside her head that she remembered from last night, and she knew she tried to explain, 'which I had no right to administer. You are my guest, and not my daughter. I offer apology.'

'I am laughing,' came a mandible message; but the background was a quick shiver of fear. Daydanda tried to soothe the fright away, and the laughing stopped, to be replaced by a sturdy mandibled denial of the fear that was, truthfully, already considerably lessened. And then an apology! 'I am sorry,' the child said. 'It was most improper of me to laugh.' And the background message was no different, but only more specific: 'It was very rude of me to be frightened at the idea of being your daughter.'

This time Daydanda repressed her reflexive irritation. 'Laugh when you like, child,' she said; 'perhaps it is a good way to release your fear.'

Promptly, she was rewarded by a clear, unmandibled, but strong reply: 'You're good; I like you. I don't care what you look like.'

The woman's vanity quivered, but her curiosity triumphed what Mother-bug thought.

'I am not scared,' she said emphatically. 'What do you think I do? Laugh when I get scared?' Then she thought it over and decided it wasn't very nice of her to laugh at an idea like that—about being the Mother-bug's child—if the big bug really could read her mind, so she apologized.

'I'm sorry,' she said. 'I guess it wasn't very nice of me to laugh at you.' And she had a feeling as if the Mother-bug knew she had apologized, and was telling her it was all right.

The big old bug was ugly, all right, Dee thought, but so were a lot of people she'd seen . . . and the bug was really pretty nice. Good, sort of, the way a mother ought to be . . .

Just the same, Dee realized, she didn't want to stay here. She didn't want to stay in the rocket either, though. I don't know which is worse, she thought mournfully; then she decided this was worse—even though in a lot of ways it was better—just because she didn't know whether she could get out if she wanted to.

She had to find that out

umphed. The child, at long last, was receptive to communication. Daydanda withdrew from contact entirely, to calm her wounded feelings, and to formulate carefully the question now uppermost in her mind: how to gain more knowledge of the Wings-House in which the Strangers had arrived.

first. She had to get back to the rocket. Once she was safe inside again, with Petey, she could make up her mind.

XVII

'I HAVE TO go back to the rocket,' Dee said out loud. 'I have to go and get us some clothes, anyhow, if we're going to stay here.'

Then she thought she felt cold, but there was a question-y feeling in her mind; she decided the Mother-bug must be *asking* her if she was cold, and finally realized that that was because she had said they needed clothes.

'No, I'm not cold,' she said. 'We have to have some clothes, that's all. The ones we wore yesterday are dirty. Unless . . .' Unless they had a soil-remover. Then she'd have to think of some other reason to go back to the rocket. 'Unless you have some old clothes around,' she finished up craftily. But it sounded silly, and her voice sounded too loud anyhow, every time she said anything, as if she were talking to herself . . . and how did she know she wasn't, anyhow? How did she know she wasn't making it all up?

The feeling she got was so exactly like the sound of her own mother's little impatient sigh when Dee was being stubborn, that it was suddenly impossible to go on doubting at all.

When the Mother-bug laughed, it tickled in her mind; when the Mother was angry it prickled. When the Mother called to her, it was a feeling that came creeping; when she didn't want to hear, it came seeping anyhow.

Trickle-prickle; creep-seep. I spy. I speard you. It was

like seeing and hearing both, if you let it be, or just like knowing what you didn't know a minute before. It could be without the seeing part, as when she thought she heard Petey's voice; or it could be without hearing, just a picture full of meaning, without any words. You didn't *really* see or hear; you really just *found out*.

And if you let yourself know the difference, you could tell what was coming from the Mother-bug . . . such as thinking she was cold for a minute a little while ago. You could tell, all right, if you wanted to . . .

It was a lot smarter to make sure you knew the differences to watch for when the Mother-bug was putting something in your head, so you wouldn't get mixed up and start thinking you wanted something yourself, when it was really what *she* wanted. Or like thinking *Petey* wanted her to open the door in the rocket, where it was really the Mother-bug . . .

No it wasn't either . . . Petey *did* want her to, because he heard the Mother-bug calling them from outside, before Dee heard it . . . or he understood better what it was, or . . . *she's telling me all this; I'm not thinking it for myself!* Up to that part about Petey being the one who wanted her to open the door, she *had* been thinking for herself; after that, it was the bug. It was getting easier, now, to tell the difference.

'How do you know Earthish?' she asked out loud, but there wasn't any kind of answer except the question-y feeling again. 'I mean the language we use. I mean how do you know the words to put in my head . . . ?' She stopped talking because her head was hurting; then she realized the Mother-bug was trying to explain, only it was too complicated for her to understand. Part of it was that the bugs *didn't* know Earthish, though. She understood that much well enough, and lost the hope she'd had for just an instant that other *people* were here already. She didn't try to understand the rest. 'How do you make Petey put things in my head?' she asked instead.

It felt as if the Mother was smiling. She didn't *make Petey say things* at all. He was always saying things, only mostly Dee didn't know how to listen—except, somehow, when the Mother-bug was around, it was easier . . .

Her head was starting to hurt again, so she stopped asking questions about that. 'Listen,' she said, 'I still have to go back to the rocket.'

She didn't know whether she wanted to come back here or stay there. No—that was true, all right, that she didn't know; but right now it was the Mother-bug *asking* her what she wanted to do.

'I don't know,' she said, not trying to pretend anything, because the Mother-bug would have spy-heard that part already. 'Only I have to get back there anyhow; so I'll wait till I get there to decide.'

She'd leave Petey behind, and return at least for a visit?

'No!' she said. That was one thing at least she was sure about. Even if she was sure she was coming back, she couldn't leave Petey all alone here with these bugs. Mommy would . . . *anybody* would get mad at a kid for doing a thing like that!

'No!' she said again. 'I've got to go, and Petey has to go with me; that's all there is to it.' She thought she sounded very firm and grown-up, until she felt the Mother smiling again the way that made her remember her . . . somebody she used to know.

XVIII

THE MORE SHE learned, the less she seemed to know. The Strange child, though still inexplicably frightened, was at last being communicative and co-operative. Yet each new piece of information acquired during the morning's interview had only served to make the puzzle of the Strangers more complex or more abstruse.

How and why they had come here . . . even *whence* they had come . . . their habits, customs, biology, psychology . . . the nature of the *ship* in which they lived, and flew . . . the very fact of the existence of the older child's continuing fear and doubt . . . and Strangest of all, perhaps, the by-now irrefutable fact that *neither of the children knew whether their Mother was alive, inside the Ship, or had departed* . . .

None of these matters were any easier to comprehend

now than they had been the day before; and most of them were more confusing.

However, there was now at least some hope of solving some parts of the puzzle . . . two parts, in any case. The Strange daughter had agreed, after only slight hesitation, to allow a flying son to come inside the *ship* with her, and to explain to the Mother, watching through her son's eyes, as much of what was to be found there as she could. The child apparently had felt that by permitting the exploratory visit, she was securing the right of the babe to accompany her on the trip . . . a right she would in any case have had for the asking. And there was some further thought in the girl's mind of perhaps not returning . . . but Daydanda was not seriously concerned about it. She had refrained carefully from proffering any insistent hospitality, since the daughter's fear of remaining alone with her sibling seemed even greater than that of remaining with the Household, provided she did not feel herself to be a *captive* in the House.

It still remained to be seen, of course, whether it would be possible to provide for the two Strangers within the biological economy of the Families. That, however, was the other part of the puzzle that was already on the road to a solution. The daughter had most fortuitously, before leaving the Lady's chamber, expressed an urgent need to perform some biological functions for which, apparently, a waste receptacle of some sort was required. Daydanda had issued rapid orders to one of the more ingenious of the mason sons, to manufacture as best he could a receptacle conforming to the image she found in the child's mind. Then she had seized the opportunity to ask if she might have a nursing daughter take some samples of the *milk* and other food that had come with them from the *ship*, and of such other bodily by-products as she had already observed the Strangers to produce; the *tears* that came from the eyes in the release of grief, and the general bodily exudation for which the child's symbol was *sweat,* but whose purpose or function she seemed not to understand herself.

Once again, as she had had occasion to do many times before, the Lady regretted the maternal compulsiveness of her own nature that had stood in the way of producing a

Scientist within the Household. As matters now stood, the samplings she had secured from the Strange children would have to be flown two full days' journey away, to the Encyclopaedic Seat, for analysis. If she had been willing—just once in all these years—to inhibit the breeding of a full Family in order to devote the necessary nutrient and emotional concentration to the creation of a pair of Scientists, she would be able to have the answer to the present problem in hours instead of days, and without having to forgo the services of two of her best fliers for the duration of the trip there and back. Then, if it appeared necessary to utilize the more varied facilities of the Seat, she could submit her samples with the security of knowing that her own representative there would keep watch over her interests; and that everything learned about the Strange samples would be transmitted instantly and fully from the brother at the Seat to the twin in the Household. Daydanda knew only too well how often in the past the Seat had seen fit to retain information for its own use, when the products for analysis came from an unrepresented House . . .

No use in worrying now, either about what might be, or about what had not been done. *One* matter, at least, would be resolved before the day was done . . . the baffling question of what lay inside that double-arched opening in the wall of the Wings-House . . . and along with it, the answer, perhaps, to the puzzle of the Strange children's Mother.

XIX

THIS TIME THEY rode in the litter; and the trip that had taken a long afternoon the day before was accomplished in a short hour of trotting, bouncing progress. Yesterday, the pace had been slowed as much by the litter-bearers' efforts to spare their Lady any unnecessary jostling, as by the shortness of Dee's legs; today Daydanda's labouring sons were inhibited by no such considerations.

At the edge of the clearing they paused, their eyes averted from the shiny hull.

Dee laughed out loud, and ran out into the sunlight. It

felt good. She knew she was showing off, but it made her feel better just to stand there and look straight *up,* because she knew there wasn't one of them that would dare to do it.

'Sissies!' she yelled out, there was no answer ... not even a scolding-feeling from the Mother-bug.

She went back to the litter, got Petey out, and parked him on the muddy ground near the airlock, wondering if it was safe to leave him out there while she went inside. They wouldn't do anything like grabbing him and running off, she decided. The Mother-bug wanted to know about the rocket too much; and the Mother-bug wanted *her* to come back, too—not just Petey.

Still, she didn't make any move to go inside. It was good standing there in the sun, even without the show-off part of it. She watched Petey grab big chunks of yellow mud and plaster himself with them, and felt the sun soak into her shoulders and warm the top of her head.

This place wouldn't be so bad, she thought, if it wasn't for the trees everyplace, cutting out the sun. Inside the forest, it was always a little bit drippy and damp, and the light was always dimmed. But when you got out into it, the sun here was a good one—better than on Starhope. It felt like the sun used to feel, she thought she remembered, when she was almost as little as Petey, before they went away from Earth.

She wished she could remember more about Earth. Mommy always told her stories about it, but Mom . . .

Don't think about that!

She wished she could remember more about Earth. It was green there, green like in the forests here, where the treetops lent their colour to everything? That wasn't what Mom . . . what the stories meant, she was sure. For just an instant, there was a picture in her mind; and because it came so suddenly, she suspected at first that the Mother-bug put it there, but it didn't *feel* that way. Then she wasn't sure whether it was something she remembered, from when she was very little, or whether it was truly a *picture* —one she'd seen at school, or on the T-Z. But she was sure that that was how Earth was supposed to look, wherever she was remembering it from.

The trees there were called Appletrees, for a kind of fruit they had, and they grew separated from each other on a hillside, with low branches where the children could climb right up to the tops of them like walking up steps. Then you'd sit in the top, and the breeze would come by, smelling sweet and fresh like Mom . . . the way lavender looked. And you would eat sweet fruit from the swaying branch, and . . .

She jumped as a hairy arm brushed her hand. It was the one with wings who was supposed to go with her into the rocket. It . . . *he,* the Mother said it was her *son,* pointed to the airlock, and Dee got the question-y feeling again. Then there were words to go with it.

'Go inside now?'

It was surprising at first that his 'voice' 'sounded' just like the Mother-bug's. Then she realized it *was* the Mother-bug, talking through his mind. Dee understood by now that the words she 'heard' were supplied by herself to fit the picture or emotions the other person—*that was silly, calling a bug a person!*—'sent' to her; but she was pretty sure that the words or the sort-of-a-voice-sound she'd make up for one person—bug—would be different from the way she'd 'hear' another one.

Anyway, the Mother wanted her to go inside. She decided against leaving Petey outdoors by himself, and picked him up and lifted him in before she climbed through the airlock. The bug with wings came right behind her.

The playroom was a mess. Living in there all the time, Dee hadn't realized how everything was thrown around; but now, when she had a visitor with her—even if he was just a bug—she felt kind of ashamed about the way it all looked. Maybe he wouldn't know the difference . . . but he would. She remembered how the inside of their big House was neat and clean all over; and not just the inside . . . even the woods were kept tidy all the time. She'd seen a bunch of bugs out picking up dead branches and gathering leaves off the ground on the way over here.

This bug didn't seem to care though. He looked around at everything, with his head bent down backwards so he could see, and Dee got the idea he wanted to know if it was all right to touch things. She picked up a toy and some clothes, and put them into the hands on his front legs. After that, he went around looking and touching and handling things all over the playroom, while Dee hunted up some clothes to take back with them.

She couldn't find very much that was clean, so she took a whole pile of stuff from the floor, and went to the back to put them into the soil remover. The bug followed her. It—*he*—watched her put the clothes into the square box; he jumped a little when she turned the switch on and it started shaking, as it always did, a little. Dee laughed. Then she went around turning on all the machines that she knew how to work, just to show the bug. She wished she knew how to use the power tool, because that made a whole lot of noise, and did all kinds of different things; but Daddy never let . . . but she didn't know how to, that's all.

The bug just stood still in the middle of the room, look-ing and listening. He didn't even *want* to touch anything in here, Dee figured; so she asked him out loud, didn't he want to feel what the machines were like? And then she found out she *could* tell the difference in one bug's voice and another's, because the Mother said a kind of eager, 'Thank you—are you sure,' the son-bug said at the same time, kind of nervous-sounding, 'No, thank you; these devices are very Strange . . .' and then he must have realized what his Mother wanted, because he said, 'I am afraid I might damage them.'

Dee felt the Mother's smiling then, and with the smile, a question: 'Where do they breath? With what do they eat?'

'Who?' Dee said out loud.

'Those others . . . the *machines*, is your symbol for them.' And at the same time, she saw inside her head a sort of twisty picture of the room all around her. She saw it with her own eyes, the way it really was; and at the same time, she was seeing it the way the Mother-bug must be seeing it—which was the way her son was seeing it, and 'sending' the picture to her. It wasn't *much* different, mostly just the colours weren't as bright. And somehow, all the machines, the way the Mother-bug saw them, were *alive*.

Dee laughed. Those bugs were pretty smart, but there were lots of things she knew that they didn't.

'They *don't* breathe,' she said scornfully; 'they're just machines, that's all.'

'?????'

'They're machines; they do things for people. You turn 'em on and make them work, and then when you're done, you turn them off again. They run on electricity.'

'?????'

She couldn't explain electricity very well. 'It's like . . . lightning.'

But the Mother didn't know what she meant by that either.

'Don't talk,' the big bug told her; 'make a picture in your head. Stand near the machine-that-cleans, and make pictures, not words, in your own head, to show how it works for you.'

Deborah tried, but she'd never seen what the machinery looked like inside the soil remover. There wasn't very much of it anyway. Da . . . somebody had explained it to her once. There was just a horn—or something like a horn—that kept blowing, without making any noise; at least not any noise that you could hear. The blowing shook all the dirt out of the clothes, and there was a u-v light inside to sterilize them at the same time. That was all she knew, and she didn't know what it really *looked* like, except for the u-v bulb; and she didn't even know what made *that* work, really.

'I'm sorry,' she said. 'I'd make a picture for you if I could.'

'Is there one of these creatures . . . machines . . . you have *seen* inside?'

She'd seen inside of the freeze unit when it was being fixed once. She tried to remember just how that looked; but it was complicated, and the Mother still didn't seem to understand.

'The little pipes?' she asked, and Dee wasn't sure whether she meant the freezing coils or the wires; but then she was sure it was the wires. 'They bring food to the creature so it can work?'

'No, I *told* you. It's not a "creature". It doesn't even *ever* eat. The wires just have electricity in them, that's all. Don't you even know what an electric wire is?'

'Where do the pipes . . . wires . . . bring the *electric* from?'

Dee looked around. The generator was . . . it was in . . . 'There's a generator someplace,' she said carelessly. 'It makes electricity; that's what it's for. I can show you how the T-Z works, because somebody I know showed me once.' She went out to the playroom, and started talking, describing her favourite toy, and making pictures in her mind to show the Mother-bug how it worked, and what some of the stories looked like. She talked fast, and kept on talking till she had to stop for breath; but then she realized she didn't have to talk out loud to the Mother, so she went on thinking about stories she'd seen on T-Z, and she decided she'd take it back with some of the film strips, so the Mother could see for herself how it worked.

Machine! An entity capable of absorbing energy in one form, transmitting it to some other form, and expending it in the performance of work . . . work requiring judgment, skill, training . . . and yet the Strange child said these things were not alive! Daydanda rested on her great couch, but felt no ease, and wished again that she had the fortitude to go out with the small group. To *see for herself* . . .

But she could never even have got through the narrow double-arch entrance to the *ship*. The ship . . . that too, then, was a machine! It was a structure; a builded thing; *not-alive;* yet it could fly . . .

These two Strangers were very different creatures from a very different race; she began to understand that now. The striking similarities were purely superficial. The differences . . .

The thought of the babe tugged at her mind, asking warmth, asking food, and she could not think of him as Strange at all. There were differences; there were samenesses. No need now to make a counting of how many of which kind. Only to learn as much as could be learned, while she determined whether it was possible or desirable to keep the two Strange ones within the Household.

Very well then: these *machines* are not alive . . . not all the time. They live only when the Strange daughter permits it, in most cases by moving a small organ projecting from the outside. Not so different, if you stop to think of it, from the Bigheads, who might be counted not-alive most of the time. It was hard to adjust to the notion of working members of a Household existing on that low level, but . . . these were Strangers.

And still the child maintained the *machines* were not alive at all, not members of her Household, merely structures, animated by . . .

By what? The things absorbed energy from somewhere. Through the little pipes . . . apparently almost pure energy, the stuff the child called *electric*. What was the source of the *electric*?

The Strange daughter had a symbol and not-clear picture in her mind: a thing with rotating brushes, and a hard core of some kind. A thing kept under a round shelter, made of the same fabric as the ship . . . *metal*. From under this *metal* housing came *wires* through which *electric* flowed to the *machines* . . . much as cement flowed from the snout of a mason, or honey from the orifice of a nurse.

Into this machine, food was . . . no, the child's symbol was a different one, though the content of the symbol was the same; food designed for a *machine* was *fuel*. Very well: *fuel* was fed only to the . . . the *Mother-machine!*

Now the whole thing was beginning to make sense. The *machines* were comparable—in relationship to the Stranger's Household—to the winged or crawling creatures that sometimes co-existed with the Household of Daydanda's own people, sharing a House in symbiotic economy, but having, of course, a distinct biology and therefore, a separate Mother and separate reproductive system.

The *generator*, said the child, supplied warmth and nourishment and vital power to the other *machines;* the *generator* was fed by the *humans* (the child's symbol for her own people); the *machines* worked for the *humans*.

'Is the generator of machines alive?' the Lady asked.

'No. I told you before . . .'

'Am *I* alive?'

'Yes. Of course.'

The wonder was not that the Strange daughter failed to include the symbiotes in her semantic concept of 'life', but rather that she *did* include Daydanda, and Daydanda's Household. The Lady abandoned the effort to communicate such an abstraction, and asked if she might be shown the Mother-machine.

Wavering impression of willingness, but . . .

The thing was on the other side of a door. The daughter went through one doorway into the room she had first entered, approached the far wall, and turned sideways, to demonstrate in great detail a mechanism of some sort (not one of the *machines;* no wires connected it to the Mother-machine) whose function apparently was educational. It created visual, auditory, and olfactory hallucinations, utilizing information previously registered on strips of somehow-sensitized fabric . . . roughly analogous to the work of a teaching-nurse, who could register and retain for instructive purposes information supplied by the Mother, and never fully available to the nurse in her own functioning, nor in any way necessary for her to 'know'. Thus an unwinged nurse could give instruction in the art of flying, and the biology of reproduction. But, once again, the Stranger's mechanism was—or so the child said—simply an artifact, a *made* thing, without life of its own, and this time it was even more puzzling than before, because the object in question was self-contained—had its own internal source of *electric,* and needed no connecting *wires* with the Mother-machine.

Mother-machine . . . *Mother!*

Daydanda reacted so sharply to the sudden connection of data that Kackot, asleep in the next chamber, woke and came rushing to her side. Smiling, she shared her thoughts with him.

Machine-Mother and Stranger-Mother both . . . behind a door! The *same* door?

'The source of *electric* is behind the other door?' The Mother-bug's question formed clearly in her mind this time. Dee looked up from the T-Z. There *wasn't* any other door. She looked all around but she couldn't see one. There was just the airlock, and the door to the workroom and kitchen in the back, but the Mother didn't mean either of those.

'I don't know what you're talking about,' she said, and went back to get the clothes out of the soil-remover, and thawed out a piece of cake from the freeze.

Daydanda looked at one and the same time through the eyes of her son in the Strange ship, and through those of the Stranger. Both focused on the same part of the same wall. Through the son's eyes, the Lady saw a rectangular outline in the surface of the wall, and a closure device set in one side. Through the child's eyes, she could see only a smooth unbroken stretch of wall.

'There is no door,' the child informed her clearly . . . then turned around and left the room, once more broadcasting meaningless symbols, and accurate, but inappropriate, arithmetic.

Dee made sure she had enough clothes for a while. She didn't want to come back here right away. Maybe later on. She'd have to come back later on, of course. She couldn't really *stay* with the bugs. But . . .

She took a long strip off the roll of bottles, and a lot of milk, and all the powdered stuff she could find that looked any good. They probably had water there, anyhow. Things out of the freeze would spoil if she took them, so she left them for later, when she came back to the rocket.

She had to make a couple of trips to get everything out to the litter: the clothes and food and the T-Z and Petey and some toys for Petey; and the Mother-bug or the son-bug, one of them, kept trying to say things at her, but she wouldn't listen. She just started saying the Space Girl oath again; and when she couldn't remember it, even some of the silly multiplication, because she didn't feel like talking right now.

XX

DAYDANDA WAS SHORT of time, and entirely out of patience. The Strange child's antics had gone from the puzzling to the incomprehensible, and the Lady of the House had other concerns . . . many of them now aggravated by inattention over the preceding days. She simply could not continue to devote nearly all her thought, nor nearly so much of her time, to any one matter.

The children had brought back with them provisions sufficient for a few days at least, and the Mother was satisfied that their presence in the Household for that period represented no menace to the members of her own Families.

There was no purpose to thinking about their continued stay until the Encyclopaedic Seat completed a biological analysis. Nor could she determine how much responsibility she was willing to take for possible damage to the Wings-House in further exploration and examination, until she knew for certain that she could offer the Strange children a permanent home in her own Household.

The flying son who had accompanied the two of them on their trip to the *rocket,* had informed her that the barrier on which the daughter's fear seemed centred was, like the rest of the Strange structure, composed of *metal,* and that this *metal* was the hardest wood he had ever seen. It could be cut through, he thought, but not without damage to the fabric that might not be repairable. As for discovering the secret of the mechanism that was designed to hold the *door* closed or allow it to open, he was pessimistic.

There was nothing to do, then, but put the matter from her mind until she had more information.

Accordingly, the Mother gave instructions—when all her children were in communion, after the evening Home-calling—that every member of the Household was to treat the Strange guests with kindliness and respect; to guard them from dangers they might fail to recognize; to cooperate with their needs or wishes, insofar as they could express them; and to offer just such friendship—no more and no less—as the young Strangers themselves seemed to desire. She then assigned a well-trained elder daughter (a nurse might have done better in some ways, but she wanted a written record of any information acquired, and that meant it had to be a winged one) to maintain full-time contact with the Strange daughter, so as to answer the visitors' questions and to keep the Household informed of their activities.

With that, she turned her mind to more familiar problems of her Household.

Dee was glad she'd decided to come back. Of course, they couldn't really *stay* here, but just for a little while, it was interesting.

The bugs were really pretty nice people she thought, and giggled at the silly way that sounded . . . calling bugs *people*. But it was hard not to, because they thought about themselves that way, and *acted* that way: and once you got used to how they looked, (And how they looked at you, too: it still felt funny having them turn their backs to you when you talked to them, so they could see you) it was just natural to think of them that way.

Anyhow, they were all nice to her, and especially nice to Petey. She could 'talk' to them pretty easily now, too; but she had an idea she wasn't really doing it herself. There was a . . . *big-sister?* . . . bug who was sort of keeping an eye on her, she thought. Not a real eye, of course; she giggled again. Just the kind of an eye that could see pictures in somebody else's head. But any time she wanted to know something, such as whether it was all right to go out, and where could she find some water to mix the food with, and—as now—how to get to one of those gardens— the big-sister-bug would start telling her almost before she asked. And Dee thought that probably most of the other bugs she talked to were at least partway using the big-sister's mind—the way the Mother-bug had helped her 'hear' what Petey 'said'—because now they all seemed to have pretty much the same kind of 'voice'. But it was different from the Mother's, or from the one who went to the rocket with her.

That gave her a strange feeling sometimes . . . thinking that maybe the big-sister one was *listening in* on her all the time, but at least it wasn't like with the Mother-bug, who'd make that prickly hurting if you thought something she didn't like. The big-sister-bug didn't try to tell her what to do or what not to do, or put ideas in her head, or anything like that. So if she wanted to just listen all the time, Deborah supposed it didn't matter much. And it certainly was useful.

Petey was stuck in the mud again; Dee helped him get loose. She couldn't carry him around all the time, so she'd finally settled for not putting any clothes on him except a diaper, and just letting him go as gucky as he wanted to. He'd learned to crawl pretty well on the soft surface; it was just once in a while that he'd put an arm in too deep, or something like that. But he didn't mind, so she didn't either.

She still couldn't see any garden; just the trees and the mud. 'How far is it?' she asked or wondered.

'Not much more,' Big-sister told her. 'Walk around the next tree, and go to . . . to your *right*.'

Just a little farther on, after she turned, Dee saw the sudden splurge of colour. It was a different garden from the one she'd seen the first time; at least the big-sister-bug said it was. The other one was for the tiny babies—the ones who were really about the same age as Petey, but about half his size. This one was for the next oldest bunch, but they were all just about Petey's size, so maybe he could play with them.

It looked just the same, though; the same kind of crazy combinations of colours and shapes. Everything was just as she remembered, except for not being scared now; and when she got right up to it, she saw these bugs weren't nursing on the plants the way the others had been doing. Once in a while, one of them would stop and suck a little while on a tendril; mostly, though, they were chasing each other around, and kind of playing games—just like kindergarten kids any place.

There were two big bugs—the kind that had dark-coloured skins, and had eyes, but didn't have any wings. These ones were nurses, Dee figured. There were others just like these, with different kinds of noses—and some with different kinds of hands—who did other things; but these ones had to be nurses, because they were watching the kids. They were sitting outside the garden, not doing anything, and Dee felt funny about going inside, partly because it was supposed to be for *little* kids, partly because she was afraid she'd step on one of the plants or something like that. So she let Petey crawl, and she sat down next to the nurses, and just watched.

It was warm in the forest. It was always warm there, but she was getting to like it. She wasn't wearing anything except shorts now, and the only thing she minded was always feeling a little bit *damp,* because the air was so wet. But altogether, she had to admit it was better at least than being in the rocket all by themselves; shut up in there as they had been, Petey was always cranky and fussing about something. Now he was having a good time, so he didn't keep bothering her. And she had the T-Z set back in their room, now, and you didn't even need a light on to work that. Of course, she didn't have very many film-strips for it; she'd have to go back to the rocket pretty soon and get some more.

They'd need some more food, too, and she'd have to get Petey's diapers clean again. She wished there was some way to take along frozen food; then she wouldn't have to fuss around with mixing things with water, and all that, but . . .

The big-sister-bug was asking her what she meant by 'frozen food', but she'd tried to explain that before.

Anyhow, she had to go back there pretty soon, if she and Petey decided to stay there for a while, because she had to leave a message, so that when somebody came to rescue them, they'd know where to look.

'You wish to visit the Wings-House *now?*' Big-sister asked.

'It's kind of late today,' Dee said; 'tomorrow, I guess.' Sometimes she talked out loud like that, even though she knew it didn't make any difference. All she had to do was *think* what she meant, but sometimes she just talked out loud from habit.

'The litter goes swiftly,' said Big-sister. 'If you wish to make the visit now . . .'

Tomorrow! This time she didn't say it . . . just thought it extra hard. Big-sister stopped bothering her about it, and she sat still and watched Petey crawling around and grabbing at the pretty colours.

XXI

DAYDANDA RECEIVED THE report personally, and trusted not even her own memory to retain it all, but relayed to three elder daughters, so that whatever errors any one might make in transcription, the records of the others could correct. There was so much technical symbology through- out the message—even though the clerk at the Seat tried to keep it intelligible—that she could not try to com- prehend it entirely as it came. She would have to study and examine the meaning of each datum, before she could fully determine what it meant in terms of the questions she had to answer for her Household and the Strangers.

If she had *only* had a pair of Scientists! Communicating with each other, they would have known the purpose of the analysis; communicating with her, Mother and sons, there would have been no problem of translation of symbols. But it was hardly possible to give full information to the Scientists at the Seat, when many of them were from neighbouring or nearby Households, whose best interests were by no means identical with her own. Of course, they vowed impartiality when they took up Encyclopaedic work, but . . .

The next breeding, *definitely* . . . ! (Kackot, daily more sensitive, came to the archway and peered in. He had taken to working and napping in the other room these few days. She sent a gentle negative.) The *very next* breeding would have to be limited to a pair of Scientists! Though now that she had put it off so long, and the youngest babes were already growing too big for fondling . . .

Scientists it would be! The Household needed them. All very well to follow easily along the drive to procreate, but it was necessary, also, to safeguard those already born. And right now, the problem was not one of breeding, or breeding inhibition, but of making enough sense out of the message so that she could come to some decision about the Strangers.

She had the three daughters bring her their copies, and lay for a long while on her couch, studying and comparing and making rapid notes. Finally, she called to Kackot, and thought as she did so that it would perhaps do something to soothe his wounded feelings, if he felt she was unable to make this decision without his help.

He listened, soberly, and did what she knew she could count on him to do: reformulated, repeated, and advised according to what she wished. Since the report clearly established that the Strangers represented no biologic danger to the Household—their exudations were entirely non-toxic, and some of the solid matter was even useable, containing large quantities of semi-digested cellulose—it was clearly her duty to keep them in the Household, and learn as much as possible from them. Since the report further indicated that normal food would be non-toxic to the Strangers (and Mother and consort both tended to avoid the question, unanswered in the report, of whether normal feeding would supply *all* nourishment the two Strange children needed), it was possible to extend indefinite hospitality to them.

(After all, if there were elements of nourishment they required beyond what the fungus-foods and wood-honey offered, they could continue to make use of their own supplies . . . which would last longer if supplemented by native food. So Daydanda eased her conscience.)

The question of how far to go in examining the *rocket* was more complicated. The ethic involved . . .

'There is no ethic,' Kackot reminded her stiffly, 'above the duty of a Mother to her Household. The obligations to a Stranger in the House are sacred, but . . .' He dropped his formality, and ended, smiling and once more at ease '. . . *non-biologic!*' So, again, Daydanda soothed her conscience.

Still, it would be better at least to try to get the child's agreement, even though it was a foregone conclusion that they could not expect her co-operation. The Lady summoned the Strange daughter once more to her chamber.

'I could write the message here, I guess,' Dee said thoughtfully. 'If you're going to send somebody to the rocket anyhow, there's no reason for me to go.' It wasn't as if she couldn't trust them; they wouldn't hurt anything. And anyhow, the Mother said she wanted to keep showing Dee what the son was doing, so they could ask questions whenever they didn't understand something.

Right now, the Mother-bug was feeling a question. 'Write a message?' Dee stopped thinking herself, and then she understood. The bugs only used writing for keeping *records* of things. When they wanted to tell somebody something, it didn't matter how far away the person was; so they didn't write things down for other people. Just for themselves, and to make a kind of history for other bugs later on. The Mother wanted to know: wouldn't she 'be aware' of the rescue party when it came.

She shook her head, and didn't try to explain anything, because it was just too *different*. 'I've got some crayons in my room,' she told the Mother-bug, 'but I used up all the paper already.'

'We have paper.' The funny jumpy Father-bug jumped up in his funny way, and went over to a kind of big table full of cubby holes, even before the Mother was done 'talking', and got a piece of their kind of paper, and gave it to Dee. The Mother was asking about crayons, what they were and how they worked, but Dee was asking *her* at the same time for something to write with, and what kind of paper was this?

The paper was made out of tree bark, and covered with a kind of waxy stuff that they made in their bodies. They seemed to make everything right inside themselves—as if each bug was a kind of chemicals factory, and you could put in such and such, and turn some switches inside, and get out so-and-so. It was certainly useful, Dee thought, with vague distaste, and then realized nobody had given her a pencil or anything yet.

But you wouldn't use a pencil on this kind of paper. You'd use a stylus, or something sharp.

'Very soon,' the Mother-bug said. 'My daughter brings you a sharp thing to write with.' Then she raised her arm to show Dee where a little sharp horny tip was, on the back of her elbow, that she used herself.

'But how can you see what . . . ?' Dee started to ask, and then she felt the Mother-bug laughing, and then she laughed herself. It was so hard to get used to people with eyes in the backs of their heads.

One of the nurse-type bugs came in, bowing and crawling the way they always did if they got near the Mother-bug, handed Dee a pointed stick, and crawled out again.

'I am staying with some bugs in a big house,' Dee scratched as clearly as she could through the wax. The bark underneath was orangy-coloured, and the wax was white, so it showed through pretty well. 'My baby brother Petey is with me. Please come and get us.' Then she signed it, 'Deborah (DEE) Levin.' And then realized she hadn't put anything in about *how* to find them. She tried to ask the Mother, but so far they hadn't been able to get together on that kind of thing at all. The bugs didn't use measurements or distances or directions the same way; they just seemed to *know* where to go, and how far they were.

'We will know if Strangers come,' the Mother promised her; 'we will go to them.'

Dee thought that over, and added to her message: 'P.S. If some big bugs come around, don't shoot. They're friends; they're taking care of Petey and me.' And put her initials at the end, the way you're supposed to do with a P.S.

'When is he going?' she asked. 'I mean, should I stay here, so you can ask me questions, or do you want me to come back later?' Petey was getting kind of restless, and he wanted something, but she wasn't sure what.

'The brother wishes to return to the garden,' the Mother explained. 'He understands what I told you about the food. He wanted to suck on the sweet plants before, but was afraid. Now he desires to return to the garden and to the other children, and suck as they do.' Then she said her son was going to the ship right away; but if Dee wanted to go to the garden with Petey, that was all right; the Mother-bug could talk to her just as well that way.

'I'd rather . . . I'd kind of rather *look* at you when we

talk,' Dee said. She knew it seemed silly to them, because they weren't used to it, but she couldn't help it. Anyhow, she got a kind of good feeling being in the Mother-bug's room. The first time she came in here it was *awful,* but right now she felt nervous or something. She didn't know why, but she *did* know she'd feel better if she stayed here with the big old bug.

'Stay then, my child.'

One of the ones with wings came in; this kind just bowed, they didn't crawl. He took the message from Dee, and went back to the garden; then they just waited for a while.

The mother was busy, thinking some place else, and the Father-bug gave her a funny feeling when she tried to talk to him, because he wasn't like a Daddy at all. Not the way the big fat bug was like a real Mother. The skinny, jumpy one was nervous and fussy and worried; and Dee thought he probably didn't like her very much. So she just sat still, squatting on the floor with her back against the wall, and thought maybe she'd go get her T-Z set and look at something till the Mother-bug was ready. But it was warm and comfortable and she didn't want to go away, out of this room, where the Mother was just like a Mother—so she sort of rolled over a little bit, and curled up right on the floor and closed her eyes. If she didn't *look* at the piled-up mats and the ugly old belly on top, it felt more like a Mother than ever before for a long time since it was so warm, hot, glowing red, and the voice said, *fire . . . fire . . . fire . . .*

That was on Hallowe'en, all black and orange, witches and ghosts, and the witch said, 'Fire! Fire! Run! Run!' but the ghost looked like a big fat bug, only white, except the white ones don't have eyes; and this one had two great big hollow eyeholes; and it was crying because it couldn't find the little girl who should have opened . . . opened her eyes, so she could see, why didn't she open her eyeholes, so she could see the little girl? Because the little girl had no eyes, only it didn't matter as long as the door was closed, the ghost couldn't get through a safety safety safe; the little girl is safe, on Hallowe'en when the ground is black and behind the door is black, black, black you can't see, and black it's

all burned up, and the ghost is white; so there's no ghost
there in the black, only a great big ugly bugley belly all
swell up with white dead long time . . . *No!* . . . all black
for Hallowe'en, black, black. . . .

XXII

THE LADY HEARD; and by her lights, she understood. It was
a sick and ugly thing to hear, and a terrible sad thing to
comprehend.

A Mother of fourteen Families is, perforce, accustomed
to grief and fear and failing; she has suffered time and
again the agonies of flesh and spirit with which her children met the tests of growth: the fears of battle, terror of
departure, pains of hunger, the awful shrinking from death.
The time they almost lost their House to swarming hos-
tile Families; the time the boy died in the ravenous claws
of their own Bigheads; the time the rotten-fungus-sickness
spread among them . . . time after time; but never, in all
the crowded years of life-giving and life-losing had Daydanda known a sickness such as now shouted at her from
the Strange girl's dream.

Even her curiosity would have faltered before this outpouring, but she *could* not turn away. One listens to a
troubled child's dream to diagnose, to find a remedy . . .
but *this!* If it were possible to invade the barriers of a full-
grown Mother of crime, one might find sorrow and fear
and torment such as this.

As the sunlight had seared her eyeball, so the hellfires of
the childish dreaming burned her soul.

The girl desired that they should find her Mother dead!
There was no other way to make sense of it. Daydanda
tried. Everything in her fought against even the formula-
tion of such a statement. It was not only evil, but impossible . . . *unnatural.* Non-biologic.

*The child wanted to know that her Mother had been
burned to death.*

Within the shining rocket, Daydanda's son moved curiously, feeling and touching each Strange object cautiously, examining with his eager eye each Strange and inexplicable shape. He waited there, unable to be still in the presence of so much to explore; too fearful of doing damage to explore further till his Mother's mind met his. But the Lady could not be disturbed, the sibling at relay duty said; the Lady was refusing all calls, accepting no contact.

Wait!

He waited.

Non-biologic . . . But what did she know of the biology of a Stranger? Even as much as the clerk at the Seat had told her, from the analysis of scrapings and samplings— even that much she did not fully understand, and that could not be more than a fractional knowledge in any case.

She could not, would not, believe that the Strange daughter's Strange complex of feelings and fears and desires was as subjectively *sick* as it seemed, by her own standards and experience, to be. A different biologic economy—which most assuredly they had—or a completely different reproductive social organization . . .

It *was* possible. The child's independence and resourcefulness . . . her untrained awareness of self and others . . . her lack of certainty even as to whether her Mother still lived . . . the very existence of two siblings of such widely divergent age and size, without even a suggestion of others who had departed, or been left behind . . .

Till now, the Mother had been trying to fit these two Strange children somehow into the patterns of her own world. But she remembered what she had considered at the time to be childish over-statement, or just a part of the confusion of the girl's mind as to place, time, and direction.

From another world . . .

From above the treetops, but that had not been startling. A nesting couple always descended from above the trees, after the nuptial flight. From above the treetops, *but not from below them. From another world* . . . *!*

Kackot was hovering nervously above her. The daughter on relay was asking on behalf of the son at the Strange ship. The daughters in the corral wished to report . . .

To Kackot and the son both, imperative postponements. She clamped control on her seething mind long enough to determine that it was no emergency in the corral, then closed them all out again, and tried to think more clearly.

The dream was still too fresh in her mind. And now there was more data to be had. Don't think, then . . . just to regain one's sanity, detachment, ability to weigh and to consider. One cannot open contact with the child while looking upon her as a monster.

(*A monster!* That's how *I* seemed to her!)

Perspective returned slowly. She groped for Kackot's soothing thoughts, refusing to inform him yet, but gratefully accepting his concern. Then the son, waiting restively inside the Strange Wings-House. And last, the child . . . Strange child of a Strange world.

'Very well,' she told them all calmly, or so she hoped. 'Let us commence.'

Dee was getting tired of it. For a while, it was sort of fun, looking at things the way the son-bug saw them, and watching how clumsy he was every time he tried to do anything the way she told him. Even if these bugs didn't have any machines themselves, you had to be pretty dumb not to be able to just turn a knob when somebody explained it to you.

She realized she was being rude again. It was hard to remember, sometimes, that you shouldn't even *think* anything impolite around here. It would be pretty good for some kids she knew, to come here for a while . . .

'Other children . . . others like yourself?' the Mother felt all excited. 'Of your own Family?'

Dee shook her head. 'No; just some of the kids who were in the Scout Troop on Starhope.'

'Others . . . brothers and sisters . . . from your Household then?'

She had to think about that, to figure out the right answer. A town or a dome or a city was kind of like the Household here . . . but of course, the other kids weren't brothers and sisters, just because you played with them and went to school together. 'Petey's the only brother I have,' she said.

She didn't think she'd made it very clear, but she had a

feeling that the Mother was kind of glad about the answer. She didn't know why; and anyhow, it had nothing to do with the rocket. The son-bug was waiting for his Mother to pay attention to him again.

For a minute, everybody seemed to go away. *Telling secrets!* Dee thought irritably. She was beginning to get very bored now, just sitting here answering a lot of silly questions. They'd already put the message on the waxbark up where anybody who came in could see it, and the son-bug had a batch of diapers cleaned for Petey, and a lot of food picked out of the dry storage cabinet. She hoped it was stuff she liked. She couldn't read the labels when she was looking through his eye; anyhow they didn't need her around any more.

'Don't be silly,' she said out loud. 'There isn't any door to open; they're both open.' *Now what did I say that for?* 'Listen, I better go see how Petey's getting along. I don't like him trying out that fungus food all by himself. I better . . .'

She started to stand up, but the Mother said quietly, 'Soon. Soon, child. Just a little more. You did not understand; we wish to know how to *close* the door . . . just how to operate the mechanism. My son is eager to try his skill at turning knobs to make machines work.'

'You mean the airlock? You can't close that from outside. But if he just wants to try it out while he's inside, I guess that's all right. It's kind of complicated, though; he might get stuck in there or something, and . . .'

'No child. The airlock is the double-arch opening in the outer wall, is it not?'

'. . . yes, and I don't think he better . . .'

'He does not wish to experiment with that one. My son is brave, but not foolish. Only the other, the inner door. If you will . . .'

'Okay, but then I want to go see Petey, all right?'

'As you please.'

'Okay. Well, you have to turn the lever on the right hand side . . .'

'No, please . . . make a picture in your mind. Move your own hand. Pretend to stand before it, and to do as you would do yourself. Think a picture.'

No! It won't open again! That was a silly thing to think. *But all the food's in there!*

'He will not close it then, child. Only show him *how* it works, how he *would* close it if he did. He will not; I promise he will not.'

She showed him. She pretended to be doing it herself, but she felt strange; and when she was done showing him, she took a good look through the Mother and through him to make sure he hadn't really done it. The door was still open though.

'Thank you, my child. You wish to go to the garden now?'

Dee nodded, and felt the Mother go away, and almost ran out. She felt very strange.

Wearily, the Lady commended her son for his intelligent perception, and queried him about his ability to operate the mechanism. He was a little doubtful. She reassured him: such work was not in his training; he had done well. She ordered two of her mason-builder sons to join their winged sibling in the ship, and left instructions to be notified when they were ready to begin.

She tried to rest, meanwhile, but there was too much confusion in her mind: too much new information not yet integrated. And more to come. Better perhaps to wait a bit before they tried that door? *No!* She caught herself with a start, realized that she had absorbed so much of the Strange daughter's terror of . . . of what lay beyond . . .

What lay beyond? Because the child feared it, there was no cause for *her* to fear as well. It was all inside the girl's subjective world, the thing that was not to be known, the thing that made the door unopenable. It was all part and parcel of the child's failure to be aware of her own Mother's life or death, of . . .

Of the *sickness* in the dream. She, Daydanda, had brought that sickness into her Household. It was up to her now to diagnose and cure it—or to cast it out. Such facts were communicable; she had seen it happen, or heard of it at least.

When a mother dies, there is no way to tell what will happen to her sons and daughters. Even among one's own people, strange things may occur. One Household she had heard of, after the sudden death of the Mother, simply continued to go about the ordinary tasks of every day, as though no change were noticed. It could not last, of course, and did not. Each small decision left unmade, each little necessary change in individual performance, created a piling-up confusion that led at last to the inevitable result: when undirected workers no longer cared for the food supplies; when the reckless, unprepared winged ones flew off to early deaths in premature efforts to skim the tree-tops; when nurses ceased to care for hungry Bigheads, or for crying babes, the starving soldiers stormed the corral fences, swarmed into the gardens and the House, and feasted first on succulent infants; then on lean neighbours, and at last— to the vast relief of neighbouring Households—on each other.

For a time, Daydanda had thought the Strange child's curious mixture of maternal and sibling attitudes to be the product of some similar situation—that the girl was simply trying not to *believe* her Mother's death, and somehow to succeed in being daughter and Mother both in her own person. But the dream made that hopeful theory impossible to entertain any longer.

Nor was it possible now to believe that the two children were the remnants of any usual Household. The girl had been too definite about the lack of any other siblings, now or *in the past*.

What then? Try to discard all preconceptions. These are Strange creatures from *another world*. Imagine a biology in which there is no increase in the race—only replacement. The Lady recalled, or thought she did, some parasitic life in the Household of her childhood wherein the parent-organism had to die to make new life . . .

The parent had to die!

Immediately, her mind began to clear. Not sickness then . . . not foul untouchable confusion, but a *natural* Strangeness. Daydanda remembered thinking of the fires of the landing as a ritual . . . and now more fire . . . the Mother must be burned before the young one can mature? Some biologic quality of the ash, perhaps? Something . . . if that were so, it would explain, too, the child's persistent self-reminder that she *must* return to the *rocket*, even while she yearned to stay here where safety and protection lay.

It was fantastic, but fantastic only by the standards of the familiar world. Mother and consort bring the young pair, male and female, to a new home; and in the fires of landing, the parent-creatures die . . . *must* die before the young pair can develop.

She thought a while soberly, trying this fact and that to fit the theory, and each Strange-shaped piece of the puzzle fitted the next with startling ease.

Perhaps if a world became too crowded, after many Households had grown up, some life-form of this kind might evolve, and . . . *yes, of course!* . . . that would explain as well the efforts at migration over vast distances across the glaring sky.

The Lady was prepared now to discover what lay behind the door; her sons were waiting on her wishes.

XXIII

PETEY WAS CHASING a young bug just a little bit bigger than he was round and round a mushroom shape that stood as high as Dee herself. Out of the foot-wide base of the great plant, a lacy network of lavender and light green tendrils sprouted. Deborah watched them play, the bug-child scampering on all sixes, Petey on all fours; and she didn't worry even when they both got tired and stopped and lay down half-sprawled across each other, to suck on adjoining juicy tendrils.

One of the nurses had already told her that Petey had tried some of the fungus juice when he first came out to the garden. That must have been a couple of hours ago, at least. Dee wasn't sure how long she'd been asleep, there in the Mother-bug's room, but she thought it was getting on towards evening now. And she knew that a baby's digestion works much more quickly than a grown-up's; if the stuff was going to hurt him, he'd be acting sick by now.

Probably she shouldn't have let him try it at all, until she tested some first herself. She still didn't really want to, though; and when the Mother said it was all right for him, she hadn't thought to worry about it.

She couldn't keep on fussing over him every minute, anyhow. Besides, that wasn't good for babies either. You have to let them take chances or they'll never grow up . . . *where did I hear that?* . . . somebody had said that . . .

She shook her head, then smiled, watching the two kids, Petey and the bug, playing again. Petey was chortling and laughing and drooling. She decided it was probably pretty safe to trust whatever the Mother-bug said.

The Strange Mother and her consort were indeed inside the *ship,* behind the door the child wouldn't see; and they were most certainly dead.

'It is . . . they look . . .' Her son had not liked it, looking at them. 'I think the fire's heat did as the teaching-nurse had told us might happen when we go above the tree-tops, if we fly too long or too high in the dry sun's heat.' He had had trouble giving a clear visimage to her, because he did not like to look at what he saw. But the skin, he said, judging by that of the children, was darkened, and the bodies dehydrated. They were strapped into twisted couches, as though to prevent their escape. That and the locked door . . . the *taboo* door?

Each item fitted into the only theory that made sense. For some biologic reason, or some reason of tradition on an overcrowded home-world, it was necessary that the parents die as soon as a nesting place for the young couple was found. And the curious conflict in the Strange daughter's mind—the wish that her Mother was burned, with refusal to accept her Mother's death . . .

After all, many a winged one about to depart forever from the childhood home—not knowing whether happiness and fertility will come, or sudden death, or lonely lingering starvation . . . many a one has left with just such a complex of opposite-wishes.

But Daydanda could not tell, from what her son had said, or what he showed, whether the parents were *burned,* within the child's meaning of the word. The son was not too certain, even that the heat had been responsible for death, directly. The room, when he first opened up the door, was filled with a thick grey cloud which dispersed too quickly to make sure if his guess was right; but he took it to be smoke . . . cold smoke. No one could breathe and live through a dozen heartbeats in that cloud, he said.

Whether the cloud formed first, or the heat did its work beforehand, the two were surely dead when their children came back from the first swift trip into the forest, that much was sure.

Whether they had themselves locked the door, and placed a taboo on opening, or whether the daughter had obeyed the custom of her people in sealing it off, was also impossible to determine—now.

This much, however, was clear: that the children had had ample opportunity to learn the truth for themselves if they wished, or if it were proper for them to do so. There had been no difficulty opening the door, not even for her sons who were unused to such mechanisms. The daughter knew how to do it; the daughter would not do it. Finally: the daughter had been *purposefully* set free to develop without the protection of her Mother.

If Daydanda had been certain that the protection of a foster-Mother would also inhibit the growth of the Strange children, she might have hesitated longer. As it was, she asked her consort what he thought, and he of course replied: 'It might be, my Lady, my dear, that these Strange people live only as parasites in the Houses of such as ourselves. See how their Wings are a semi-House, not settled in one location, but designed for transport. See how they chose a landing place almost equidistant from ourselves and our neighbours, as if to give the young ones a little better chance to find a Household that would accept them. It would seem to me, my dear, my Lady, that our course is clear.'

Daydanda was pleased with his advice. And it was time for the Homecalling. The Lady sent out her summons, loud and clear and strong for all to hear: a warning to unfriendly neighbours; a promise and renewal to all her children, young and old.

Dee lay on her mat in the chamber she still shared with Petey, and watched the T-Z, but she did not watch it well. Her mind was too full of other things.

The Mother wanted them to stay and . . . 'join the Household.' She wasn't sure just what that would mean. Doing chores, probably, and things like that. She didn't mind that part; it would be kind of nice to *belong* some-place . . . until the rescue party came.

That was the only thing. She hoped the Mother under-stood that part, but she wasn't sure. They couldn't just *stay* here, of course.

But it might be quite a while before anybody came after them, and meanwhile . . . she looked at Petey, sleeping with a smile on his small fat face, and on his round fat bottom a new kind of diaper, made by the bug-people the same way they made the sleeping mats, only smaller and thinner. That was so she wouldn't have to bother with cleaning the cloth ones any more.

Petey was certainly happier here, but she'd have to watch out, she thought. If the rescue party took too long to come, he'd be more like a bug than a human!

She went back to watching the T-Z set. She had to learn a lot of things, in case she was the only person who could teach Petey anything. Tomorrow, the very next day, she was going to start really teaching him to talk. He could say words all right, if he tried. And with the bugs just in and out of your head, the way they were, he'd never try if she didn't get him started right away.

She turned back the reel, and started the film from the beginning again, because she'd missed so much.

The Lady of the House was pleased.